THE SKI LODGE

Nina Manning is the author of ten psychological thrillers, including worldwide bestsellers *The Daughter in Law* and *The Bridesmaid*. Her most recent is *The Beach Holiday*. Nina is also the author of *The 3am Shattered Mums Club* and the sequel, *The 6pm Frazzled Mums Club*.

Nina studied psychology and criminology and is a trained chef; she has worked in private households and catered an intimate afternoon tea for HRH, King Charles III.

After moving from Dorset to Inverness, Scotland, Nina is inspired by the dramatic backdrops of The Highlands.

When she is not writing, she can be found romping in the woods with her dog and family, plotting more books.

Also by Nina Manning

The Daughter in Law
The Guilty Wife
The House Mate
The Bridesmaid
Queen Bee
The Waitress
The 3am Shattered Mums' Club
The Beach House
The 6pm Frazzled Mums' Club
Her Last Summer
The Dinner Party
The Beach Holiday

THE SKI LODGE

NINA MANNING

HODDER &
STOUGHTON

First published in Great Britain in 2026 by Hodder & Stoughton Limited
An Hachette UK company

The authorised representative in the EEA is Hachette Ireland,
8 Castlecourt Centre, Dublin 15, D15 XTP3, Ireland (email: info@hbgi.ie)

1

A CIP catalogue record for this title is available from the British Library

Paperback ISBN 9781399745628
ebook ISBN 9781399745611

Typeset in Sabon MT by Manipal Technologies Limited

Printed and bound in Great Britain by Clays Ltd, Elcograf S.p.A.

Hodder & Stoughton Limited
Carmelite House
50 Victoria Embankment
London EC4Y 0DZ

www.hodder.co.uk

To my three children, Savannah, Bodhi and Huxley.
I love you all the most.

1

JOLIE

'Gable, please don't just throw your soggy salopettes on the floor,' Jolie called after her nine-year-old son as she looked at the trail of water on the wooden floor of the lodge. She cast her eyes across the rest of the space in front of her, the large open-plan sitting area and kitchen, and wished she had asked for a maid to be included in the cost of the holiday. Maid, that's what they called them up here now. It was nothing like when Jolie was here, working in Cil del món, which was named after the high mountain that made you feel as though you were on top of the world.

Just as his mother had asked him to, Gable trudged back, lifted the soggy trousers from the floor, and took them to the bathroom, where Jolie had put a clothes horse with a huge towel underneath as a makeshift drying station. She didn't really feel as though she were on holiday, with the constant feeding, tidying up and drying clothes. Gable walked out, and she winked at him. He gave her a wry smile, and Jolie felt her heart expand; her little boy was growing up. Just a year away from double digits and already wavering between trying to be cool in front of his mates and still needing his nightly reading book and cuddles before bed.

Jolie went to the kitchen to prepare a snack for them. They would eat out for dinner again later, as they had every night, but the children would be hungry now after their many hours on the slopes and would need to bridge the gap.

When she had worked here twenty years ago, the maids were called hosts, which sounded a lot more dignified. Jolie had never imagined that two decades would pass and she would return to the same resort where she had worked in her twenties, for two reasons. One: she was a terrible skier and snowboarder, and no matter how many lessons she'd had, she had remained flat on her back, adding further injury to her already incredibly bruised coccyx. The second was far more complicated and involved many poor decisions and painful memories she had attempted to bury, but which of course would surface from time to time. She had hoped when her husband, Idris, dropped it on her that they were heading here as a family on an all-expenses-paid business trip, those memories would stay where she had filed them, that she could somehow keep them from returning, as though the messy experience she'd had here years ago had all been a bad dream, and not a very harsh reality. And she had done well so far. She was enjoying being with her husband and children, albeit only having limited time with Idris; this was a work trip after all, and amongst all the mountain adventure and après-ski, work had to be done.

It had been the thought of what happened here that had distressed her the most and she had never recovered from it. She doubted she ever would. As they had travelled here, Idris had taken her hand during the coach transfer, thinking she was having one of her anxiety attacks that she experienced and managed occasionally, but she had shaken it off as quickly as it arrived, and things had been okay since. She knew she needed to stay strong and focused in front of her family.

Now, in the lodge they had been gifted for the week, she was amongst the same mess she remembered when she had worked as a host. Some mornings she would come to work and gasp at the disorder. It was always unbelievable; it was as if the guests had completely forgotten who they were and had become animals, leaving every little thing in their wake for her to clean up. Jolie did not want her two children to think they could leave their rubbish and mess for someone else to tidy away; come to think of it, she could add her husband to that. When they'd left the mountain today, Idris had gone for a final run with the colleagues who had joined them for the first half of the trip and were leaving the next day. Jolie had brought the children back to the lodge as the weather began to turn. She had hoped that the visceral effect of the claustrophobic weather had not been obvious to her two children. The mountain didn't give her the same comfort or thrill that it gave others, and when the sky had turned white, she had fought past the memories that had threatened to terrorise her, gathered the children and headed back down to the village where she felt instant comfort from the smell of the log fire and the sight of the red wine. She had detested the mountains the first time, and she was not going to love them this time.

When Jolie had worked here, she preferred shopping or going to a nice bar or café after work. However, this was a free work trip, a little bonus for Idris, and it presented a good opportunity for the children to try skiing for the first time. Many of her and Idris's friends visited the mountains several times a year. But Jolie had never caught the bug. You had to love the mountains to feel comfort in their presence and she did not love the mountains. And she could feel that they did not love her either.

When Idris told her they would be going to Cil del món, her mind had become a jumble of emotions. Once it sank in, she realised that, of course, one of the most luxurious skiing resorts on the planet was precisely where Idris would be sent for a work retreat to bond with his colleagues and future partners. As Idris was just months away from securing a partner position at his firm, this perk was the company's way of demonstrating how well he would be looked after once he was in. Depriving him of that would have severe repercussions for his career, and Idris had looked after Jolie too well for her to repay him with such a blow at this stage. The firm was all about 'the family'; they were included in everything from the Christmas parties to naming some of the newest software they used.

So she had smiled and said that it would be amazing. She had never been skiing before, she told him, a little white lie to make the whole trip that much easier for her. How could she possibly have told him about that time of her life? Jolie barely knew how to deal with the weight of the daily guilt she carried from back then, and there was just no way she would find the words to talk about it with Idris. So here she was, a novice on the slopes. And when she appeared overwhelmed by the sheer size and encompassing feeling of the mountains around her, to her husband, it seemed as if this was the first time she had been here. It had literally taken her breath away to be back here again, to be reminded how much the mountains could make one feel so small and insignificant.

At dinner last night, Idris had put an arm around her and whispered how well she was doing. Idris knew that sometimes life was challenging for Jolie. Of course he didn't know all the reasons. When he met her, she was on antidepressants. But Idris had breathed life into her otherwise stagnant world. He'd provided her with a home, a place of safety and security, and she had been allowed to come out of herself again, slowly, and the tiny spark that Idris had recognised as the real Jolie had reignited. The death of her father a year into their relationship, then the death of her mother six months after that, was a much-needed cloak that disguised her nerves.

'Muuuum,' came seven-year-old Vita's voice from the bedroom she was sharing with her brother for the duration. She was more than happy to be bunked up with her big buddy.

'Yeeees,' Jolie called back.

'I don't have anything else to watch.'

Jolie let out a sigh. There was no Wi-Fi in the lodge – a technical issue had prevented them from downloading films. Now Vita had finished her last one.

'Can you just come out here and have your snack and we'll do colouring?' Jolie called again.

'Yeeesss! Colouring!' Vita shouted, running in from the bedroom, her damp hair curling in the heat of the chalet. Jolie smiled and pushed a colouring book and pens towards her daughter.

'We'll download some more films at the restaurant tonight, yes?'

'Are we eating at the Italian tonight?'

'Yes, we are.'

'Yippee!' Vita put her hand into a fist and pulled her arm downwards. Jolie laughed inwardly at her daughter's innocence, not realising how sweet and funny she was, but knowing she hated it when her mother giggled at her.

Jolie had the children bathed and dressed, ready to eat out, when Idris came through the lodge door at six. His hair was wet around the edges, his face ruddy and pink from the fresh air, or perhaps from a cheeky beer on the top of the mountain.

'The children are starving,' Jolie whispered as he headed to the bathroom.

'I'll have a really quick shower and we're out of here.'

Vita sat on the stool at the kitchen counter. She and her mother exchanged a glance and both rolled their eyes.

Half an hour later, the children were tucked up at a table, huge white napkins stuffed down their collars, the restaurant buzzing with music from a guitar duo. Jolie had seen the lads a few times, and a gentle reminder returned to her of when she was working in the resort and would come out to Mak's bar. It was a fond memory of the band that had played out at the bars each night, one she held and cherished. But she knew she couldn't cling to even one happy memory as everything she knew of here had been tarnished with the same brush of fear and guilt. She had come here the first time, with a purpose: to prove to her parents that she was more than what they thought she was and to build her character, to become stronger. But what had happened in the end had only made her weaker.

Jolie must have been staring intently at the band because Idris's voice came through her thoughts a little too loudly as though he were repeating himself.

'Pip and Austin are off tomorrow.' He leaned in towards her.

'I know,' she said, picking up her wine and taking a slow sip.

'So I was thinking, I might go back with them.'

It sounded to Jolie like a question, yet she knew it wasn't. Her heart picked up speed. He definitely said 'I' and not 'we'. She swallowed but her throat was dry. He was going to leave her alone here.

'Go back to London? Tomorrow?' Jolie said to him, the heat rising through her chest into her cheeks; her mouth was now so dry she took a long glug of water to lubricate her tongue. She had just about managed being back here knowing that Idris was always close by, but if he left, she would be alone and the memories would reach out and grab her. The guilt would resurface; it would be too overwhelming. How would she keep all of that from the children? How would she cope?

'Yes, it's the bloody Wi-Fi, Jo. We have this presentation, and I can't get a thing done. I was hoping I could have worked evenings, but I've done nothing.'

'Except to enjoy your wife's company,' she said, arranging the napkin in her lap, trying to add light to the dark that had filled her up.

Idris kissed her gently on the cheek.

'Of course, there is that, and I have enjoyed it. I don't want to fall behind; the other two have worked so hard to get us where we are already, and this was supposed to be a half-work and half-leisure trip.'

Jolie nodded. 'I know.' The Wi-Fi had failed in multiple areas around the resort and even for those lodges who had it, it had been very up and down. It had been a constant source of frustration; she had seen how it had bothered her husband. At least there was plenty to do to distract Gable and Vita.

'They think they can switch my flight; Pip's been talking to Angie.'

An image of the company secretary popped into Jolie's mind. She was competent and could always deal with any situation at a moment's notice. Idris worshipped the ground she walked on. Jolie felt the jab of envy towards a woman she barely knew but who'd raised her children by herself after her husband had walked out on them after the birth of their second daughter. She always felt that Idris might compare her incapability to the wonderful ways in which Angie could handle any situation and was always so calm in any crisis. But he never did.

'Of course she'll be able to sort it. She always can,' Jolie said haughtily.

Idris looked at her and blinked slowly. He either pretended he didn't hear the contempt, or he didn't suspect that – now and again – she felt as though she were not the most important woman in Idris's life. Or at the very least, not the most capable. There had been occasional jibes from Jolie in the past about the glamorous woman who practically ran the company and was adored by all. But Angie, who had been in Jolie's company on a few occasions, had always been incredibly kind and gracious, and of course Jolie had no reason to think she had anything to worry about. Idris had been the one who allowed her to grow again. She knew he wouldn't ever do anything to crush her, like the limpet he had discovered clinging to the glass of vodka and tonic in the bar that day they met.

'So you're okay if I go? The kids are making great progress, coming on leaps and bounds.'

'They are children, not kids,' Jolie scolded. It was pathetic, a little bugbear she clung to, and it felt like the right moment to mention it again. She had no other control over the situation. 'They're children, Idris, not baby goats.' It was a phrase she had heard her mother repeat countless times during her childhood. She berated herself for adopting that expression from a woman she had not regarded particularly highly in her youth. Yet, it had stuck, and she found it irritating when people referred to her two beautiful children as 'kids'.

'Children,' Idris dragged the word out to mock her. 'Listen, it's only three days without me, and the children will be pro skiers by the time you get home. And the firm will be so happy that you stayed and enjoyed the rest of the trip. They are generous, but they hate waste.' He rubbed her shoulder, a subtle way to tell her she could do this without him and that she would be okay. But already Jolie felt as though she were tumbling. She couldn't imagine being here without Idris. What could she do? In Idris's mind, she had come on leaps and bounds these last few years. But he didn't know what she kept locked away in the deepest crevices of her mind, the memories that were sure to take their grip once he was gone.

'I can't believe we haven't done this before.' Idris picked up his wine and knocked it back before leaning in front of Jolie for the bottle and topping up both their glasses. She brought a smile to her lips, and kept it there to appease her husband, hating how he could relax when she was the one who had to continue on here for three more days.

Jolie glanced at her children as their food arrived: two steaming bowls of spaghetti Bolognese. They had raved about it and would no doubt expect the same quality at home; she could already feel the weeks of comparisons any time she cooked it or they ate out at a restaurant. She managed to smile, and now it was genuine. The children were making core memories. Jolie was proud of herself for getting through four days. She made a decision to take away these fond memories of Cil del món and hope they would keep away the dark memories of the past. Because being here would always be marred by the tragedy on the mountain that day. It was one of only a few secrets she kept from her husband. Essentially, it wasn't a lie – it was just one of those things she had just withheld from him about her past. After all, didn't everyone have secrets?

2

RONA

Rona stood outside lodge 44. She had just watched the last guests leave and had opened the door to begin airing the rooms. There was a level of expectation with these five-star lodges and guests anticipated having nice things around them when they arrived. That was what *Tranquil Lodges* stood for and had been drummed into her since she began working here twenty-three years ago. A home-from-home experience for those whose houses resembled boutique hotels. These people had money and paid the highest prices for the most luxurious lodges in the village close to the lifts. Cil del món was a resort located at the highest peak in the Pyrenees mountains, featuring only a few restaurants and hotels in the village. In all of these places, the service was impeccable and the customers were given the five-star treatment.

But Rona hadn't needed it drummed into her. It was part of her daily mantra to keep things tidy. She was adept at tying up loose ends, especially at a moment's notice. Always going the extra mile, and never leaving anything out of place. Her aim was to leave a place looking like she had never been there, as though perhaps a mythical brownie creature had come in and done all the work for her and left without a trace.

Rona loved the remote lodges the most, the ones that were only used a few times a year. She enjoyed going out there, feeling the emptiness, letting the nothingness embrace her. She found it quite healing. The way the mountains opened up a little, further up the road, was sometimes exactly where she needed to be to escape the claustrophobia of the village.

It was January and the busiest time of the year. Everyone was getting away after the madness of Christmas. How these people ever had the money to spend after the most expensive time of year was never a mystery to Rona. She was surrounded by wealth every day, and even though she had come from a very different upbringing, her eyes had become accustomed to another way of life. Money was not spoken of here; it was just something that the guests who entered the resort every week had.

She had arrived from Birmingham as a lodge host in 2002 and never went home. After she was promoted to manager, she didn't have to worry about getting her hands dirty, but she liked to come down and check on the girls from time to time. She had been known to step in and roll her sleeves up when someone called in sick. It had happened a lot, but Rona wasn't afraid of hard work. Rona was always where she was needed, at the exact time she was needed. To Rona, there was no other way to exist. In the same way the money kept appearing in these rich clients' bank accounts, Rona kept turning up to work on time.

'Okay, we'll take it from here, Rona.' A girl in a blue polo shirt barged past her into the lodge. Rona looked at her watch.

'You're ten minutes late,' she said as a second girl walked in after her and began hurriedly unloading her caddy. The first girl rolled her eyes whilst the second girl eyed her nervously. *Bloody cheek*, thought Rona. *These girls have no clue, no clue at all about five-star service. They rush through the job and try and get it done as quickly as possible.* That hadn't been the way before Rona was promoted to manager. She took her time, and then checked and double-checked and didn't leave until every inch of the lodge was perfect.

'Thanks for stopping by,' the eye-roll girl said and both girls started laughing.

'Well, just make sure you get it looking five-star, please. Five-star. Are you familiar with what that means?' Both girls eyed one another but said nothing.

'As I thought,' Rona said as she walked away.

On her days off, Rona liked to relax with TV shows and magazines and do some tax-free shopping in the valley.

Occasionally, Mercy would turn up and meet her so she supposed she could call her a friend now. Rona preferred her own company, but occasionally, she would see Mercy and listen to her chatter on. Mercy didn't badger Rona with questions, and Rona had grown to like the familiarity of it. The notion that she would take coffee with Mercy, enjoy the cake from the local bakery, without the underlying worry that Mercy might suddenly wish to delve into her past, try and discover who she really was. It gave her an enormous sense of structure, something Rona craved. It made her feel normal. The role of manager for *Tranquil Lodges*, whilst it had few career prospects, brought focus and a daily routine. There was nothing like the satisfaction of closing the door on a perfect lodge before the guests arrived or when she read the five-star reviews online. Which Rona did often, most nights before she went to bed.

It was a good enough life for someone like Rona; it had its advantages and kept her occupied. Rona needed to be kept busy, or her mind would whirl out of control. She rarely let it happen, but when it did, it would come from nowhere like an avalanche. Such things couldn't be predicted, and sometimes, Rona would find herself once again alone on the edge of the mountain where everything had changed forever.

3

JOLIE

'Wave bye-bye to Daddy,' Jolie said, gathering Gable and Vita at the lodge's front door. It was 8 a.m., and they were both still in their pyjamas, their hair tousled, and their eyes half closed. Jolie pulled her thick cardigan around her and shaded her tired eyes from the brightness of the morning sun as its rays began to hit the snow-drenched mountains that hugged their lodge which nestled among them. The mountain was already coming to life. In the distance she could hear the sound of the ski lift starting up and the high buzzing sound of a skidoo. Jolie spotted a few hosts in light blue logoed polo shirts under their heavy jackets, their boots crunching through the snow as they headed to some of the other lodges to begin cooking breakfasts.

The memory of when Jolie was the one doing that grabbed her and, for a moment, she was back there, walking up the hill to greet the family she'd been assigned to and make their space clean and tidy again. And then that memory was once again stamped out, and she felt the fear and the loss of someone she had cared for return.

'I'll see you all in a few days.' Idris's voice pulled her back to the present. He bent down and kissed both children tenderly on their cheeks.

'I can't believe Angie managed to get you a flight within a few hours,' Jolie said as he stood back up. The children were yawning and rubbing their eyes. However, Jolie was merely making conversation, as of course Angie would have sorted it. A flutter of nervous energy built in her stomach, threatening to consume her entire body if she didn't manage it.

'Gable, Vita, you can go back to bed if you like,' Jolie told her children, and they slowly turned and walked back to their bedroom.

'Bye, Dad,' Gable called back, and her heart tugged at the way he said it so sweetly.

'You'll be okay,' Idris said with a hint of a question in his voice, but not enough that she thought he was that worried about her. She always managed to get it together. He knew she had her problems, but nothing that ever stopped her functioning day to day.

'No racing down those black slopes now I'm gone,' he added for some light relief. Jolie noted he had not responded to her comment about Angie. Good old Angie, who'd saved the day again. She knew she had probably sounded churlish, and it was good that he didn't engage with her. She would only regret Idris leaving on a sour note. She couldn't stop the recurring thoughts that she was being abandoned on the mountain once again; someone she loved dearly was leaving her behind.

'See you in three days, then,' he said, bending down and picking up his suitcase and cabin bag. He leaned in and kissed her on the lips.

'I love you,' he said.

Jolie took a moment before she repeated it back to him. 'I love you too.'

He opened the door, and a skidoo was ready to take him to the main road where he would meet Pip and Austin.

'At least you're not travelling alone,' Jolie said as he reached the door.

'We'll get some work done in the business lounge,' he said.

She nodded. 'See you in three days.'

Just three days, she told herself.

'I'm a phone call away; don't forget to do your breathing if—'

'I know.' Jolie cut him off. She didn't need to think about breathing. She had managed so far and was now two-thirds of the way through the trip. He was right. She had done well. Under exacerbating circumstances, which Idris had very little knowledge of. Sometimes Jolie wished he did know, that he understood her more, so that she had someone to share the burden with.

'The kids are having an absolute riot. Thanks for staying for them.'

Jolie tutted and rolled her eyes.

'Sorry, *the children*,' Idris said.

She didn't have much choice but to stay with them. She didn't want to ruin the children's holiday or chase after her husband. *Just three more days*. She would be on that plane and back home before she knew it.

Idris stepped out into the snow, and a man jumped off a skidoo and attached his luggage to the back. A small gust of wind rushed at Jolie and grazed her cheek. She looked up at the sky. White clouds were already blocking the recently risen sun, and she felt her stomach grip. She really didn't fancy another day on the mountain.

Idris blew her a kiss, mounted the back of the skidoo and was away.

She watched their backs for a moment until they were at the top of the hill leading to the road.

The thought of going out again and climbing the mountain today was weighing on Jolie. But Vita was already dressed and waiting for her in her bedroom.

'I said go back to bed, not get dressed!' Jolie longed for a coffee, another hour in bed undisturbed then a long hot shower.

'I'm dressed, Mummy.' Vita swung her legs as she lay on her back.

'I can see.'

She wished she could have gone home with Idris, but he was right: Gable and Vita had taken to the snow like ducks to water and it would have been cruel to deprive them three more days on the slopes because of her own selfish desire. But was it truly selfish to want to leave somewhere with such bad memories, to have not wanted to come here in the first place? Jolie didn't honestly think so, but she had been suppressing her own feelings and emotions for years now, what difference did a few more days make?

She looked up at the mountain just outside the window. She had felt safe within the boundaries of the nursery slopes this week, but the top of the mountain was not far enough away. It was always there, watching her and reminding her, judging her. How on earth had she ended up here, so close to the same place she had been all those years ago? Of course, Cil del món had changed considerably and grown, with more accommodations, a new hotel and plenty more bars and restaurants. But the very thing that made it what it was, that surrounded her wherever she turned, the mountains, they had never moved and it disturbed Jolie how they had seen everything yet remained silent.

The lodge she had once served in was just far enough away that she didn't need to think about it, but they hadn't spent any time in the village yet. The lodge she had been staying in this week was right on the slopes, like a hotel with a swim-up pool; you just threw on your salopettes and off you went. Each day was so busy: skiing, eating lunch and then more skiing, then après-ski, then back to the lodge, then dinner. Each day took it out of Jolie, but she had been glad of the distraction. Maybe she needed to just go to the village, be closer to the lodge she had worked at. If she went with the children in tow, they would distract her from any negative thoughts. Sometimes, all it took was one of her children to touch her and any unpleasant feelings would disintegrate. Jolie wondered if being closer to everything might help her with closure.

Perhaps a trip up the mountain was what she needed as well. Maybe she just needed to embrace it all, face all her fears at once. But no sooner had Jolie considered it than she realised it would be a step too far; she could easily push herself too much, and how would that affect the children? She was intrigued to see the bar, Mak's, she had frequented when she worked here and maybe her lodge and the café she had eaten breakfast in, hungover and hungry for grease and salt. It had been a comfort, in a way, that she hadn't had to pass the places every day. Yet deep within her was a yearning to visit it. Just briefly, to see how it looked through the eyes of a woman twenty years older. Perhaps now Idris had gone, she could do so without any questioning. She could have a visceral reaction and she wouldn't have him ask if she were okay, if she needed to do her breathing exercises. She and the children could eat at one of the restaurants there, and they would relish a new adventure.

'Mummy.' Vita sat up.

Jolie turned to face her.

'I'm hungry.' Vita hugged Pooky, her teddy. A beautiful, shaggy bear that Vita took everywhere.

'Of course, darling, let's make some breakfast.'

The children excelled later that morning and they took their lunch break in their favourite haunt to the side of the nursery slope. Jolie got herself and the children comfortable at a table on the balcony overlooking the rest of the resort, which stretched out behind it, slopes of varying difficulty going off in different directions. She could see three other large cafés and bars situated around in a semicircle and a few smaller food vans. The sun's rays reflected off the snow, and the surface sparkled like diamonds. Jolie put her sunglasses on to shade her eyes from the glare. The clouds that had threatened to stay earlier had long passed and the whole morning's skiing had taken place under a bright blue sky. She looked at Gable and Vita in their glasses she had bought them specifically for the mountain. She hadn't even prompted them to wear them.

Jolie addressed the children. 'Instead of going back on the slopes, I thought we could go to the village. There are shops and cafés there; we haven't done any shopping since we've been here; we've been so busy skiing.'

'We're so good – that's why, Mummy,' Vita said, echoing her father's words of praise.

'That you are.'

'Can we buy Daddy a present?' Gable asked and Jolie noted how Idris was 'Daddy' again in his absence.

'We sure can. We can buy everyone presents. And you two can choose something to take home too.'

'Oooh really?' Vita asked. 'Like what?'

'Well, we can look and see. It could be clothes or more sunglasses or a teddy.'

'I love Pooky too much.' Vita squeezed her bear, which came in her rucksack each day to the slopes.

'I know you do.' Jolie stroked Pooky's soft brown arm. Vita didn't know that this was the third Pooky bear she'd had. He had been lost twice and had to be rebought twice, each time being told that he had been miraculously rescued and refreshed. Pooky the third had joined their family, and Idris had said firmly that it was the last time, but how would he know? Jolie thought, thoroughly expecting to pay the high cost of the vintage-looking teddy bear again.

After lunch, Jolie and the children walked the short distance into the heart of the village. It took less than ten minutes, her heart raced and she began to sweat profusely. She was surprised at the strength of the involuntary response to the places she had lived and socialised all those years ago. But she needed to do this. Perhaps if she normalised it in her mind, she could go home to England and finally come to terms with the past.

As they stepped out into the bustle of the village through the snowless paths that had been trodden by so many, Jolie felt a strange sensation come over her. Was it nostalgia? she wondered, as she remembered the walks she took each day from her flat to the lodges.

Immediately, she saw it: Mak's, the bar she had gone to regularly. It had a different name now, but she peered through the window. It was closed. Back in the day it would often open at lunchtime, or maybe that had been just for staff like Jolie. She noted it would open this evening and a part of her longed to go in there and sit at the bar, to remember it all, maybe conjure up some happier memories, to balance out how she felt about Cil del món.

She strained to see through the glass into the place where she had spent so many nights – the layout was the same, and she felt her stomach flutter at the memory of it all, the long nights after a morning working, an afternoon up the mountain, then another shift in the lodge, before heading off to this place to meet her friends.

Their names drifted through her mind now, but she was too scared to let them come too close to the surface. She had kept pushing them back down to the depths; that was all she could do. It was so long ago. But one name always remained there, no matter how hard she tried to push it away. And their face, the sound of their voice, when they knew it was all over.

Christ, Jolie. She pulled herself away from the window and brought herself back to the present. It was all in the past, yet the ghosts seemed to echo around her.

Why had she allowed Idris to bring her here? She could have dug her heels in and said no, but Idris would have questioned it.

She was never one to say no for the sake of it. She would have had to have given him a plausible excuse, or told him the truth.

What could she have said to deter him from allowing Angie to book the flights? If she had said that skiing was not for her, he would have suggested she stay in the spas and cafés all day and hire a nanny to care for the children on the slopes. Jolie would have hated that. She would have wanted – no, needed – to be around her children. She could never have let them be up on the mountain without her.

'What are you thinking?' Gable asked and Jolie almost laughed at the way he sounded just like Idris when he said it. But her stifled laugh was quickly followed by the sudden realisation that maybe Gable wasn't just mimicking his father, he had actually begun to sense when Jolie was feeling not quite herself. Had he begun to see the signs? She felt sick at the thought of her little boy having to deal with things that were far beyond his years. She turned and placed her arm around his neck and ruffled his hair.

'I am just fine. I was thinking how this place used to be such a popular resort, even back then . . .' She trailed off. She had almost started to tell her children about when she had worked here.

Gable looked at his mother with confusion.

'I read all about it before we came,' Jolie added and she knew it would be enough for Gable. 'I think there is a lovely little café down here somewhere. I bet they do yummy food. Who's ready for a chocolate milk?'

Both children whooped and trotted off in front of her.

That was too close for comfort. She had thus far managed not to get herself into trouble, but now that she was nearer to where she spent most of her time, it had all become too much to contain.

'Is that the café, Mummy?' Vita asked.

'Yes, it is. Let's cross over the road; be careful of the buses and cars,' Jolie said, realising that both she and the children had already become accustomed to the quietness of the mountain with only the odd skidoo to navigate around whilst the village was much busier.

She looked across the street and there it was: the very first café she had gone to when she had arrived here in early 2004. Her hand went automatically to her chest as if to try and steady its rapid beating.

You're fine, she said to herself. *Why not go in and see how it's changed.*

She took Vita's hand, and Gable followed, walking across the road to the café.

Jolie pushed open the door, eager to be inside, but equally terrified of going back in time. She ushered Gable in front of her and pointed out an empty seat to the children, and they raced over to it.

Her skin tingled at the sight of the place. A memory of a friendly face shot through her mind, and then it was gone, the same way she had gone in real life. The café hadn't changed much at all. She gazed at the pictures on the wall – skiing scenes, all faded but very much the same ones she had often stared at while hungover. The counter remained in the same spot; the only difference she noticed was that the coffee machine was bigger and fancier.

She glanced at the menu behind the counter. It seemed familiar, too, with some additions of bagels and paninis. The seating had changed, though. Where before it had been canteen-style chairs and tables nailed to the floor, these were round tables and comfy-looking bistro-style chairs.

Jolie joined Gable and Vita at the corner table by the window. It was a spot where Jolie had often enjoyed sitting and observing the passers-by as they made their way to the bank and the pharmacy. People-watching had always been one of her favourite pastimes. However, she had not realised in those early days that she would soon need to start watching her back as well.

A waitress approached her table and smiled down at them all. She ordered café con leche for herself and hot chocolate for the children.

Gable and Vita bickered over the number of their marshmallows, eventually wandering over to the games and bookshelf. They both returned, thrilled to have found Connect 4, and began playing together without any further fuss.

That would keep them quiet for twenty minutes, Jolie thought, but no sooner had she taken her first sip than her mind began to wander again, and those names she had so wanted to suppress managed to squeeze themselves into her conscious thoughts. All the people she had known before were there in the room with her. And she saw the beautiful face of the one person she had thought she would remain friends with forever. Before she knew what was happening, Jolie was transported back here, twenty years ago.

4

JOLIE
TWENTY YEARS AGO

Jolie dragged her two suitcases off the busy path and into the café, perching them in the corner. She didn't want to upset the locals by taking up too much space with her luggage. And she had brought a lot. Two full suitcases and a backpack; it was an embarrassing amount, really. She had wanted to appear free and bohemian, arriving with just a beanie hat and a rucksack, but Jolie couldn't deny who she was and where she came from. She was not the type to throw a few belongings into a bag and set off without knowing when she might return or having a big plan.

This trip had been planned meticulously; she was going to stay for the full five months of the ski season. She hadn't ever thought she would want to go somewhere like Cil del món. It was a luxury resort that was far out of her comfort zone, not the kind of place she felt she would fit in at all. But once she realised she had to go, that she was no longer welcome at home, she began her research. She read up about Cil del món online and discovered that there would be an eclectic mix of staff staying and working there; some traveller types who live out of a rucksack for years between here and hotter places in Europe during the summer, and people like her, whose parents had paid for this experience. But not in the kindly way that some people's parents do when they are excited to see their children off into the big wide world to begin their life experiences. This was more of a payoff. Thank you for your time; that will be all now.

'But where will I go?' Jolie had asked.

Her parents must have presumed she would use the money wisely, put it down as a deposit on a rented property plus her first month's rent.

But Jolie was mad, and her anger fuelled her to begin researching places where she might go to get away from it all. Start again, become someone new. *Where was the best place to go and have an adventure?* were the words she had googled in the end.

Cil del món was fairly high up on the list. *Come to the top of the world and forget all your cares.*

She began looking for jobs and found a lodge host position. It sounded perfect, working mornings and early evenings with one day off each week, plus every afternoon to tackle the slopes. Jolie had wanted to learn to ski, as so many people she knew could already do it. Her parents had never taken her on a skiing holiday. They had flown once to Spain when she was nine but had never been back again, opting instead for camping holidays in Norfolk and Wales. Those had been quite nice, but Jolie always remembered feeling cold at night and her back aching from the hard ground. Then she went to college and university, and somehow the last few years just slipped by. She had spent her weekends and all her money in pubs and nightclubs at university. However, she ultimately didn't come out with that degree. And that wasn't because she failed the work. It was as though her parents had always been waiting for the moment when they could use their constant disappointment in her and direct it at one thing. And on this occasion, she had no excuses to give.

At twenty-two, she needed to gain some direction. This job would be a good start for her, look good on her CV, and demonstrate she could stay somewhere for longer than a few weeks. Who knew where she would be drawn to after that? The world truly was her oyster. She had taken the leap; she just hoped she was up to it. She had the money in her account from her father, but what had been lacking were the words of encouragement. Where had been the 'go get 'em, kid'? Wasn't that how parents saw their children off when they left home for the first time? But her mum had popped her head around the door the night before and told her they would be letting out her room, so not to expect it back. It was their way of making it permanent without actually saying so. But Jolie was determined to make this work, to show her parents she was strong and capable. But most of all, now the time had come to show them that she didn't need them.

A lady approached her table and asked her something. She could have been speaking Spanish or Catalan; she wasn't familiar with the language yet. But she hoped to be.

'Erm, coffee?' Jolie asked and the lady let out a sigh. It was the beginning of the season, and Jolie expected the lady came across many who were completely unprepared or unable to speak the language. Jolie felt stupid and ill-prepared. If she'd had more notice, perhaps she would have taken some time to learn some of the basic language. But then she reminded herself that she was never one for studying. She hadn't done very well in school, and university had its challenges, and learning was one of them, especially when there were so many other distractions. But already, despite the language barrier, Jolie had a feeling about this place; she felt like it was the sort of place someone could become accustomed to living. It was smart, clean, there was plenty of work by all accounts, there were nice bars and restaurants, it was a tax-free haven, and then there was the lure of the mountains. Although right now, there was barely any snow, just the high, imposing bare mountains all around, towering over the village, staring down at her, making her feel just a little bit claustrophobic. But she would get over that; she was sure.

'Café con leche?' the lady asked, pointing to a picture on the menu that resembled a milky coffee.

'Yes,' Jolie said. '*Sí*,' she corrected herself.

Jolie spied a picture of eggs and bacon and pointed to it. '*Sí*?' she asked the woman.

'*Sí*.' The lady scribbled on her pad and swept away back to the counter.

Five minutes later, Jolie was tucking into a plate of eggs and bacon, washed down with a delightful cup of coffee.

She had just finished her food and pushed her plate away when the café's door burst open. A young man and woman bustled in, talking loudly.

'I just don't see why you had to do it, that's all,' the woman said, with what Jolie thought sounded like a Spanish accent.

Jolie thought she looked about her age. She had long, dark hair, a beige coat with a fur hood, and what appeared to be pink, sparkly leggings and beige, furry-trimmed boots. As it hadn't snowed yet down here in the village, Jolie was going to get away with trainers for a few more days, but she knew she would need to buy herself a good pair of snow boots to get around in.

She tried to avoid looking at the couple who were clearly having an argument, as the woman had taken a seat very close to where Jolie was sitting. The man was also roughly Jolie's age and didn't seem as vocal as the woman; he was attempting to calm her down, and his voice wasn't as raised. But this woman was furious.

'Sometimes, I think you don't even care at all, Adam. I came out here to support you.'

The man, Adam, looked forlorn, but the woman continued. Jolie stared back down at her table.

'It's just not good enough; I want a bigger apartment, not to be cramped in that one-bedroom place.'

Jolie thought she had caught the thread of their conversation and dared to look up, briefly checking Adam's expression. But instead, she was shocked to catch the eye of the young woman, who gave her a quick smile and a wink.

A wink.

Jolie wasn't sure whether to laugh out loud.

She ordered more coffee in an attempt to stretch out another hour until she had to meet Estelle, her new employer, who would drive her up to the lodges to give her the tour and then take her to her apartment.

'Anyway, we'll leave it for now, because I am sure this girl doesn't want to hear us bickering on,' the woman said loud enough for Jolie to hear, and Jolie smiled to herself. She wasn't ready to engage in conversation just yet. If she was being honest with herself, she felt a little intimidated.

Once her coffee arrived, she took out a paperback she had been reading on the plane and briefly on the bus. She tried to re-immerse herself, but kept picking up strands of conversation from the neighbouring table. Jolie couldn't help but think that the woman had chosen to sit so close that Jolie was compelled to listen to what she had to say. She didn't know the woman, but from what she had seen – and heard – of her, she seemed a bit of an exhibitionist, as though she enjoyed being listened to and watched. Jolie couldn't imagine anything worse than having anyone eavesdrop on her private conversations.

Jolie had just ended a relationship with a guy before she came here. Well, he had ended it. But she wasn't going to dwell on that. Just as she wouldn't let herself get angry about how everyone else had disowned her right before she left the country. She eyed the woman surreptitiously, but the woman was already looking at her, and when their eyes met, she smiled again. Jolie looked away, embarrassed.

She sipped her coffee and tried not to look at her neighbours again. They had calmed down, or at least the woman had. They had ordered coffees but Jolie could sense she was being observed. She would occasionally glance up, only to see the woman seem as though she were looking away, as though she had just been looking at her.

Glancing at her watch, Jolie saw she was to meet her host along the street in half an hour. She could drag her luggage for a short time and pop into a shop. She felt the need to leave this café. Standing up, she moved towards her suitcases. As she began to pull one towards the door, the woman suddenly appeared behind her.

'I just need to get past you to the bathroom,' she said quietly. Jolie looked at her luggage, then at a small door; she hadn't noticed she had been blocking it with her two suitcases.

'Oh, sorry, I didn't realise I was . . .' Jolie struggled to move the heavy luggage.

'Here, let me,' the woman said, taking the handle of one and lifting it to the right. Jolie followed suit.

'Thanks. I didn't see the door to the toilet there.'

'That's a lot of luggage,' the woman noted.

Jolie examined the suitcases, assessing them as though she were seeing them for the first time. 'Yes. Yes it is.'

'So, you put a body in there?' the woman said a little too seriously and Jolie wasn't sure whether to laugh.

'I . . . it's my first time.'

'You don't say,' the woman said, with a little more humour in her voice this time, and Jolie let out a breath she had been holding. She laughed, and the woman laughed too.

'I'm Martina. And this is *not* my first time,' she said and looked around at the table where Adam was holding a Nokia mobile phone, which looked similar to the one Jolie had bought herself before she left because she'd had a vague notion that she might need to call someone. Or that someone might want her to call her, maybe. It was still in her bag switched off, and she had meant to turn it on and call her parents on their landline, but something had stopped her. A sort of sadness that had started in her throat when she had left the UK was now buried deep down in her stomach.

'I'm Jolie,' Jolie said to Martina. 'I'm meeting my new boss. I start as a host in a few days.'

'Oh, right, so you'll be working for Estelle?'

'From Tranquil Lodges?'

'Yes, that's her,' Martina said and swung her long brown hair over her shoulders. Jolie noticed that she was wearing blue eyeshadow.

'She's okay I suppose.' She flicked her hair again.

Jolie felt disheartened, and her expression probably showed that. She had hoped to get a good boss, but hadn't had great luck in the employer department. Maybe she just wasn't that employable.

'I'm sure you'll be fine.' Martina looked Jolie up and down. 'Sometimes we just don't see eye to eye.'

Jolie absorbed the information and would need to think about that later; she hadn't even met Estelle yet. Once bedded in, she could return to Martina's comment about her new boss.

'Do you work for Tranquil Lodges?' Jolie asked.

'I suppose you could say that,' Martina said vaguely, and Jolie thought it was a strange way to answer. You either did or you didn't – but Jolie wasn't about to delve into the specifics with Martina when they had just met.

Martina looked over at Adam. 'He's fine there for a little while; I'll help you pull one of these monstrosities up the road.'

Before Jolie could protest, Martina had taken the handle of one of the suitcases and was wheeling it out the door.

'The toilet,' Jolie blurted.

'What?' Martina spun around.

'I thought you needed to go, to the toilet?'

Martina glanced around at the little door Jolie had just been blocking.

'Oh, yes. I can hold it in.'

Jolie quickly grabbed the handle of the other bag, looked over at Adam, who was still staring at his phone, and followed Martina.

As Jolie walked behind her, she felt a happiness begin to unfold inside her. It had been such a long time since someone had come along and said hi, and she'd been able to have an easy conversation with them. Something told her that Martina had somehow befriended her, and that she was about to become an essential part of her life.

5

JOLIE

NOW

They left the café, the children with hot chocolate moustaches, but Jolie was too distracted to look for wet wipes in her bag. Sitting in the café had brought back so many memories of when she had first arrived and of course when she had met Martina, someone she thought she would end up knowing for a very long time; but that was never to be. Then there were all the times she had spent in the café. Hours of her week when she had been hungover and needed a hearty brunch before heading up the mountain or sleeping the rest of the day. Days became nights, nights became days, and a lot of the time Jolie hadn't known how she had managed to function. But that had been the way of the seasonal life. Work, play; work, play. There was not a lot else in between.

Jolie had been sure she wanted to come here into the village, to put to rest the nagging feeling that had been plaguing her since she arrived, since Idris had announced they would be holidaying here.

It had been difficult to pretend that everything was new to her, agreeing with Idris while he pointed things out to her with awe. At least the children were here; their mere presence completely diverted Jolie. She had noticed that Idris had begun to back off a bit; he was less protective and asked her less about her general sense of well-being. He could tell when she was having a turn, and they worked through it together; it had become a routine for both of them, part of their domestic existence, like doing the dishes or folding the laundry. And during that time, even Jolie had seen improvements. Now that both her parents were dead, she had managed to make some peace with herself and had done well in her various therapies, discussing the fractured relationships she had endured with both her mum and her dad.

What she never discussed was her time in Cil del món. She understood that holding on to those emotions made her easily vulnerable to being triggered. However, there was simply no way she could ever speak of what she had done during her previous life here. She supposed she would need to take it to her grave, and she was prepared to do so. Besides, her anxiety was nowhere near as severe as it had once been. She was less jumpy, had more patience, and was a lot more sociable. Idris had attributed it to a lack of confidence when he first met her, as she had barely been able to look anyone in the eye, like a terrified and timid Princess Diana, peeking at everyone through the gap in her hair and using it as a shield the rest of the time.

Of course, she could have used her parents as a reason for most of her anxiety, but it ran deeper than that. A place that Jolie had not dared to go.

Idris told her regularly what a wonderful woman she was and never drew attention to her faults; he didn't see them as faults, but rather as slight flaws that she had inherited and had managed to iron out when he met her. But in Idris's eyes, Jolie would always remain a little fragile. So in that sense, it was almost unbelievable that just as she had begun to thrive, she should find herself back in the very place that had robbed her of her confidence.

She tried to shake away the dark memories that had begun to consume her and focus on the fact that very soon she would be going home and that she would never have to return. If Idris ever suggested they return to this location, she would remind him of the hundreds of ski locations worldwide that they had yet to visit as a family. They did not need to come back here as a foursome again. But Jolie knew, even as she had the thought, that it didn't matter which continent a mountain was situated in; they would always haunt her.

She took the children's hands. Jolie was pleased how freely Gable offered his as they were so far away from home, a different story on the street of the borough in London, where he might bump into a school friend. They walked along the little path, and Jolie saw a sunglasses shop, which had not been there when she'd worked here. This felt new, and she felt the familiar buzz she got when she would occasionally go shopping for clothes or underwear. She fancied a new pair of sunglasses and the children would enjoy trying pairs on for a while.

She steered them into the shop and they pushed the rotating shelf, picking out pairs and showing them off to one another. Jolie was wearing a pair she was considering buying when she felt the presence of someone very close to her. She was still wearing the glasses when a lady, who looked as though she were in her late seventies thrust a piece of paper her way. Jolie took it and smiled. She wasn't sure she should encourage touting on someone else's premises, so she stuffed the paper in her pocket, embarrassed to have accepted it.

Both children held up the sunglasses they wished to purchase, and Jolie took them to the counter along with the pair she was wearing. She wanted to say to the sales assistant, 'You can never have too many pairs of sunglasses,' but she wasn't sure if she spoke English. The woman smiled at her, scanned her items, and Jolie handed over her debit card. Once the items were bagged, she took the children's hands and walked out into the sunshine.

Jolie felt a rush of joy, partly from the spontaneous purchase and partly from feeling thankful she was with her two children. The sun was high in the sky, and she was not, for once, on the slopes. In three days, she would be home, and she could focus on booking a summer holiday somewhere far away and very hot.

She was imagining sun-kissed skin on white sandy beaches when she felt a tug on her sleeve.

She looked down, and Vita was holding a piece of paper that was slightly scrunched up.

'This fell out of your pocket, Mummy,' Vita said. Jolie took it from her and began to uncrumple the paper, which she could see was the advert handed to her just a moment ago in the store.

She began examining it, imagining it might reveal where she could sell all her gold or direct her to the cheapest taxi service, but instead, she found herself looking at a face. She stopped and tried to steady her breathing. She must have made some sort of sound because Vita touched her arm and asked if she was okay. Jolie looked briefly at her daughter and then nodded. But she felt far from okay. The coffee she had just drunk rose in her throat and tasted bitter and acrid. The children stopped outside a gift store and pleaded with their mother to go in. Jolie waved them on and watched them through the window. Then, she tentatively looked down at the flyer in her damp hand. Her whole arm was shaking as she raised it enough to look at it properly, hoping that by some minor miracle, she had imagined it and it had been some cruel flashback, a slip of her imagination. But there was no denying what she was looking at. A photograph of a very beautiful young girl, so bohemian, so free. With pink streaks in her dark brown hair and glittery eye shadow.

Underneath were the words:

Still missing.
Last seen 15th February 2004.

And then the name:

Martina Acosta. Aged 23.

6
RONA

Today, Rona would be meeting her friend Mercy at the main café in the village, where they met most weeks whenever Rona fancied getting out of her flat. Rona remembered what the café had been like when she first arrived here over twenty-three years ago; it barely had three dishes and just basic tea or coffee. Now, it was the hub of the village, offering a full breakfast and lunch menu and every barista drink imaginable. They even served bubble tea!

Rona arrived before Mercy, the way she did every week. She liked to arrive, take her seat, and acclimate to her surroundings before Mercy eventually showed up. Rona didn't get out much; she had her routines and liked sticking to them. The village was much different now to how it had been many years ago. She recognised a few faces, but still, she preferred to keep herself to herself; she didn't speak to these people. She didn't know them;

they didn't know her. It was better that way. She didn't have to forge friendships or fake greetings. She could just come and get what she needed and then leave again. Back to work or home to her little flat where everything was quiet and calm. Where she was safe.

She wouldn't come at all if it weren't for Mercy's insistence. She could hear her voice badgering her, telling her she needed to get out, that they needed time together, to talk. Rona knew she was one of the last of those who had worked here twenty-odd years ago. She had never really tried to make friends back then, apart from one or two occasions, and she certainly didn't need to try now. But Mercy was insistent. She plagued her if she didn't respond. It was easy to just go along with what she wanted.

Rona took a seat by the window. Sometimes, Mercy was on time; other times, she was late. It didn't bother Rona; she had nowhere else to be, and she was ready for Mercy when she arrived.

Rona thought about a time when she did try to make friends with someone. It was so unusual for her, and so outside of her everyday behaviour that she shocked herself.

The girl had knocked her back; she hadn't asked again. She didn't ask anyone else again. She wasn't sure what it was about that particular girl, but for a moment, she had felt a secure connection.

Yet here she was, in the same village she had lived in for over two decades. It wasn't that there weren't other options out there for Rona, but she couldn't leave the Pyrenees. There was too much that was holding her here; her soul had become part of the place. Nowhere else would do now. Not after everything.

Amongst the business of her thoughts, Mercy had arrived and began talking. She would often just show up, begin speaking as though she and Rona had been chatting away for hours, already halfway through a conversation. Mercy was telling her one of her funny stories, but Rona felt distracted today and wasn't really in the mood for listening. Mercy was a lot younger than Rona, in her early twenties. She had so much energy. Rona just smiled, nodded, and made the right noises in the right places. When the waitress approached the table, she narrowed her eyes at Rona.

'Is everything okay with you, madam?' she asked Rona in Catalan.

Do I know you? Rona thought to herself. She ignored the waitress's comment and glare and glanced at Mercy. She was still talking and hadn't even noticed the waitress.

Rona thought Mercy would like to try the special, the escudella. Mercy said it sounded delicious – a warming winter stew – so she ordered that along with her usual coffee.

The waitress wrote down the order all the while glancing between Rona and Mercy.

Rona ended the interaction with a hard stare and the waitress retreated. This was why Rona didn't like to come out very much. The locals could be so unwelcoming.

Soon, the plates were being cleared, and Rona noticed some commotion in the doorway. A lady was trying to get in, but the waitress who had served them their lunch was not allowing it. Rona knew enough Spanish and Catalan to understand the conversation.

The woman held some flyers and mentioned that she needed to come in to distribute them.

The waitress told her she was not allowed and was not welcome. The commotion was distressing and upsetting for the customers.

Rona could still hear Mercy, who was quite unaware of what was going on around her and continued with her chatter, which was more of a monologue now. But Rona felt a growing sense of unease, and eventually the sound of Mercy's voice faded to barely a whisper. She wanted the woman at the door to leave; she didn't like how she persisted with her requests. There was too much happening, a sensory overload that Rona didn't know how to handle. She scraped her chair back, and Mercy suddenly became silent. Rona stood up and looked towards the door. The woman with the pamphlets was finally quiet, too, and she turned to leave. But just before she did, she gave Rona a long, lingering look and in her eyes, Rona could see anguish.

She threw some euros on the table, grabbed her bag and walked towards the door. The lady was already walking along the road. Rona looked down, and just by the door, she saw that one of the pamphlets had dropped to the floor. She stooped to pick it up. Her heart lurched when she saw the image on the paper, and she screwed it up tightly in her fist and stuffed it into her coat pocket. She hurried out of the café, her mind a whirlwind of conversations and images.

7
JOLIE

'I told you, we're all fine,' Jolie said, holding her phone to the children so Idris could see their happy red faces.

'I can see, you all look lovely and healthy.' Idris grinned.

Jolie and the children had just had their final day on the mountain, and Jolie was quite frankly relieved. The image she had seen on the flyer a few days ago had brought everything hurtling back. Martina, the friend she had cherished, still missing after all these years. Even though she was only messing around with the children on the nursery slopes, she had been on edge the whole time, fearful that she or the children would fall and hurt themselves. The unease had lingered all week but now it was at full throttle and Jolie was tired of it all. She was desperate to leave and feel the familiarity of her home, to get the children back to their daily routines, where she would find solace in the monotony of it. The mountains seemed to have closed in even more around her and she had felt a compression on her chest for most of the day, which she hoped would lift with a large glass of red wine at dinner time.

Jolie could see the flyer in her mind's eye, as well as the look of distress on the face of the woman handing them out, who she now realised was Martina's mother. Jolie had never met Martina's mother, but she had hoped that one day their friendship would blossom further so that she could have met some of Martina's family. She appeared to be a woman who was worn out by it all – two decades of searching for her daughter. Jolie felt her gut tighten at the prospect of it happening to her. She imagined Vita missing, not knowing where she was or what had happened to her, and she felt the terror grip her as though it were real and not just imagined. Jolie had wanted to run after Martina's mother, to touch her arm and tell her how sorry she was. What else could she say that would carry any meaning? She had always carried this doubt with her, a fragmented part of herself she had tried to file away under 'Martina', but it refused to stay where she placed it. As much as Jolie wanted to offer Martina's mother a nugget of information to help ease her hopelessness, she knew she couldn't.

There was a loud crash from the kitchen, and Jolie jumped. The glass of wine she had just drunk had done nothing for her frayed nerves. She looked around the restaurant, her body in a state of hypervigilance. She should feel more relaxed than this; it was done. She had survived. She just needed to get home now, and while travelling could often be stressful, especially with young children, she was looking forward to it more than anything. She still had all the packing to do when they got back from the restaurant, which she had left until the last minute because she wanted to have something to keep her mind occupied tonight. She wanted the evening to pass quickly. They would all be on the coach in a few hours, travelling to Barcelona and then flying home.

'I guess I'll see you tomorrow then,' Idris said through a yawn, and Jolie felt that pang of envy. The lodge they'd had for this last week had been more than ample and some people would have given their right arm to have what she'd had. But these weren't usual circumstances. If Jolie had been anywhere else on the planet, she could have appreciated what she was experiencing; she would have taken time to pause and feel the moment, burn the memory in.

'I guess I will.' Jolie felt a jolt of tiredness and a longing to be out of the noisy restaurant.

'Goodnight.' Idris blew her a kiss and rang off.

Jolie turned to her children as they scooped up the final dregs of their ice cream. She took both of their iPads and downloaded a few new films for the coach and the plane.

Once she had done that, she paid the bill and left the restaurant for the final time.

It was dark back at the lodge, and when Jolie reached for the key in her coat pocket, she felt the flyer rub against her hand. She hadn't been able to get rid of it; it was a weird fascination, that a time in history she had been a part of was still being thought about every year. Although she didn't doubt that Martina's mother thought of her missing daughter daily, Jolie was intrigued by her dedication, how she had continued to search for her daughter for all these years. Jolie recollected that Martina is . . . was an only child. It was something that Martina had made a big deal about, 'only child syndrome' she had called it, and they had laughed about it and aligned it with Martina's tendencies to be quite selfish and spoilt occasionally. Perhaps it was why she had thrown such fantastic tantrums and made such a spectacle of herself.

Martina had often found herself in trouble, often pissing people off. Jolie felt a shudder as she remembered how Martina could be. They may have laughed about it, but it had annoyed Jolie. The whining, the way she had to make everything about her. But they had been friends, and so Jolie chose to overlook the annoyances and focus on the things that she did like and admire about Martina.

'I can't wait to see Daddy,' Vita said quietly as they entered the lodge.

'Me too,' Gable agreed.

Once the children were inside the lodge, Jolie turned in the doorway and a sharp cold wind whipped at her body. She shivered. She really could not wait to get back home, away from the endless cold and snow. Whilst there had been times at the top of the mountain when she had felt the heat, she was now tired of traipsing through snow and wet clothes and generally feeling quite cold and then going into a café or bar and getting too warm. And here the memories of her past and the mistakes she had made were too close for comfort. It was as though the mountains that surrounded her were looking down at her and pointing their fingers. Because they knew; they had seen it all.

'Me three,' Jolie added and the children giggled as she closed the door and locked the lodge.

She thought they would be too tired to miss him, but alas, no amount of distraction, exercise, and time outdoors could stop them from pining for their daddy.

Jolie tucked Gable and Vita into bed after their showers. Gable wanted to read, so Jolie left the side lamp on. She would let him stay up all night and read if he wanted to; she wanted him to love books that much.

Jolie went into the living space where she had piled all the clothes, toiletries, and cases and began squeezing everything back inside them again.

Just after 10 p.m., she had everything stacked by the door, ready to get on the bus at 7 a.m. She could hardly believe she would be back in London in less than twenty-four hours and that she could put the last week behind her. She had been strong to come here, she realised now, and to see out the last few days alone without Idris around, but she had lost all of her strength now, and she was managing on just her last frayed nerves. Since she had seen that flyer, she had allowed herself to crumble, as though she had given herself permission. It was enough. It was too much. Although she hadn't looked her in the eye when she had accepted the flyer, once she had realised that it was Martina's mother who had pressed it into her hand, she was overcome with a slow-burning terror that had spread through her and gripped her a little harder with each passing day.

Then came the flashbacks and the memories, everything she had vowed to forget, because why would she want to carry such a monumental event around? She had a very nice life now: a five-bedroom townhouse in Kensington was where she called home; she drove a Mercedes GLA SUV, did her weekly shop in Waitrose and took regular spa days with her friends.

But most of all, she didn't need to work, which had its pros and cons. After her first time here in Cil del món, she returned to England, moved to London, sofa surfed for a few months, flat shared for a few years even though the proximity of virtual strangers pained her. She tried to hold down various jobs until she took on a job as a host at a Soho club, where Idris had found her, after an arduous shift, staring into the bottom of her glass. After that, she didn't need to work again. And whilst she had attempted several times to dip her foot back into the world of employment, Idris always insisted she was doing the best job where she was, at home raising their children whilst he was at work.

And whilst each day bore its challenges from playground politics to PTAs, she was content.

Jolie took out the flyer again and clutched it tightly in her hand. She studied Martina's face: her smooth olive skin, dark eyes, and luscious brown hair streaked with colour and sparkle. She would be forty-three now, a year older than Jolie.

She wondered what she would be doing with her life. Martina's mother obviously thought that she was still alive somewhere; otherwise, why else would she be here all these years later, searching for her?

Jolie scrutinised the image of the girl she had known so well, so long ago, and she thought that after what had happened, her mother was fighting a fruitless mission.

Because back then, Martina hadn't stood a chance.

8

JOLIE

TWENTY YEARS AGO

'I expect you to be here at exactly 8 a.m. every morning. You make the muffins; we use this pre-pack. They rarely notice, and it smells fresh and home-made.'

Estelle, the CEO of Tranquil Lodges, was Catalan. She had lived in the Pyrenees mountains all her life. To Jolie, Estelle oozed glamour. She wore a white trouser suit; her hair was dyed a golden brown – Jolie could just about see the dark roots appearing – and she wore dark red lipstick that was perfectly applied and matte on her full lips. Estelle picked up a packet of muffin mix; her long red fingernails stuck out comically as she tried to grip it. Jolie realised that those fingers wouldn't be stuck in a washing-up bowl or scraping muffin mix from a bowl; they would only be seeing the keys of a computer or the receiver of a telephone.

Estelle had worked hard to make the business a success, as she had explained in her opening speech when Jolie met her outside the bank an hour ago. There had been an awkward greeting between Estelle and Martina. Martina had left her to it, and Estelle had taken her straight to one of the lodges where Jolie would be working each day for the next four or five months, driving her there even though it was a mere five-minute walk from Jolie's apartment.

'Next, you fry the bacon and eggs and leave the bread here for toast next to the toaster.' Estelle went on in her Catalan accent. She would work between 8 a.m. and 1 p.m. and then 5 and 9 p.m., six days a week. That gave Jolie four hours to herself in the afternoon. Estelle explained that she would usually finish work by 9 p.m. at the latest. During those shifts, she would be expected to make the beds each morning, change bedsheets halfway through the week, cook breakfast, prepare and serve dinner and keep the kitchen and communal areas tidy.

'Do not touch the bedrooms other than to make the beds,' Estelle told her and then looked at her for longer than Jolie thought was necessary.

'Okay, I understand,' Jolie said. 'I get it,' she added under her breath, and Estelle gave her a sidelong look. Was Estelle thinking she needed to watch this one? It wasn't as though Jolie's true destiny was to be here; she should be at home, finishing her degree. She was here because her parents had forced her out of the house. It was clear her parents were so disappointed with her that she was not welcome. Would she ever be welcome again? She wasn't sure. She had never been given the chance to explain the circumstances to them. In a way the truth was worse than them believing she had simply flunked a course.

This had to work out for her; she had to start building a life for herself now. She had no support from her family, and she couldn't name one person she could still call a friend – someone she could reach out to in a crisis. She was officially on her own. But that was fine; she was new here, and she was going to start again. Make new friends and be a good friend. Yet as she stood listening to Estelle drone on about which pan to use for what dish and how to dry and stack the plates, she felt deflated and wondered why she hadn't gone to Bali instead.

She had been attracted to a ski season because of the social scene. She knew that every night the staff gathered in the bars to celebrate. Working with hangovers was a common occurrence here. She had read and also heard from people she knew who had undertaken similar trips, but that was fine because Jolie was a professional at managing a hangover.

The tour/induction finally ended, and Jolie got back into Estelle's white SUV – she sensed a fashion pattern here – and Estelle drove her to her apartment in the village. There were about thirty individual apartments in her block, and already, as she entered the foyer, she could smell the vibe. It was like arriving at university two years ago. Another year and she could have maybe scraped by with a 2:1 in sports psychology, but she had only come away with a first in partying. She had enjoyed quite a lot of the theory, but she had struggled to focus her mind a lot of the time, and that wasn't always to do with the remnants of alcohol in her body. Towards the end of her time at university, she could no longer control her spiralling thoughts. There was a nagging feeling that had taken up permanent residence around her body, pulling her down, and a voice that was whispering to her, 'You're not worth anything. You're unlikeable.' Jolie was adamant she would overcome that now, and even become someone who had as much confidence as Martina.

And she didn't need to just rely on the voice in her head. Her phone had told her that she was no longer welcome, as each day she received fewer and fewer texts for invites out to the café or bars. When she finally left, realising she wasn't going to pass her course and the pain of losing touch with everyone she had got to know there became too much, her parents had little to say about her apparent failings, but they didn't need to use words. She would see it in their eyes and the shared looks they gave one another when they thought she wasn't looking. She had let them down. Their only daughter, who had meant to amount to so much more. She wondered, in the end, if they had cared if she had succeeded or not? They had been quick enough to say goodbye to her, to be the ones to instigate it.

Jolie was determined to have a good time and enjoy herself, because when she thought of her parents, she would instantly see those looks, followed by a burning shame that she had yet to amount to anything. However, that didn't matter because no one knew her here; she could be whoever she wanted.

Estelle watched as Jolie pulled both her suitcases, but she didn't offer to help. But then, with those nails, why would she risk breaking them on one of the mammoth cases? Jolie's room was on the first floor, a short flight up in the lift and along the corridor.

The space was small. There was just one room with a sofa bed, a kitchenette, and a bathroom, which surprisingly had a bath and a shower. This was not what she had been used to at home, or even when she had been studying and had lived in halls. This was far more luxurious and a lot quieter. It was all hers, and she didn't have to answer to anyone or share anything. Finally, she felt so wonderfully free.

The best part about the apartment was the balcony. It was large enough that she could sit out and look over the street, take a beer or a glass of wine, and relax. That was all Jolie wanted from this trip: to enjoy herself without feeling guilty, not to have to look at faces filled with displeasure, and maybe make a couple of good friends.

'Now I leave you,' Estelle said and extravagantly twirled – holding out her hands – around the room as though she were highlighting just how fortunate Jolie was to receive this brilliant accommodation as part of her working package – that and a ski pass for the entire season.

'Okay. Thank you, Estelle.'

'You will be at lodge 15 at 8 a.m. sharp. Okay?'

'Of course!' Jolie said with a smile, thinking that she had the rest of the afternoon and evening to herself and that as soon as Estelle left, she was going to go out and find a bar. In the back of her mind, she was thinking of the girl, Martina, she had met at the café earlier. She seemed fun, and just the sort of person Jolie wanted to get to know.

9

JOLIE

NOW

The skidoo took them and all their luggage up to the main road, where the coach was waiting to get them to the airport. It had been a stressful morning with Vita losing Pooky, her beloved teddy, meaning Jolie had to empty two of the three suitcases until she found him buried in the bottom of the second one. What had she been thinking? She had been thinking about Martina Acosta and the damn flyer she had taken off her mother. She had barely slept either, as thoughts and images and even voices came at her from her past in vivid, enigmatic dreams. No matter how she had tried to get Martina out of her head, she had come in and made herself comfortable amongst her conscious thoughts. It was all there coming back to her in great waves, and Jolie found it difficult to concentrate and do her usual immaculate packing. She must have unconsciously grabbed the teddy and stuffed it into the suitcase.

By the time they had left the lodge and reached the road, Jolie was feeling flushed and frantic. She took deep breaths as the skidoo driver took all their luggage and left it by the coach.

'Thanks, Anthony,' Jolie said, and he gave them all a salute and bounded off.

Her mind was still reeling. She was tired, her brain buzzing, and every little noise from her children set her already frayed nerves on edge. So, when she stepped inside the coach, initially she didn't notice the driver waving her off or that there was no one else on the bus.

'Cancelled, cancelled,' he said and waved his hand as Jolie began to make her way down the aisle. She looked back at the confused expressions on her children's faces, and then she looked through the window, where a group of people were standing around clutching their phones, faces to the screens.

'Is *this* coach cancelled?' Jolie asked. She did not speak enough Catalan to ask him if another coach was coming. But the driver just looked away from her and waved his hand to dismiss her.

'Come on, children.' She ushered Vita and Gable off the coach and moved towards a circle of men and women.

'Is there another coach coming?' she asked, aware of the time and how long it would take to drive from here to Barcelona.

'No, apparently not,' a woman said in a shrill American accent. 'The God damn flights are cancelled.'

'What?' Jolie's heart raced; she was having a strange out-of-body experience. This wasn't happening. This couldn't be happening, and she wouldn't believe it. 'Which flights? Your flights?'

'All the flights, honey,' she said, tapping away furiously on her phone.

'That's why this man won't take us to the airport; there are no flights leaving Barcelona,' the man standing next to her, also with an American accent, said.

'What do you mean no flights?' Jolie was aware she sounded mildly hysterical but she didn't care. She just wanted it all to be wrong, and for another coach to come and get them immediately.

'I mean every single flight has been cancelled. For the foreseeable,' the American woman told her.

Jolie felt gripped with panic. 'Is it a terrorist attack?' she whispered so her children wouldn't hear.

'I don't think so,' the American man said, looking at his phone for confirmation. 'From what I am getting, there has been a major disruption with the air traffic control systems, some huge failure, and so no flights will be heading out today from any airports. Or tomorrow, I very much doubt.' The man looked at Jolie and smiled. 'I have a friend who works in security at Barcelona airport. He's seen this sort of thing before. It will cause major disruption for days if not weeks.'

Jolie's mouth went dry, and her heart felt as though it might burst right out of her chest. She needed to sit down and put her head between her legs. The attack she was usually so ready to tackle was proving too much. She was tired, and she had barely slept. Both of which were aiding the anxiety. Days. Weeks. Why did this man look and sound so upbeat? He was clearly not fazed by being stuck in another country with no way out.

'Looks like it's a few more days' skiing for us,' he said, looking over at the woman who Jolie presumed was his wife.

'Oh God, I am so done with the snow,' she said and pulled her face into an exaggerated expression of exasperation. 'Get me to a beach.'

Jolie would have chatted along with her if it weren't for the massive ball stuck in her throat, preventing her from speaking and restricting her breathing.

'What's happening, Mummy?' came Vita's voice. Gable's face wore a strained expression, much like Idris's when he was trying to work something out. He was always striving to be brave and grown-up.

'I just bought a lodge here last year. This is my wife's first time skiing. I think I might have to sell it.' The American man laughed. 'I think she actually hates it.'

Jolie tried to smile, but her mouth barely twitched at the edges. She was focusing hard, thinking what the hell she was going to do.

She looked around at the others crowded around the coach, bewildered and staring at their phones.

'Mummy?' came Vita's voice again.

Jolie looked down at her daughter. 'Erm, it looks like the airport might be closed today.' Jolie forced the words out.

'So do we stay here?' Gable asked. Jolie's gut wrenched at the slight tremor in his voice. He tried to hide his worries and insecurities so hard, but Jolie could hear and feel them. He may not have a Pooky bear like Vita, but he sought security in other ways.

'I'm not sure, Gable. Let me try and call Daddy and see what he thinks.'

Jolie took her phone and noted the pathetic reception. How were all these people getting such good coverage?

'What to do,' she said quietly. The cases were too big and heavy for the children to carry themselves. Suddenly, she heard the comforting sound of a skidoo up ahead and she waved her arms as though she were flagging down a taxi.

The driver stopped and lifted his goggles.

'Hi, we just left our accommodation; I wondered if you would mind returning our luggage. Our flight has been cancelled, and I need to leave it there until I know what we're doing.'

The driver nodded and loaded the luggage onto the skidoo.

'It's number 70,' Jolie added.

'Our luggage is going back on this again,' Vita said, always the one to comment on their minute-to-minute activities.

'Afraid so.'

The children watched as the skidoo disappeared down the mountain.

'Race you back down the hill,' Jolie said, thankful they were all still wearing their snow boots.

When they arrived outside the lodge, Jolie felt a flutter of panic as she saw the door was already open and a second skidoo parked outside, full of cleaning equipment.

'For the love of God.'

Jolie walked to the door, and a maid dressed in a blue polo shirt with the Tranquil Lodges logo on it looked at her curiously.

'Hi, we just checked out of here a little while ago,' Jolie told the maid.

'And did you forget something?' the maid asked in a Spanish accent.

'We didn't, but it turns out our flight has been cancelled, so, well, I guess we might need the lodge for another night or two.'

'I am afraid that is not possible,' the maid replied.

'What? Why not?' She glanced at both of her children, who were looking up at her with anticipation, waiting to hear how their mummy was going to solve this problem. She calmed herself and her words came less flustered this time.

'I have two children, my flight has been cancelled, and I need to leave my luggage here for a few hours. I can pay extra. How much?'

'I cannot, I'm afraid. This is booked for someone; they will arrive soon, so I am cleaning.' The maid held her cloth aloft to demonstrate.

'Someone is coming now, another family?'

'Yes, a family.'

Jolie felt herself go cold. She looked around at the mountains, and they seemed to be moving in towards her. There was a sudden cold blast that seemed to envelop her, and she was reminded of how she had shivered outside the lodge last night, feeling as though the resort was trying to keep her here, pulling her in and holding her hostage. She shook her head, tried to focus on what needed to be done, even though a tightness in her chest and throat made her feel as though she couldn't breathe. Everywhere would be fully booked. It was the busiest time of the season. This was a tiny resort with two hotels and lodges.

Just think, Jolie, she told herself as she began to take a few deep breaths. Perhaps there might be a spare room at one of the hotels for a night or two. But first, she would need to do several things. She would need to check the airline on her phone to find out if the flights were indeed cancelled and when she would be able to get another one, then she would need to call Idris. He might have another view on this, and maybe he could book their flights and transfer his end while she concentrated on finding somewhere for them to stay for a night or two, or however long the flights were cancelled for.

'Right, come on then, you two.' Jolie gathered Gable and Vita and ushered them away from the door. She sighed and turned and looked at the maid. 'Thanks,' she said, although she wasn't sure what she was thanking her for.

Jolie settled Gable and Vita in the café with chocolate milk and a croissant each and ordered herself a latte. She felt sick and probably wouldn't finish it; it was more of a token drink as she checked her phone. The café was busy, everyone staring frantically at their phones. Jolie pulled hers out and opened the airline app. There it was: a notification.

> We're sorry. We have had to cancel this flight.

'Where is the button to book another flight?' Jolie muttered anxiously under her breath.

'What, Mummy?' Vita asked; a chocolate moustache had appeared on her upper lip. Part of Jolie's brain wanted to search her bag for a wet wipe; another part was too focused on the flight app. There had to be an offer of another flight or a link to take her somewhere to book one. But there was nothing.

Jolie went to another flight website, but again, nothing. She tried another and then another until she had tried them all, and there were none. There were no flights leaving Barcelona or Toulouse, or other airports in France. There was not a single airport that was taking flights back to the UK.

She googled 'flight cancelled Barcelona'. Her phone filled with news reports about cancelled flights. She clicked on one and saw words that didn't make much sense.

Hundreds of flights cancelled in fallout from UK air traffic control failure.

'This is the fucking UK's fault,' Jolie said but not quietly enough because a small voice said 'Mummy' and she glanced up to see Vita glaring at her. 'Bad word.'

'Sorry,' Jolie said. And she looked back down at her phone. 'Right, shall we call Daddy?'

'Yay!' came the joint response from both Gable and Vita.

'I've tried everything,' Idris said to Jolie after they had spent five minutes trying to have a conversation as a four until Jolie lost all patience and sent the children back to their seats and ordered more pastries.

'Everything? Are you sure? Can you get Angie on it? Get her to keep checking. Everyone will be trying to get flights home; it will be like getting tickets for Glastonbury. We need someone on the flight apps all the time.'

'Angie doesn't get paid to help me with my personal life,' Idris said quietly.

'Angie and your firm are the reason I am stuck out here in the first place!' Jolie raised her voice loud enough to attract the attention of her children and a few diners on neighbouring tables.

'I didn't mean that . . . I just meant she can't be assigned to the task twenty-four-seven. Of course, we will all be doing everything we can to get you home.'

Jolie took a few calming deep breaths.

'Are you feeling okay?' Idris asked tentatively.

'As well as I can be,' Jolie said.

'Of course. You're doing great. This will all be over soon, I promise.'

Jolie wanted to cry, but she pushed down the tears for the sake of her children and because she didn't want Idris to worry and think that she was going to fall apart. It was just a cancelled flight. Well, hundreds of cancelled flights. But she would see it through. The way she had seen the last week through.

'I can't be calling around hotels and checking flight apps and looking after the children, Idris.' Jolie's exasperation evolved into anger. Jolie said her husband's name with such contempt that the woman on the next table shot her a look.

'I don't expect you to,' Idris said and then he was silent for a few seconds. 'Is there a forum, on Facebook, somewhere you could put out a post?'

'I suppose.' Jolie wasn't really listening anymore. She was beginning to think she would be spending the next few nights on the streets and she felt a small spike of terror jolt through her.

'Ask who has availability, there must be lodges free or rooms somewhere,' Idris continued.

'The Wi-Fi is horrendous.'

'No, Jolie. Your coverage is horrendous. I told you to switch suppliers months ago, but you wanted to remain faithful.'

'I've been their customer for twelve years.'

'Yes, and you have had zero coverage since you got there. You only get any reception when you connect to someone's Wi-Fi. It's like living in the Dark Ages with you. It's not as if I can't afford to put you on a better contract. You should have moved over with me—'

'Idris, please stop talking now. I have a headache. At this rate, your children and I will be sleeping on the streets tonight. Do you even care?'

'Of course I care, Jolie. I can't do much else but look in the same places as you. Do what I suggested: get on a forum; you're on enough ones at home.'

Jolie looked around the café and heard the tiredness in Idris's voice.

'I'm going to go.'

'Okay, sweetheart, call me back as soon as anything changes,' Idris said.

'Will do.'

Jolie hung up without saying goodbye.

She looked over at Gable and Vita, tucking into another round of pastries, watching something on Gable's iPad, and giggling together, and she opened up Facebook. She quickly found a forum for Cil del món, the one she had joined before they arrived here. She began typing a post.

> Due to the air traffic control failure, my children and I are stranded here. We need accommodation for at least tonight and until we can get flights back to the UK. If anyone has anything or knows anyone who has a lodge or a room for a few days, please get in touch with me here or on the following number.

Jolie typed in her number and pressed post.

Then she set down her phone and looked around her at the chaos, listening to the noise. She tried to shut it all out, but all she could think was that she was stuck back in the very same café she'd frequented twenty years ago, trapped in her past, and right now, there was no way for her to escape.

10

RONA

Rona stood outside on the village path, watching the flurry of people coming and going. Every single lodge was booked out. People were arriving, and the resort was packed with those who couldn't get back to the airport or get on a plane due to all the flights that had been cancelled in the UK.

Watching so many people move around the resort was stressful, but at least it was good for Tranquil Lodges. As long as the business was thriving, that was all that mattered.

Rona stood outside the lodge that had just been vacated. She watched the girls rushing in with their caddies of cleaning products.

She nodded at one of them, acknowledging their hard work. Rona knew how exhausting this part of the job was. But she liked to come down to the lodges to check on the girls and make sure they were leaving them like the five-star accommodation they were supposed to be.

Rona turned and headed back down the hill to her apartment. Once inside, she flicked the switch on the kettle and then collapsed into her desk chair.

She opened up Facebook. She was part of many forums for Cil del món. She liked to see what everyone was saying. There was usually a lot of advice seeking. Were the resorts child-friendly, how much snow was there at the moment, what were the restaurants like? People would also chat about their holiday experiences, and Rona went full voyeur, picking up on any slight bit of negativity about the lodges and addressing it immediately. This was part of her daily routine, to check in on what customers were chatting about, and in a way, she enjoyed it as much as the other aspects of being a manager of a busy hospitality company. It was another box ticked at the end of the day. Another way to satisfy her otherwise busy brain.

She browsed through the latest posts. Many people were panicking over the latest news about the flights, so there was a lot of discussion about that. The kettle boiled, and so Rona stood up and made herself a coffee. She took it back to her seat and carried on scrolling. She stopped when she saw a post with a name that made her heart lurch a little. It was an unusual name and one she rarely came across. On the few occasions she had seen or heard it in the last twenty years, she had recoiled. And that was the same response she was having now because, somehow, she just knew. The profile picture was of a woman with two small children, an older man who looked in his mid-forties, with one arm placed on the shoulder of the older child, a boy, and the other arm placed tightly around the arm of the woman.

Jolie. She didn't need to look for long before she realised that it was *the* Jolie. Jolie Morgan. But this wasn't the surname she was using now. She was obviously married now as the surname on the profile was Holloway. She clicked on the post.

> Due to the air traffic control failure, my children and I are stranded here. We need accommodation for at least tonight and until we can get flights back to the UK. If anyone has anything or knows anyone who has a lodge or a room for a few days, please get in touch with me here or on the following number.

Rona noted that it was posted early this morning. Underneath were a handful of comments apologising that they couldn't help and suggestions of places she might try, but Rona knew all too well that they would all be full at this time of year. Rona thought this was a fascinating situation. She knew all the lodges were booked, but she just might be able to find something special for Jolie.

Twenty years might have passed, but Rona was intrigued. It was fate, Rona thought. After all this time, Jolie was back in town. And Rona was going to help her.

11

JOLIE

TWENTY YEARS AGO

The bar was heaving, hot and sweaty. A band, consisting of two guitarists, sang a range of classic sing-along songs. Jolie recognised Adam as one of the guitarists. He seemed to catch her eye, and she lifted her hand to wave, but he looked away, not recognising her. Of course, she thought, trying not to feel deflated. He had barely seen her in the café earlier. The middle of the bar was full of people dancing. Jolie had utterly lost all sense of who she was. She couldn't believe she had only arrived here a few hours ago. She had no cares; she only had herself to worry about.

As much as she was throwing off the shackles of her old life, the memories weren't going anywhere just yet. She could still see the tired and disappointed faces of her parents, she could still hear the frustrated voices of her friends from university, and then there was silence – the unanswered calls and ignored text messages. That was worse than any of it. She would rather be screamed at and called every name they could muster, but when they ran out of words, that was when it hit the worst.

Jolie knew that these memories would fade; soon they would just be a murmur in the back of her mind and, eventually, she could live her life without being reminded every day of who she had been, what she had done and how many people she had upset. Her parents had been frustrated with her from the moment she was able to talk; she was sure of it. It still hurt how they had been so quick to say goodbye, to make her departure official and to ensure that she understood she wouldn't be welcome home anymore.

She tried to recall a few words that had resonated and felt vaguely as though she were being wished well, but she couldn't. She did this because they were her parents. Her mother had given birth to her; they had to still love her. But just like her friends, once their anger had subsided, they were almost neutral when she had left. Emotionless.

So she used what little energy she had left that day to dance and forget about England and the life she'd so suddenly had to leave behind. She would find safety and happiness amongst the cold of the mountains, and warmth and claustrophobia in the bars. Here, she could be anyone she wanted. It was a fresh start. She would make new friends. She would reinvent herself.

Jolie knew it was late. She had been in the pub for many hours. She thought of her new job starting tomorrow and how she was a little nervous. She wanted to make a good impression on her first day, but she was bound to make a few mistakes to begin with.

A small group had very quickly surrounded her, and she was trying to remember all their names: a young bloke from Argentina called Arnie, a petite girl from France called Sabrina, and another guy called Paul from Bristol. Jolie hadn't laughed so hard for such a long time. How was it that people could be so happy? At university, she'd had a good time, but people were stressed with exams and assignments, and she was never quite sure where she stood with most of them. But here, she felt everyone was genuine, and they had no hidden agenda; they just wanted to live, be free, have fun, make a little money, and ski or snowboard. She could sense that after just a few hours.

'Let's sit down,' Sabrina shouted across the music. Jolie nodded and they found seats at a table near the bar.

The boys joined them.

'Who wants a shot?' Arnie asked.

'Yes!' Sabrina shouted.

Jolie gulped and looked down at her feet, hoping she would get overlooked or they might disregard the idea. Maybe someone would look at their watch and realise it was almost midnight and they all needed to be up in a few hours. Jolie so wanted to be different this time. She wanted to be mature and responsible and, mostly, she wanted to be refreshed for her first day and she didn't want to let Estelle down; of course she didn't. She intended to keep her job until the end. But she needed to ensure she made friends and kept them, and if that involved having a few extra shots, what was so wrong with that? An image of Estelle came to her mind. Behind that pristine exterior, she was certain her new boss had claws and teeth, and she could destroy her.

Jolie looked at Sabrina hopefully. She was a housekeeper for the hotel; did she not need to turn in soon, so she could be as fresh as a daisy for work? But Sabrina didn't need to work face to face with her clients; she could plug her earphones in and not be bothered by anyone. Whereas Jolie could be hosting up to ten guests and needed to be sociable and vibrant.

'I still cannot believe you work for Tranquil. You are so lucky.' Sabrina had been sick with envy earlier when Jolie told her she worked for Tranquil Lodges.

'You wouldn't last five minutes in that job,' Paul, a ski instructor from Bristol said. Then he looked at Jolie. 'But you look a bit more robust.'

Jolie spat out a laugh. 'Robust? What is that supposed to mean?'

Sabrina was looking at Paul with intrigue. Jolie studied his face too. He wasn't bad-looking, but Jolie had already noted that he took himself far too seriously.

'I just mean, the workload, the people you work for, I heard it can get . . . challenging. That's all.' Paul sounded as though he were backtracking.

'Well, I like a challenge.' Jolie lifted her glass as if to toast herself.

'I'm sure you do.' Finally, Paul managed to crack a smile that seemed quite genuine. 'I think you'll do great. Cheers.' He held his glass of beer out and clinked Jolie's vodka and Diet Coke. Jolie smiled and he looked at her for a few extra seconds before Jolie quickly looked away. She wasn't sure if there was some sort of meaning to his words; was she really being warned or was it just a bit of friendly advice?

Jolie didn't care how challenging the job might be; she was here to succeed and do her very best.

The final person in their small party was Arnie. He worked in a hotel at the top of the village as a chef.

'Jolie?' Arnie asked. 'Shot?'

Jolie recoiled at Arnie's words but she contorted her face into a smile and looked up. 'Absolutely,' she replied. She didn't want to risk missing her opportunity to secure friendships. These early interactions were crucial in showing people that you were laid-back and likeable.

'Good girl,' Arnie said.

'No more for me,' Paul said. 'I've have an early morning class on the nursery slopes. Need to be focused for the little terrors.'

Why couldn't Jolie just say no like that and walk away guilt-free, not worrying if her new-found friends would think her a lightweight on her first night here?

Then Paul surprised Jolie by leaning in and kissing her on the cheek. Suddenly, everything distorted around her, and she felt as though it were just her and Paul, and all his attention was on her. Her surroundings blurred, and the music seemed to slow and fade. Then Paul stood back from her and moved towards Sabrina. He did the exact same, kissing her on both cheeks and then shook Arnie's hand. Jolie must be drunk if she thought someone might fancy her on the first night. Besides, she reminded herself, she was here to work on self-love. She wasn't seeking the distraction of a man.

'Look after these ladies,' Paul said to Arnie and then he leaned in and whispered to Jolie, 'I'm here if you need help with anything.'

Jolie looked at the others to see if they had noticed. He definitely wasn't bad-looking, Jolie thought again, and noted that he hadn't given Sabrina a final look before he left. Jolie felt a sudden thickness in her throat as though she might cry. She was tired. It was late. She had been travelling most of the day. Now Paul had excused himself; perhaps she should just follow suit. But first, there was the shot to deal with.

Arnie arrived back with a tray of six shots.

Jolie's heart fluttered, and her stomach tensed. *Just walk away*, her mind was telling her; the other part of her brain was saying it would be fine. She was in a new place; no one would judge her on the first day at work.

Arnie handed her a shot and she took it and downed it.

The alarm on Jolie's watch went off at 7 a.m. She sat bolt upright. She was instantly filled with regret. She could feel the alcohol still in her body; she would feel it until at least lunchtime. She couldn't remember much about the last part of the evening. But she had told herself that she would take the shots and then leave. Just walk out. People did that when they were drunk; it was like a homing beacon. Jolie had done it enough times. She hoped and prayed that was precisely what she had done last night.

Please, please, please, Jolie chanted to herself. *Please don't let me have said anything.*

She needed to get to lodge 15 in an hour, so she got in the shower and afterwards dressed in jogging bottoms and a thin woollen long-sleeve top. She applied some light make-up and tied her hair back. She assessed herself in the mirror and silently told herself it was going to be okay. She was going to be okay.

She put on her trainers – she still needed to buy herself snow boots – and snow jacket and walked the short distance to the lodge. She had a key and let herself in, which felt weird. Inside, the first thing she noticed was the mess. Then her eyes were drawn to the living area, where a small child was curled on the sofa, watching a film on the TV. It was a Disney film that Jolie loved. She moved closer to the child, who briefly looked up and then turned back to the TV.

'Hi,' Jolie said, 'I love this film. Is this your favourite?'

The girl, who Jolie gauged to be about four years old, looked at her again and shrugged.

'Not a morning person, huh? Me neither. I stayed up late last night.' Jolie leaned on the arm of the sofa. 'So I'm pretty tired.'

The girl was looking at her with interest and anticipation now, as though she were a magician and she might perform a spur-of-the-moment trick.

'Hello, can I help you?' came a clipped female voice. Jolie looked up, and a woman in a pink and orange kimono, her hair long and wavy down to her shoulders, was walking across the living area towards the child, trying to tie the kimono up at the front as she walked.

Jolie jumped to her feet. 'I'm the lodge host.'

The woman looked at her with confusion. She sat beside the little girl and put her arm around her, smoothing her hair against her forehead.

'Oh, that's right. I didn't want one but the other family insisted.'

Jolie was taken aback.

'Oh, don't be offended; it will be a nice help. There are five children here, seven if you include the men. It will be busy. And messy. I'm Ali.'

'Hi, Ali,' Jolie said brightly, still feeling perturbed and confused by the initial reaction from Ali. Didn't she know that these lodges came with the hosts, that it was part of the luxury element?

Jolie cast her eyes around the space, which comprised a living area, open-plan kitchen, and dining area.

'Don't mind me.' Ali waved her hand about. 'I'm not very good with strangers. Especially around the kids.'

'Well, I had my disclosure thing done,' Jolie said, trying to remember the name of the document she brought with her from England to show she wasn't a paedophile or a convicted murderer.

'Oh yes, I understand, but anyone can forge those things. They don't prove anything really do they?' Ali looked at Jolie.

'I suppose not. No,' Jolie said to appease the woman. She was sure it was easy to fake anything if you wanted to.

Jolie felt a pang in her gut, a sudden regret that she had come here, or maybe it was just the remnants of alcohol buzzing around her body, making her feel paranoid and anxious.

Ali stood up. 'Well, you look okay.' She walked past her to the kitchen. 'As you can see, everyone settled in very well yesterday.' She gestured to the mess.

'Er, yes,' Jolie said. 'Would you like me to start breakfast?'

Ali let out a massive sigh as though life was just one colossal inconvenience right now.

'I suppose. I'm not hungry. I never eat in the morning, but the others will be, I presume.'

Ali looked at her as if she were still trying to accept her presence, filled a glass with water from a bottle on the kitchen work surface, and returned to the sofa to rejoin her child. There, she began fussing with her hair unnecessarily again, until the girl gently lifted her mother's hand and moved it away.

Jolie took a deep breath and began cleaning the kitchen.

An hour later, her workspace was sparkling. Fresh American pancakes, a fruit platter, and jugs of orange juice were on the dining table. Jolie had set it for nine, with cutlery, plates, and glasses. The muffins were in the oven and she was about to start frying eggs and bacon. She had just turned on the kettle to make a cafetiere of coffee when she heard some commotion coming from the doorway, and four young boys came running in, followed by a striking man dressed in a white Stussy T-shirt and green combat trousers. Jolie, still near-inebriated, felt a tingling in her stomach. She wondered if she were still drunk as the words 'Now aren't you a sight for sore eyes?' were on the tip of her lips.

She had to press her mouth together to stop them from coming out. The man's eyes rested on her long enough for Jolie to recognise the interest. A tall blonde-haired lady followed him out, looking pristine in a white turtleneck and tight blue ski pants. Actual ski pants, Jolie thought. She had only seen those in images from the 1980s.

'Don't just stand there, Duncan,' the woman said and gave Jolie a quick glance up and down. 'You must be the maid,' she said as she arrived next to the table. Jolie went to correct her and tell her that she absolutely wasn't the maid. She was the host, but the woman was speaking again.

'This all looks fantastic. Thanks so much. Are you here all week, or do we get a new one halfway through?'

'I will be your host for the entire week,' Jolie said, inserting her correct job title into the sentence. But the woman was picking at blueberries and didn't appear to have paid much attention.

'And do you have a name?' Duncan had also made his way to the table.

'Jolie,' she said, wondering if her initial thoughts of him might be betrayed by her face, which she could feel reddening. It was warm in the lodge and she had been working hard for the last hour.

'Jolie, that is an awesome name,' he said. 'And I'm sorry my wife called you a maid.'

The woman in ski pants looked at him.

'Did I?' She glanced at Jolie. 'I've spent a lot of time in America, and it's a thing there.'

'Jolie is our host,' Duncan said. 'I'm Duncan; this is Rebecca.' Rebecca made a little faux smile, and then Duncan pointed to the end of the table where the boys were tucking into the buffet.

'And three of those are ours,' he said. 'I don't even know which ones.' He waved his hand around.

'It's fine. It's my first day, so you're forgiven.' Jolie laughed a little and Rebecca eyed her.

'Your first day?' Duncan said. 'How does that work? Do they train you for this job? Do you just know everything?'

'I . . . well I know enough. I can cook and clean and organise, and they are the three main components to the job.'

Duncan nodded. 'I'm impressed. And slightly jealous. You get to live in the mountains for six months. I wish I could live in the mountains for six months,' he said, a little quieter to Jolie, but Rebecca's ears were pricked up, and she had heard.

'I'd say four weeks is just fine.' Rebecca rolled her eyes. She sidled up to Jolie. 'I would love him to be away longer; believe me, sharing a house with four males is not fun. He riles them up mostly. Absolute savages. And anyway, I get two weeks in Marbella with the girls for letting him come out here another few times during the season.' Rebecca sounded as though she was trying to impress Jolie. Jolie raised her eyebrows.

'Two weeks in Marbella. Wow,' she said to appease Rebecca.

But Jolie was really intrigued by Duncan's four holidays to the same resort. Why would he want or need to come here four times a year?

Jolie and Rebecca watched as the boys shoved pancakes into their mouths, practically whole, and guzzled orange juice.

'Hey, how about a little bit of fruit down there?' Rebecca pushed the bowl of blueberries towards the boys.

'Morning!' a pair of voices chorused, and Jolie looked up to see another man walk in with Ali.

'That's Ali and Mark,' Duncan said.

Jolie smiled at Ali as she glanced her way, but it was not reciprocated. Jolie felt a sharp pang in her stomach.

'I can't believe you got us rowdy lot for your first shift,' Duncan said, not looking as though he were ready to move away from the island and join his family. Jolie felt the relief wash through her; at least someone was willing to be polite.

'And on a hangover.' The words were out of Jolie's mouth before she even had time to consider them. It was that in-between stage of still drunk and a little bit hazy from a night of drinking that allowed those words to form and then make their way into the room. Her stomach tensed as she thought about the repercussions of what she had just said. She felt foolish. Would they go and speak to Estelle, tell her what an incompetent drunk they had as a host? How had this happened? On day one, she had already done the thing she had promised herself she would not do. Drink. And now she was boasting about it.

But there was something about Duncan that made her feel as though she was able to open up, tell him things that she wouldn't necessarily consider telling other people. She knew how mad it sounded even in her own head. She had known Duncan for five minutes.

Duncan let out a loud laugh. 'Celebrating your first night here, and why not. I doubt you'll be able to keep it up every night, but that is one of the job's perks.'

Jolie still felt utterly ashamed, even though Duncan was making a real effort to help her feel better about her misdemeanour. However, Jolie thought, he didn't seem to be trying at all; instead, it appeared he was being sincere. Which was refreshing.

Jolie smiled at Duncan, and he grinned back at her.

Suddenly, the door burst open, and there, in the doorway, bringing in all the cold with her, was the same girl she had met yesterday and who had helped pull her suitcase up the road.

Jolie looked at her.

'Martina?'

Martina was looking around the lodge, her gaze clouded. Her eyes finally rested on Jolie.

'You're working here?'

'Yes,' Jolie said. She went to the door, closed it, and Martina stepped forward.

'I thought I was working here. I mean, I thought this was my lodge.' Martina's expression was slack. 'Shit. What number is this?'

'Fifteen,' Rebecca called vaguely.

Martina looked at Jolie. 'Is that right?'

'Yes.' Jolie nodded.

Martina glanced across the room, rubbing her hands together as though dry-washing them. Rebecca was distracted from the children and was staring at her. Martina was looking back at her.

Duncan turned and his eyes rested on Martina.

'So, we've established this isn't your lodge then,' Duncan said loudly and brightly.

Martina pulled out a crumpled piece of paper from her jeans pocket. Jolie noted how Martina was dressed: not in comfortable working clothes like Jolie's, but as though she were going out. Jolie suspected that she had not yet been home to change, judging by the smell of cigarettes and alcohol on her and the faintest hint of body odour. She hadn't seen her in Mak's bar last night, so where had she been?

Martina looked down at the piece of paper. 'Sixteen, I'm sixteen.' She glanced over at Rebecca one more time. 'I'd better go; I'm late.' Martina turned and opened the door. Jolie followed her.

'I'm glad we didn't get that one,' Jolie heard Rebecca mutter to Ali, and Ali agreed with a low, all-knowing humming sound.

Martina stopped just before she stepped over the threshold. 'Are you around this evening?' she asked, and Jolie noticed that Martina wasn't really looking at her. Her eyes were darting over towards Duncan, who was now busy with the boys.

'Yes,' Jolie said quickly. When she met Martina yesterday, she was intrigued and had enjoyed listening to her broken Spanish accent, the way she had involved her in her conversation with her boyfriend almost immediately, and the way she had helped with her luggage. Jolie wanted to spend more time in this girl's company, get to know her. It had been so long since she had enjoyed the company of a female acquaintance with whom she felt a connection – not since university. There was a swirl of images in her head, faces of those she had considered to be her friends, their faces taut and dismissive.

'Great, I'll meet you at Mak's bar?' Martina said. 'About nine thirty?' she added, and it sounded too loud for the room.

She swept out of the lodge as quickly as she had arrived.

Jolie turned back to her families.

'Easy enough mistake to make,' Duncan said.

'Yes,' Jolie agreed and returned to the island counter.

'They all look the same,' Rebecca said.

'What, the maids or the lodges?' Ali hooted.

'We're hosts,' Jolie added coolly, and Ali, looking sheepish, busied herself pushing food at her non-compliant daughter.

Biting the side of her lip to hide her triumphant smile, Jolie turned to the kettle to re-boil the water. She had managed to stand up for herself, on her first day. It was definitely the alcohol remnants that had given her the courage. She felt she might need to be a little stronger here, set the standards, and start as she meant to go on if she wanted people to take her seriously. She wasn't sure why she felt she needed or wanted Duncan to see or hear that side of her. But somehow, it felt right.

It was clear these women were snobs, that they somehow felt threatened by Martina, and her youth and bright clothing. But Jolie had been instantly drawn to her and with every passing minute she was desperate to get to know her more.

12
JOLIE
NOW

Jolie drained her third coffee of the day. She placed the mug on the table and stared at it, as though it might be able to help her out of this situation, like a magic lamp she might rub and gain three wishes. Just one would be good, she thought. *Get me home.* She had been in two cafés and one restaurant with the children, trying to figure out a plan. The children were becoming tetchy, and as the extra shots of caffeine wore off, exposing the raw tiredness, so was she. Earlier that morning she had called all the local hotels. One room was available, but it had been given to someone else by the time she arrived.

'We were considering opening up one of the conference rooms. If you leave your number, I will call you if and when we do.' Jolie had written down her number on the compliment slip the receptionist handed her, and had tried hard not to cry or get cross in front of the children, but she was desperately losing hope. She had remained composed and, instead, handed over her number, smiled at the receptionist and then ushered her children away, trying not to think about where they would stay that evening. Now she was back in a café, this time feeding the children something a little more substantial and rereading messages on Facebook.

One message had come in from someone called Rona.

> Hi Jolie, I might be able to help you with some accommodation for a while. Can you meet me in the village at the main café?

When Jolie had seen the reply, she'd messaged back immediately. Yes, she was interested. Of course she had prayed for the airport to sort itself out, reopen, and open up a flight to get her, Vita, and Gable home to England. But maybe that wasn't going to happen today – not from what she could see on her phone or from what the locals and tourists were telling her. Jolie was terrified. She hadn't known what to do. Should she have waited to see if the conference rooms opened? But that might have meant another day at least and then she would be sleeping on the floor with other families next to her. It seemed this Rona was her only option right now. Rona had messaged back a few minutes later, and they arranged to meet at this café.

Now Rona was late, which was why Jolie was rereading the message exchange, to make sure she had got it right, to make sure she knew where she was meeting them. Jolie presumed it was a woman as her profile picture was one of those cartoon images that was supposed to look like the person. This female character had long dark hair.

Jolie was tired. She needed a shower, and then to sit by a warm fire, read a book, and not be surrounded by her luggage and her overtired, fidgety children.

But Jolie waited because right now, she had no choice; she just needed somewhere to hunker down for a day or two until the flights were back up and running. It felt strange to be receiving help from a stranger. She could only hope and presume this was someone who knew the area well, or had a spare room in her house.

She looked at her children and wondered how this had happened to her. But she knew that there were parents around the world in worse situations than her, and she felt such deep empathy for displaced families as she was faced with utter uncertainty. She had never been in a situation like this before. And she was livid with Idris for being so bloody blasé about the whole thing. She knew that if it were the other way around and it was him alone with two small children, he would be paying for a private jet to get them out of there. Not that they could afford a private jet; as comfortable as they were, that was off their radar. Jolie felt quite proud that she had been able to survive thus far. And that she had almost managed to find somewhere for her and the children to sleep. Even though it was Idris who'd suggested checking out the village forum, Jolie was still out here in the trenches, dealing with it and living it.

She only hoped that Idris would have a little more respect for her for using her initiative. Jolie sometimes felt that in his eyes, she was just a stay-at-home mum, but there was so much more involved in that than he would ever care to know or realise. But this was serious; these were his children too.

Every time the door squeaked open, Jolie's eyes shot up to see if it was Rona. Jolie rubbed her face, feeling the tension headache that had been forming release its vice-like grip for a minute. This had been the longest day of her life. She could just lie down on the floor and fall asleep. She didn't think the staff would mind; the café had become a sort of waiting room filled with people between accommodations or needing to be fed before returning to whatever accommodation they had cobbled together.

The front café door squeaked again, and Jolie looked up. A woman with shoulder-length brown hair, wearing a green snow jacket and brown snow boots walked in. Jolie looked at the shoes; they were practical but not very nice-looking. Was this the woman? Was this Rona?

The woman looked around the café, and finally, her eyes rested on Jolie. She gave a tight smile and made her way over to the table.

'Jolie?'

'Yes!' Jolie let out the word as though she were deflating.

Both women smiled uncertainly. A lump had formed in Jolie's throat; she instantly felt relief, an overwhelming sensation that this woman was here to help them. They wouldn't be wandering the streets or sleeping on a hotel conference carpet tonight.

'Oh my God,' Jolie said, and suddenly, tears were streaming from her eyes. 'Sorry, sorry, it's just been a really long day, that's all.'

Rona cocked her head curiously. Was it at Jolie's sudden display of emotion? Jolie pulled herself together. Rona looked at Jolie for another few seconds and then turned her attention to the children and looked at them for a moment, but she didn't smile or say hello to them. The children were staring at their screens anyway.

'What a pickle you've found yourself in.' Rona fell into the seat opposite Jolie.

Jolie took a tissue from her pocket, wiped her tears, and blew her nose.

'Sorry, it's been a stressful day. I guess I have a lot of pent-up emotion.'

Rona shook her head. 'I can't believe it. It's just awful. So many people stranded.' She looked out of the window. 'It's a good week to get stranded; another big dump is due.'

Jolie's stomach lurched at the thought of being surrounded by even more snow. The big dumps, when they came, always made her feel uneasy, the way any extreme weather did.

'I couldn't face another second on the mountain. Our passes ran out yesterday anyway, so I won't renew them. It might only be a day or two,' Jolie rambled. Talking made her feel mildly better. It felt good to have someone to talk to who wasn't her children.

'With any luck.' Rona gazed out of the window and Jolie looked at her and wished she had said something more positive than that, like: *Oh God yeah, I'm sure you'll be back home in forty-eight hours*.

Jolie didn't want to rely on luck. She wanted assurance, guarantees.

But what did this woman know? She didn't work for the air traffic control department or whoever was responsible for this mess. She was here, and she was going to help them. That was what she had said, hadn't she, that she could help them? Jolie felt panic surge through her again. She wanted to look at the message again to make sure she hadn't misread it. What if this woman was only here to gloat and she had nothing suitable after all?

'So you said you could help us?' Jolie blurted out. She needed to know because if it wasn't the case and she had been mistaken, then she wanted to know right away.

Rona lifted her hand to get the waitress's attention. The waitress came over, and she ordered a coffee in Catalan.

Jolie's heart sank. She had hoped Rona would walk in here, scoop them all up and take them somewhere warm and comfortable. Did she not realise how long they had been sitting around today?

'Rona, that's an unusual name, isn't it?' Jolie said, scratching around for ways to keep the conversation flowing, to keep it light, to not look like the desperate mess she felt like on the inside.

Rona smoothed her hair with her hand. 'I suppose it is,' she said, and Jolie nodded and tried to recall where she had heard that name before. One of Vita's friends had a grandmother named Rona. Old-fashioned was what Jolie had wanted to say instead of 'unusual'.

'So do you live locally?' Jolie asked, dabbing a tissue at her eyes and nose. She had felt the way Rona had looked at her just now when she was crying. Had their paths crossed already this week?

'I live in the village.' As Rona spoke, Jolie heard the slight Midlands accent in her tone. A memory nudged her, but she was already batting it away, focused on where she and her children would stay tonight.

'You speak good Catalan,' Jolie commented. Complimenting the stranger who was about to bail them out could only work in her favour.

'Well, I've been here a few years now.'

'Do you not ever get . . . claustrophobic?' Jolie looked around, feeling the mountain's presence through the café walls, the impending weather, and the snow, which would soon cover everything. The thick blanket encasing the mountains went so deep, so very deep.

'I guess I didn't choose to live here; the mountains chose me, maybe?' Rona said, and for a moment, there was a serious expression on her face, and then Jolie laughed.

'That was so profound.' Jolie laughed again, an uncomfortable feeling swirling in her tummy.

But then Rona laughed too, and Jolie felt her gut relax.

'I guess that's what living in the mountains does to you,' Rona said. 'Makes you wise.' She tapped her head.

'Well, good for you.' Jolie felt the urge to mention that she had worked here twenty years ago, but the image of Martina on that flyer was still so fresh in her mind, that bringing any of that time back to life with anyone, whether it was someone she knew or a stranger, was unthinkable.

Rona's coffee arrived, and she took her time adding sugar and stirring it.

'It's been a long day for us,' Jolie repeated to make sure that Rona understood she did not wish to stay here any longer than necessary, but Rona was focusing on her coffee. Jolie felt her mouth go dry, and she gulped down some of her water.

'You said you might be able to help us with some accommodation?'

Rona lifted her mug to her mouth and sipped; her lips pursed to avoid getting burnt. Jolie waited for a few agonising seconds and then watched as Rona placed her mug down. She looked at Jolie and then smiled.

'Of course. That's why I'm here.'

Finally, Jolie felt her body relax. She let out a breath she felt she had been holding for ages and put her palms down in the middle of the table in an act of thanks.

'You're a lifesaver. You really are.' Jolie felt herself welling up again. 'This has been an absolute nightmare; I can't believe it has happened to me, actually, I mean to us.' Jolie looked at the children, who were now looking over at her. 'This is probably one of the worst things that has happened to me,' Jolie said and then thought, *but not the worst*.

Jolie was sure she saw Rona narrowing her eyes at her.

'Who's this, Mummy?' Vita came and stood next to her mother, and Gable tutted and muttered 'Vita' under his breath.

'It's okay, Gable. Children, this is Rona. Say hello.'

'Hello,' both children said in unison and the sweetest tones.

Rona looked at them again with great curiosity. 'Hello,' she said eventually.

'This is Gable, and this is Vita,' Jolie said, smiling through wet eyes. 'My children,' she added, a sudden maternal pull just coming over her. Rona looked at Jolie.

'You're fortunate, Jolie.'

'Thank you.' Jolie wiped under her eyes; she probably had mascara all down her cheeks.

'And you, do you have children?'

Rona shook her head. 'I never did, you know, Jolie. Funny thing. I just never met the man I was supposed to be with.'

'Oh, I'm sorry to hear that,' Jolie said.

Rona frowned. 'Don't be sorry. There's more to life than children.'

Jolie smarted at her words; they felt harsh, like she had been smacked.

'You must excuse my bluntness,' Rona said, noticing Jolie's expression. 'I've been on my own for a long time.' She briefly gazed down at her lap, then looked up and pressed her hands together. 'Now, we should get going because it's already late, and you will want to reach your accommodation.'

The word 'accommodation' rang out like a choir of angels.

'Are we going?' Gable asked.

Jolie looked at Rona. 'Is it far?'

'It is a bit of a drive,' Rona said, leaning in and speaking quietly. 'It's the best I could do. A lodge that isn't being used right now.'

'Do you work for Tranquil Lodges?' Jolie asked.

Rona stood up. 'Why, yes I do.'

Jolie thought of the remote lodges just outside of the village and realised that must be where they were going.

'We must go if we're going to make it up the mountain before dark.'

'Right, right, yes.' Jolie set about gathering their bags and rucksacks. She was relieved when Rona picked up a suitcase and carried it towards the door.

Jolie thought about remote lodges reserved for clients with a lot of disposable income who didn't want to be in amongst the hustle and bustle of the après-ski. There were only five or so lodges up there, with a private lift to the top of the mountain. Each lodge was far enough away from one another so that you didn't feel as though you were right in the middle of it all. They were selected for their discreetness. For their remoteness.

Jolie stuffed the children's bags with their crafts and iPads. She felt Rona looking on, waiting at the door, and observing as she performed her motherly duties. All the while, Jolie tried not to think that instead of getting closer to home, she was about to go further up into the mountain.

13
JOLIE

The children had fallen asleep in the back of the car, and Jolie had been nodding off intermittently but hadn't wanted to fall asleep. She had been on high alert all day, a level of hypervigilance she hadn't experienced before. She'd swung around repeatedly in the car, checking on the children, gauging their expressions, checking they weren't scared. As scared as she was anyway. But children were robust, at least hers were, not a trait they had inherited from her, and they seemed to be going with the flow. For now. Though she was sure the lodge was going to bring them the comfort they had been craving all day, she didn't wish to rest until the children were safe and in their beds, and she had a glass of something alcoholic inside her. Jolie had purchased two bottles of red wine from their favourite restaurant and had intended to take them home, but she wondered if it would be such a crime if she finished them before then. After all, she had earned it; if Idris were in this situation, he would be necking it back without a second thought. But that was the joy of motherhood; it came with unequal helpings of guilt no matter what you did or didn't do.

The journey to the remote lodge was bumpy enough that Jolie was thrust in the front passenger seat from side to side. She felt a bout of nausea coming on, but she had something for that in her bag. She had packed for all eventualities. Idris had mocked her and called her a walking pharmacist. But Jolie always liked to be prepared. That was why this was so stressful; Jolie was not in control of anything anymore.

The higher they climbed in the car, the more snow there was on the ground, which wasn't giving Jolie much comfort. She desperately wanted to get away from the snow now; she was done with it. Yet here she was, becoming further immersed in the white powder. The sky had also turned a dense grey colour, a sure sign that there was more to come, as Rona had already said about the big dump. It made Jolie's body tingle and her spine twitch, just the thought of it all surrounding her. Jolie presumed Rona must know the roads well enough, which was the other ounce of comfort that Jolie took. She hoped Rona wouldn't take any risks, particularly when she had precious cargo in the back seat.

Jolie tried not to think about the way Rona had stared at the children as though they were alien objects. And she had made no effort to engage with them at all. But it was late, and they were all tired, so Jolie wasn't expecting a fizzling conversation from anyone. Still, it had played on her mind that Rona had looked straight through the children as though they weren't there. Rona didn't have children, Jolie reminded herself, and it was almost certainly a lack of maternal instinct. And because Jolie was so full of maternal love and protection for her children, perhaps she was overcompensating, and everyone else just couldn't match up. She also felt extra fragile right now, she reminded herself. She knew she shouldn't allow herself to overthink, but she was so tired, her mind was not hers to control right now.

Besides, she just needed to be thankful that Rona was here and that she was helping them. Even if it did feel a little random that this woman she had just met was stepping up and sheltering them. Jolie could never have imagined this scenario in a million years, not any of it. And somehow, here she was living it.

The car came to a sudden halt and Jolie bolted upright, realising that she must have allowed herself to fall into a light slumber for the last few minutes.

'We're here,' Rona said flatly. The drive must have taken it out of her. Jolie considered how tired Rona sounded, how dishevelled she looked, her face expressionless. A certain amount of concentration was required on these roads. Jolie wouldn't be able to do it. She would need to be a driver first and that was something she never managed to achieve. It had never been on her radar as a teenager, probably because neither of her parents offered to teach her or suggested she begin taking lessons. Once she was settled in London, driving wasn't something she ever wanted to do. And then the years had gone by, Idris drove the long distances and if she was out with the children, they took cabs or the tube. The idea of driving on the other side of the road sounded bad enough, without the elements to consider as well. Jolie would forgive Rona if she were a little unresponsive.

'We're just so incredibly grateful,' Jolie said, her voice stiff with tiredness, as she looked out the window and saw the dark silhouette of the lodge. She pulled out her phone and saw no reception. Her heart fluttered, and her gut tightened.

'You won't get much out here.' Rona confirmed what Jolie had already feared. 'The snow won't help either.'

Jolie looked at her and hoped she wasn't conveying the worry or frustration bubbling inside her. She was regretting not changing her supplier even more now. At least she might get a smidgen of reception if she had switched as Idris had suggested. She was too damn loyal for her own good.

'I can check the flights when I get back to the village,' Rona said.

Jolie thought for a moment and then spoke. 'But how would that work? You couldn't book them for us or contact me to let me know; I couldn't do it from here. I can't keep the children occupied in the village all day again tomorrow.'

Rona looked at her; her expression was empty. Jolie realised she sounded slightly hysterical.

'I'm sure you'll feel better after a good night's sleep,' Rona finally said, and Jolie almost wept again, the most positive words she had heard since the whole horrific experience had begun. Doing all this alone was so hard; she had to keep herself looking upbeat even when she was totally flat inside. She couldn't let the children know she was scared. Just as she was thinking about them, they began to rouse.

'Mummy,' came a voice, and she couldn't say whose it was. There were only two years between them, and even when Gable wanted to be grown up as he approached double figures, he would still revert to his little boy ways often, and Jolie embraced it whenever she could.

Rona exited the car, leaving the driver door open, and headed towards the lodge, her boots crunching in the snow. They were so much higher up here, and Jolie felt it. She could hear it, the way the snow absorbed all sound.

Silence.

Jolie wondered when someone had last been in the lodge and how long the building would take to warm up. She would be happy if it just had a fireplace and beds for the children. She didn't need to be in contact with the outside world right now. But she had wanted to message Idris to let him know she had found somewhere to stay. Damn it, she cursed herself, why hadn't she finished the message she had begun before they got up here, when it was likely that there would be no signal? She had been too busy thinking and worrying about the children and then trying not to fall asleep.

She would have to succumb to the remoteness, live in the moment and try and enjoy it a little if she could. She could think of it as an extended holiday. A tranquil and remote extended holiday. Jolie reminded herself she had lived for many years without a mobile phone. It was so frustrating that everything was done online these days, and ironically, they were in a place where access to a satellite signal was non-existent.

Gable let out a loud yawn and Jolie looked around at him; he looked bleary-eyed and even in the near darkness, Jolie could see how tired he was. She was envious that her babies could just sleep unaffected because they knew they were safe with their mama. At times, she prayed that this stage would go on forever.

But now she wished they were older, more competent, and less reliant on her. Her heart was going to explode with all the fierce love she had for them. What if she couldn't protect them? She shuddered at the words. Where had that come from?

Jolie looked at the lodge perched all alone, the dark silhouette of a mountain behind it. Rona had turned the lights on, so Jolie could see the exterior properly.Jolie knew how old these lodges were and this one had red wood cladding to make it look authentic. On one side was a veranda, all tucked safely under a huge slanted roof covered in a blanket of white.

She stepped out, her boots squeaking as they hit the undisturbed snow. She could see the outline of the mountains on either side of her, mere shadows in the dark now, but always there, waiting and watching. She shuddered from the sudden blast of cold on her skin, through her thin clothing, which was not nearly suitable for the surroundings, but when she had dressed this morning, it had been to travel on a plane, and she always got hot when she travelled, especially with the children. She felt the silence again, it was ringing in her ears as she tried not to think how far away she was from the village and other people. She crouched into the back of the car and lifted Vita into her arms, who buried her head into Jolie's neck. Jolie knew she was only dozing and would be excited to see where she would sleep tonight.

'Cool,' Gable muttered as he took giant steps in the fresh powder as he followed behind.

Rona stood in the doorway, and lights flooded the hallway behind her.

Inside the lodge, it was as cold as outside, and Jolie shivered, knowing it would be a while before the fire began to heat the rooms. It was a vast contemporary space with large windows at the back, a large open-plan living space and kitchen dining table to seat eight, with a huge log burner at the centre of a selection of oversized chairs and an L-shaped sofa.

'We'll get the log fire going, but once it's going, it is hot,' Rona said, a sound of reassurance in her voice, and Jolie allowed herself to relax another notch.

It had been a nightmare of a day, but she was here now, at the lodge. She would put the children to bed and pull out that bottle of red.

Rona took her through to one of the bedrooms with two beds. There were no sheets.

'Oh,' Jolie said. 'I'll need to make the beds up.'

Jolie stood frozen to the spot momentarily, unable to move from pure exhaustion. Then she put Vita down on one bed.

'Let me do it,' Rona said. 'You've had such a day of it already.'

'You're too kind. I can do it I am sure. I used to do this every day . . .' Again the words almost slipped out of her mouth: that she had been here and done this work before. But Rona didn't respond.

Gable flopped down on the other bed, and Jolie followed Rona to find the bed linen. Suddenly, the memories of working as a host were fierce in her mind, the relentless bed-making each morning and changing sheets every week. There was always so much laundry to do.

Rona stopped in front of a door and opened it. A space the size of a box bedroom greeted them, with shelves either side stacked with towels on one side and linen on the other.

'So many towels,' Jolie said.

'What?' Rona swung around.

Jolie thought she had only spoken in her head. She had been thinking of how many towels she would get through each week just for one family when she had worked here all those years ago.

'There are always a lot of towels,' Rona said. Rona walked in and picked out a stack of linen from a shelf with 'single' on a label just beneath it. She handed the pile to Jolie.

'You really don't remember, do you?' Rona said and Jolie's mind began racing, searching backwards, searching for whatever it was she had missed Rona saying.

'I, sorry, I missed what you said,' Jolie replied eventually, one hand beneath the pile, the other resting on the soft cool fabric.

'I mean, you don't remember me, do you?' There was almost a laugh in Rona's voice.

Jolie rewound her mind back to the beginning of the day when this nightmare had begun. She had encountered many people and spoken to tens of them.

'I delivered towels to you that day, helped you out of a sticky situation.'

Had she been to their lodge this week? If she had, then Jolie couldn't have been there; she would have remembered Rona's English accent in a resort full of so many foreign staff.

'Did you meet my husband?' Jolie asked.

'What? No.' Rona sounded irritated.

'I'm sorry, it's been a long day. I can barely remember details from a few hours ago let alone a few days.'

'It hasn't been days, Jolie. It's been years.'

Jolie heard the sound of her heartbeat thrashing in her ears. She tried to get a grip on the linen, but it was too soft. Years,

Rona was saying. Jolie was suddenly very aware that she was in the Pyrenees mountains, back where she had been twenty years ago. A place she had run away from in the end. A feeling of dread that had begun in her gut was filling up her entire body.

'Did you . . . did I know you, from here?' Jolie whispered uncertainly, not wanting to reveal her past unnecessarily.

'Yes, Jolie. We worked together. We both worked for Tranquil Lodges. Some, erm, twenty-odd years ago now.'

Jolie swallowed. Her mouth was dry. She thought of that red wine.

'Let me help you out a little. You knew me as Dowdy, I believe.'

Jolie's heart felt as if it had stopped momentarily. She put her free hand to her mouth.

'Oh my God.' The words slipped through her fingers.

Of course Rona was her real name, but from the moment Jolie had met her, she saw this woman as dowdy, because of the dull clothes she wore, and the way she wore her hair. And her glasses, big black NHS-style ones that were trendy now, but not back then. This was not the same woman she saw before her. Rona had grown her hair, there were no glasses, and she dressed a little better. Jolie thought of those brown boots of hers. Still not quite there.

'Oh my God, I don't know what to say.' Jolie felt a laugh creeping up her throat and she stopped it before it escaped. 'I . . . the name, Dowdy, I don't know . . . it was silly.' Jolie struggled to say the right words.

Rona looked back down at the shelves and began lifting more sheets. 'I know, Jolie. It was a long time ago. We were all different then,' she said as she bent down, no longer looking at Jolie.

Jolie cleared her throat, feeling a void opening up between them. Was Rona purposely making her feel uncomfortable about this? Or maybe Jolie had been plain awful back then.

'But you've changed. Your hair, your glasses.' Jolie wanted to say something about Rona's weight. Twenty years ago, this woman had been half the size. 'Do you wear contacts now?' Jolie asked shakily.

'I had laser surgery.' Rona stood up, her arms filled with more sheets, her face inches from Jolie's.

'Oh my . . . wow. That's amazing. This is . . . wow. I can't believe it.' Jolie wanted to take a step backwards; she could feel Rona's breath on her face.

Jolie was having trouble believing it. Twenty years had passed. Two decades. How was it that anyone who had been doing a season or two or even three back then was still here, living and working? Cil del món was not the place you stayed. Eventually it disposed of you when it had had its fill. There was nothing here, the experience was transient, and people just didn't make a life here.

After a few more uncomfortable moments, Rona moved forward and Jolie was able to finally step backwards and to the side.

'Let's get these sheets on, shall we, and then we can have a proper chat.'

Rona took a pile of towels and squeezed past Jolie. Jolie was left standing there, and as she stood, she pondered. What had just happened? Why was she here in a lodge so far from anyone, with a woman she hardly knew back then? She wondered why Rona hadn't told her that she knew her during their first correspondence. But mainly, Jolie was wondering, after all this time – when she'd had no idea who Rona was – what else did Rona remember about her?

Once the sheets were on the beds, Jolie was able to tuck the children in. Vita was back asleep in a matter of minutes. Gable didn't seem in any hurry to fall asleep and was still staring at the ceiling when Jolie left their bedroom; she hoped he was okay and just overtired and not too stressed about the cancelled flights and not being able to get home. Rona had made two coffees by the time Jolie came out of the children's bedrooms. Jolie had had her fill of caffeine and didn't much fancy another coffee, but she smiled and thanked Rona. Rona, the woman who had worked for Tranquil Lodges all those years ago when Jolie had worked here too.

As she had been lying next to Gable, stroking his hair to coax him to sleep, she had been hit with endless questions and images. She tried to recall all the times she had been in Rona's company, and it didn't amount to much. Now that Rona had identified herself, she remembered the woman who had popped up from time to time around the village. She had begun to recollect the time when Rona had come to her lodge and helped her out with something. She had been one of those people who was there but wasn't there.

Jolie took the coffee Rona handed her. She was really hankering after a nice warm glass of red. She would feign a few sips and then pour it away once she was alone.

'So you still work for Tranquil Lodges?' Jolie brought the cup to her lips but only inhaled the aroma.

'It's still very much my life,' Rona said.

'And do you still enjoy it?'

'I have always enjoyed it; the organisation and the importance of it. All the little five-star touches. It all makes a difference.'

'Absolutely, it's been a nice experience.'

Jolie saw Rona's eyes narrow. Had she said something wrong?

'How does it feel, to be on the other end of the experience, Jolie?' Rona asked, her voice piqued, with barely a smile, her eyes still locked on her. Jolie felt heat rush through her.

'I . . . it's very different. I enjoyed my time here, when I worked as a host. I know what it is to work hard. And I know what it is to appreciate such luxuries,' Jolie said firmly. She didn't like the way that Rona had asked her that question; had she meant to sound resentful, offended even that Jolie was now the one receiving five-star treatment?

Rona dropped her eyes down to the kitchen counter. 'Well, I made manager, so things changed for me.'

'You got a promotion?' Jolie said brightly.

'Manager, yes. The team are pretty hard-working. They can slack and cut corners from time to time.' She sipped her coffee. 'But I guess we all knew someone like that,' she added as an afterthought and Jolie's mind instantly went to Martina. She was sure that Rona was thinking of her too. Was this a conversation they ought to be having? Did Rona want to talk about Martina? Jolie tried to recollect the time she had spent here in the early noughties. Martina had been her friend. But where had Rona slotted into the equation? Had she been an acquaintance of Martina's before Jolie had arrived? All Jolie could remember was that Rona was never in the forefront, she had never been out to the bars with them, she had never taken coffee with her or gone up the mountain with them. But Martina's reputation preceded her. In such a small village, Jolie would have been surprised if Rona had not known of Martina. If not when she had lived and worked, then afterwards, when she had disappeared.

'Congratulations on making manager!' Jolie said, then realised how overenthusiastic she had sounded and how that might have appeared to Rona as disingenuous.

'You're lucky to work for such a prestigious company. It's only got better since I was working here,' Jolie said, still feeling awkward.

Jolie wished the ground would swallow her. If only she could get to the wine and pour herself a large glass, that would ease the mortification. But Rona was set on the coffee.

Jolie supposed to Rona she appeared just like all the other rich guests who came here every year. But how could she say she wasn't, without sounding as though she were trying to appease her? This was an elite resort for the very rich. The fact that Idris had been sent here as part of his work commitments was a sign that he would be going up in the business soon.

Rona managed a small smile and left the room. She came back with more linen.

'This is for your bed,' she said and went to walk to the other double bedroom.

'Oh, let me; you've done enough. You must be tired and ready to go home.'

Rona rubbed her eyes. 'A little, yes.' She went to the door. 'Hold on one minute.'

Jolie watched Rona walk back out to the car and go to the boot. She took out a box and then returned.

She placed the box down on the kitchen counter.

'What's this?' Jolie asked peering inside the box. She spotted brioche rolls, butter, jam, packets of crisps, a packet of ground coffee and milk.

'Just a few supplies to keep you going.'

'That's really kind of you,' Jolie said.

'Well, you'll need fresh coffee in the morning. Those log fires will keep the place warm all night, but you'll need to add more logs to them in the morning. Now, if you'll excuse me, I need to get back down the mountain.'

Jolie felt a flutter of panic. She didn't want Rona to go. She didn't want to be the only adult here alone in this part of the mountain.

'Sure, and thanks again.' Jolie forged a smile and swallowed hard, her mouth suddenly so dry.

Rona eyed her for a moment. 'You'll be fine. No one comes out here. It's just you and the kids for miles.'

This time, Jolie couldn't swallow; she felt as though all of her upper body had gone numb. If that was Rona's way of trying to make her feel more secure, she really hadn't done a very good job.

She closed the door behind Rona after she left and went back into the children's bedroom to check on them, all the while trying not to think about how far away from home she was, how she had no Wi-Fi, and how it was just her and her children on a remote part of the mountain for the entire night.

14
RONA

Rona woke up feeling drained and lacking energy. Why had Jolie returned? She was content just getting by, living the simple life she had built here in Cil del món. Now, her mind was a storm of thoughts and memories, along with her responsibilities and all she needed to do. She should have ignored that damn message, but instead she'd replied, and now she was involved. This episode was part of her life, and she had to see it through to the end, because that was what Rona did. She hated not finishing what she started. But Rona knew there had to be a reason that they had been brought back together after all this time. Perhaps fate had taken a hand and Jolie was here to pay for what she had done the first time around. Rona could not help but feel some pleasure for what that meant for Jolie. After all, she had barely acknowledged Rona the first time around, even when Rona was offering to help her.

Today, she was going to have coffee with Mercy. Rona felt some relief because this was routine, and would take her mind off the woman and two children in the lodge in the mountains. She had put them there; this was all on her now. But she couldn't let Mercy down and just because Jolie was stranded here did not mean that Rona would change her plans.

She had dreamt of the past last night. Enigmatic images of people all talking at her. Jolie had been there. And so had Martina. This was what Jolie coming back into her life had done. She was shaken up, feeling as though things were spiralling.

But Rona knew she needed to be focused. There was a lot to do.

First, she checked in on the flights. As she had suspected, they were still all cancelled. At least she would have something to tell Jolie, even if it wasn't the good news that she would be hoping for.

Rona felt a pull towards the Facebook group. There had been a few more posts about the current situation. Most people were jovial and happy to be stuck on holiday. Why couldn't Jolie be? Why did she always have to be so . . . entitled?

Jolie might have forgotten all about Rona, but it had been the opposite for Rona. She had thought about Jolie a lot. She considered how she had been with her during those few months she had lived in Cil del món, and worked as a lodge host. Rona would have liked to have been her friend, to have got to know her. She was sure the two of them could have been friends. But it hadn't worked out that way. Martina had got to her first, with her fancy clothes and wild nature. It was too tantalising for Jolie, who had come here with nothing.

It was apparent that someone like Jolie would have overlooked someone like Rona, which she did the first time she was here. But to do it again? To not even recognise her face, or even know her name? It had made Rona's blood boil; she had to hide her emotions. She didn't show Jolie that she was put out that she had no idea who she was. She was good at not showing her true feelings. It was something she had been able to do for as long as she could remember. Later on, as an adult, she understood it was something she had been forced to learn. Eventually, when no one comes at the sound of your cries, you learn to accept that you're not worth the attention and you give up.

Rona scrolled back to Jolie's post. She looked at the comments again and underneath it were a few more from other tourists and hoteliers. Rona hadn't left a comment. She had private-messaged Jolie. No one on this thread would know that she had helped Jolie out. And that was a good thing. She didn't need the attention on her right now. And she couldn't let anyone know she had used that lodge.

Rona swiped out of the app and back onto the flights, as they might have changed in the minute she had been away. They hadn't. Jolie and her kids were still going to be with her.

She felt a surge of anger run through her. In her mind's eye, she saw Jolie in the lodge, cosy and warm, rescued. Catered for. She couldn't help the rush of resentment that had been planted last night, and she was loath to admit that it had begun to grow. When she went to try and shake it off, she could feel the pull of its roots. Rona knew that when that seed of resentment took hold, it really did take hold of her, of her life, of her senses.

'Damn it,' Rona spat to herself. Things had been okay. She wouldn't have said her life was perfect. She had a lot of insecurities; she hadn't made it that far in her career, certainly not what she had dreamt of when she was a young girl, and she had no family of her own. She hadn't seen her mother and father since she left home in 2003. Just a birthday card and Christmas card each year, which Rona reciprocated. But Rona would say she was settled, her life unadventurous; she had no worries. All she had to do was keep quiet and live an unassuming life, and that was what she had been doing. And now, Jolie had come back, and things were a mess again. But what else could she do? She had no choice.

Rona glanced at the well-wishing messages.

They didn't know Jolie.

They didn't know what she had done.

The café was warm and condensation covered the windows. No sooner had one set of customers left and freed up a table then more arrived, and the café was at capacity again. Rona didn't think she had ever seen it this busy in the twenty-three years she had lived here. She heard the waitress talking to a customer in Catalan. The hotel had just opened up its conference room and any stranded guests were welcome to use it. Jolie had just missed out on that. But Rona couldn't help wondering how Jolie would have coped. Poor, rich Jolie, who had everything handed to her on a plate now, who had not really worked for anything her whole life, it seemed. She'd married a rich man. She was looked after.

Mercy appeared without Rona even noticing. Rona was in her own world when she started speaking. She smiled and listened to everything Mercy had to say. Rona thought about Jolie at the lodge, alone with just her kids, but she didn't say anything to Mercy; she nodded along to all the chatter about the resort's state. It no longer felt like the five-star resort it had been before yesterday; suddenly, everything felt completely out of sync. It was messy, disorganised. Chaotic. Rona didn't like it. She would need to check on the lodges, make sure the girls were still doing their jobs and giving each place the five-star treatment. It was easy to fall to pieces in strange circumstances, and Rona was sure half the hosts and cleaners were not up to the job anyway, let alone when facing unexpected challenges. Back when Jolie worked here, they used to have to turn the lodges around themselves for the next guests. Now they had a team of cleaners who worked around the resort. She was glad to be going further out, back up the mountain, away from it all.

Eventually, the waitress came over, and Rona ordered a coffee for herself and a fizzy water and a bocadillo for Mercy. It was a different waitress to the one who had served Rona last time. Rona noted a double take but there were no lingering looks or making her feel uncomfortable this time.

Rona checked the flights once more, only to see the same status across France and Spain's airports. That was it then. It was settled. Jolie was staying where she was. For now.

It was 11 a.m. when Rona finally asked for the bill and said her goodbyes to Mercy. She noted the concerned look the waitress gave her this time as she turned to the door to leave. She could already sense that Jolie would be getting frustrated and she knew she would probably be pacing the lodge, worrying about how she was going to get back to that beautiful Kensington townhouse she had seen on her Facebook pictures. Rona felt a smirk lift the edge of her mouth. She couldn't stop the sense of schadenfreude that had begun to creep through her.

Jolie had not been kind or hospitable back then, she had forgotten who Rona was, and now she was in a predicament that Rona was helping her with. Rona enjoyed the feeling of power. It was why she loved the host role. She felt a need to be in control.

There was a TV on in the café, and it cut to the weather. Rona looked at the swirls of cloud bringing the snow. She had predicted this.

She supposed she would have to get up the mountain and break the news to Jolie. No flights, and soon they would be totally snowed in.

As she stepped into her car, she looked up to the sky. The blue had disappeared, and now snow clouds were appearing. Rona knew the weather signs; she had lived here long enough to know when a big dump was coming. The mountain was about to get a heavy blasting, and by tonight, Rona knew no car could access the road to the lodge for days. Not even the snowplough would come up. The only way in and out was by skidoo because of what happened last year, the one thing Rona had neglected to tell Jolie before she left her last night.

Rona knew people like Jolie, and people like Jolie did not change. They were always thinking of themselves and never really thinking about what was happening around them. The dangers that lurked close by. The snow would cause Jolie a lot of frustration, but she would get used to it. She would have to. She had no choice.

Because the snow was the least of Jolie's worries.

Jolie Holloway had no idea the danger she and her children were in.

15

JOLIE

TWENTY YEARS AGO

The bar was even busier than it was the night before. Jolie found Martina at the bar; a drunk man was hitting on her, and when she turned and saw Jolie, the look of relief across her face was palpable.

'Thank God you came. I was about to throw my drink in his face,' Martina called over the music, which was provided by Adam, with another guitarist, singing the classic pop songs everyone knew and was singing along to. It was the time of night when all the staff finished for the evening and made their way to the Mak's bar. Jolie had seen a couple of much smaller bars in the village, but this was by far the most popular place, and already Jolie had fallen in love with it, the customers it attracted and the general vibe. She felt quite at home.

'Does Adam sing here every night?' Jolie asked.

'Three nights a week, usually. How was your first day?' Martina asked as she summoned the barman. 'Two beers,' she said, and Jolie nodded in agreement.

The barman handed them their drinks, and they propped themselves up at a nearby table. The man who had been trying to hit on Martina staggered away to prey on someone else.

'How was it? Did you manage okay?' Martina asked.

'It was okay.'

'What did you think of the family?'

'Families,' Jolie corrected. Martina nodded. 'The ones with the little girl were a bit strange, but Rebecca and Duncan seemed cool, Rebecca a bit *too* cool.'

'Yeah, she is,' Martina said glugging her beer.

'You know them?' Jolie thought back to the way Martina had been looking at Duncan.

'They come here every year, and Duncan comes a few times a year.'

'I know. That's weird.'

'Is it?' Martina looked nonchalant.

'Do you think he's hot?' Jolie asked, thinking about how Martina had appeared to be trying to get his attention when she was in lodge 15 this morning.

'Of course,' Martina replied as though it were such an obvious answer. Jolie presumed it was; she had thought that about Duncan the second she had set eyes on him. But there was something about the way Martina replied; there was a warning in her voice. She thought again about the look she had given Duncan when she had wandered into their lodge. Had it been an accident or had she meant to come?

'Did you host them before?' Jolie quizzed, aware she was asking lots of questions.

Martina looked at her, nonchalant.

'You looked as though you knew them. Him – Duncan.'

'Oh, yeah, I hosted them. You got them this year,' Martina said bitterly.

'Estelle?' Jolie asked, remembering how Martina had said she didn't get on with her. Had she made sure that Martina was not with Duncan this time?

'Yep. Bitch.'

'She knew you got on well with the family, so she put you in another lodge?'

'That's the kind of thing she does,' Martina said.

'Why do you still work for her?'

'Because it's easy work and . . .' Martina galloped out her words and suddenly stopped as though she were going to say something else but had thought better. Jolie looked at her and waited, but she just smiled and drank the rest of her beer.

'Hey, let's dance.' Martina dragged Jolie to the dance floor. Jolie wished she had another beer inside her so she could feel less conscious of her bumbling body. But the band were good, and she fell into an easy rhythm.

She had just begun to lose her inhibitions when she saw a familiar face in the crowd.

'Hey, is that Duncan?' Jolie shouted in Martina's ear.

Martina swung around and looked at the doorway where Jolie was looking.

'Yes.' Martina turned back around, and Jolie was sure she began exaggerating her dance moves even more.

Jolie watched the doorway, expecting to see the other father, Mark, there or even perhaps Duncan's wife, Rebecca, but Duncan was with two other men who looked to be Spanish. They went to the bar, and Jolie looked on as they ordered something that resembled whisky.

It was odd because when Jolie had left the lodge forty-five minutes ago, Duncan had been snuggled on the sofa with Rebecca. He hadn't mentioned going out, nor had he looked as though he were ready to go out. But there he was all the same. Jolie could tell that Martina was doing that thing, pretending she wasn't interested and was only dancing for herself, when all the while, Jolie knew she was hoping Duncan would look over at her.

Jolie tried to continue dancing, but the atmosphere had changed. She felt Martina's energy shift, and that affected her.

Do not drink anything stronger than beer, Jolie told herself as she indicated she was getting another drink and went to the bar. She could see Duncan to her left out of the corner of her eye, and by the time she had ordered another beer, he was by her side. She hadn't expected that and jumped as she turned and saw him standing next to her.

'This will be your local haunt then,' Duncan said.

'I guess it will be. Seems to be the best bar out of the handful.'

'It's a great place. I know Mak. He's a good lad.'

'You come here often?'

'As often as I can. I like the people, the atmosphere. I also like meeting new people,' Duncan said, and this time, Jolie was sure he leaned in a little closer as he spoke the last words, as though they were explicitly aimed at her.

'You looked pretty cosy when I left earlier. Like you were all ready for bed.'

'Rebecca and the kids will be, and Mark and Alison. But I'm a night owl.'

'They weren't as forthcoming as you. Mark and Alison. I don't think Alison even wants me there.'

'Ah, yeah, she can have a bit of a stick up her arse sometimes.'

Jolie looked at Duncan.

'Sorry, I mean they're not really our *friend* friends.'

'I get you,' Jolie said. 'You just use them. To make yourselves look good.'

Duncan laughed. 'They are a bit square. I mean, that poor little girl is a prime example of proper helicopter parenting. Rebecca likes them though.'

Jolie felt the growing intimacy of the conversation, how Duncan spoke to her as though he had known her a lot longer than a day.

'So you decided to sneak out all alone.'

'I met a couple of mates.' Duncan gestured to the men behind him, with whom he had come.

'They look more like bouncers than mates,' Jolie noted.

'It's always good to have a couple of bouncer mates.'

'Hmmm,' Jolie said.

'What does that mean?' Duncan said through a laugh.

Jolie wasn't exactly sure what she meant by it, only that there was an energy emanating from Duncan that both repelled and drew him to her. Jolie thought there was an edginess to him, but that seemed to make him all the more appealing – all the more reason to get to know him. Jolie thought people with only one side to them were so dull.

Duncan began looking around, and Jolie sipped her beer, watching him. Eventually, his eyes rested on Martina, who was still dancing, and Jolie watched as Martina turned, as though she could feel the weight of his stare, and the two of them shared a look that seemed to linger. Jolie thought back to when she was in the lodge that morning, and Martina had looked and smiled at Duncan. Martina had told her that she had worked for the family, but why had Rebecca not recognised her and said hello and why had Duncan chosen to ignore her? Rebecca had even made an unkind comment and why would she do that if Martina had been her host?

It didn't make sense, but then, in the short time Jolie had known Martina, nothing about her seemed to. She was fiery, didn't seem to like authority, and she was so bohemian. She looked like the sort of girl whose handbag would be packed with enough paraphernalia so at any time, she could bolt. Jolie was sure that if she ever did get to see inside Martina's handbag, she would be right.

Jolie wanted to ask about Duncan right then, to see what the connection was, or what hold he had over her, as that was how it appeared to Jolie.

She tried to push away the twinge in her stomach. She had been through so much, lost a lot of friends before she came here. Jolie sensed that Martina was not the sort of girl to conform to a normal friendship, and Jolie needed that more than anything right now. But she knew that if she pushed her, she might force her away and she would be gone, free to run to the next new person.

All the while she was thinking this and sipping her beer, she had missed Duncan slip away. She turned to the bar and ordered two more beers. She would take them over to Martina, and she would drop all her inhibitions and dance like no one was watching. She paid the barman in euros and turned to walk back to the dance floor. But the space Martina had previously taken up in the middle of the dance floor was now empty. She quickly scanned the room to see if she was chatting to someone somewhere else or was on her way back from the toilet, and that was when she saw them. Martina and Duncan, she leaning into him, his arm around her shoulder as they left the bar together.

16

JOLIE

NOW

Jolie paced the lodge communal area for what felt like the hundredth time that morning – and it could well have been. The children had been fed with brioche rolls and chocolate milk, but it was getting on for lunchtime, and she would need to feed them again soon. She had managed a coffee, but her stomach had begun churning from the moment she had woken up, a slow-burning anxiety that had now peaked into something far more acute.

Where the hell was Rona? Would Idris be worrying about them? She hadn't been able to contact him since last night. She reread the last message she had begun to type out to him.

> I have reached out on the forum and am meeting a woman who might have somewhere we can stay.

But she had never got around to telling him that was exactly what they were doing, or confirmed where they were staying or even hitting send. After Rona had arrived and all the commotion of gathering everything up and making sure the children had everything – including Pooky, because she didn't want him to be lost again – she realised she hadn't hit send.

At least he might put two and two together. Idris knew Jolie's phone network was rubbish and that she had a lot to contend with after the flights were grounded, but she would need to make sure that he knew they were safe soon. Idris would be worried; there was no doubt about that. Jolie and the children were his world, and he would soon want to know where they were. And Jolie wanted to tell him where she was. She wanted to share her location via what3words; she wanted to send a loving text to say she missed him and send him pictures of them all in this remote lodge so that when she got home she could look back and find some fond memory amid what had turned into the holiday from hell.

The reality was that this place was any other person's dream vacation. Someone would love camping out here for weeks alone, drinking hot chocolate and brandy and reading book after book, but she couldn't even begin to enjoy it, not for a second, when she had no contact with anyone besides the children, when she didn't know when Rona would be back and she didn't know when she would be able to feed the children next. This, Jolie realised, was the worst situation she had ever been in, made worse by the presence of the children and that underlying fear that she and this lodge were the only thing between them and a great outdoors which, by the look of the sky, was not particularly encouraging. Great for the skiers. Not so great when you are unable to leave.

The children seemed happy though; they had found snakes and ladders in one of the bedroom cupboards and had been playing it for the last hour since they had run out of their shows and movies. As Jolie was unable to download anything else, they would have to start rewatching what they had already seen. For now, she was satisfied that they were entertained by one of her favourite childhood games.

Jolie stopped pacing when she heard the sound of a car pulling up. It was almost 1 p.m. and she ran to the glass door to look out, noting the heavy flakes that were falling and settling fast. She watched Rona step out of the car and pickup a cardboard box. Jolie opened the door. She had never been so happy to see anyone.

'Do you need help with that?' Jolie called out. Rona strode to the door.

'There is one more box in the boot.' Rona walked past her to the kitchen.

Jolie was only wearing a pair of thin cotton stretchy trousers with a lightweight cardigan over a T-shirt, but she pushed her feet into her snow boots and dashed out to the car. She lifted the last box, and as she did, she saw something familiar. It was the same flyer she had been handed by Martina's mother a few days earlier. But this one was torn and a little screwed up. But through the creases, there was Martina's face, and the words about how long she had been missing. At the sight of Martina, Jolie felt the familiar pang of sadness and regret that had never really left her. But this time it was stronger. She was back in the mountains, surrounded by everything that reminded her of her time here before. Jolie reread the flyer as though she hadn't had it memorised. Her mind flew back to that day, the last day she had seen her.

Martina had always been prevalent in Jolie's memories. Even though she had only known her a short time. Jolie felt a stab in her gut. Being back here again stirred up the guilt. It was her fault Martina's mum was still searching for her all these years later. Jolie held the flyer to her chest and wept silent tears before she quickly wiped them away and carried the box into the lodge.

Jolie wondered what Rona might have thought when she was handed the flyer, because it looked as though it had simply been screwed up and she thrown it in the back of her car. She tried to remember what Rona's and Martina's relationship had been like, but she was coming up blank. Did they even know one another that well? Jolie wondered why Rona had made little effort back then to mesh herself more with the group. Did she dislike Martina, and had that dislike run so deep that she could not have brought herself to be part of the group? Jolie felt helpless for not knowing more.

Jolie put the box on the counter and ran back to close the door.

'What's the situation with flights?' Jolie said, not even trying to hide how anxious she felt.

Rona shook her head as she unpacked the box. 'Nothing. I logged onto every airline website several times, and no one is flying out of any French or Spanish airports today, and there was nothing showing for tomorrow either.'

Jolie felt her stomach sink, and her mouth went dry. 'Oh God,' she muttered.

'Mum! Is there more food?' Gable was by her side. She tried to find solace in what she had and live presently. She had food, shelter, warmth, her two children and Rona who was trying to help her.

'I need to get a message to Idris. To my husband.'

'You don't drive,' Rona said.

'I . . . did I tell you that?' Jolie questioned. Why had Rona said that? It had been a hazy twenty-four hours, and she couldn't remember much of her and Rona's conversations so far. They had been few and far between and of not much substance anyway, but at some point, Jolie must have revealed that she did not drive. Had she divulged any more information than that?

'Mum, I'm hungry.' Vita was next to her now and trying to peer up to the counter to see what Rona was taking from the box.

'Thanks for all this,' Jolie said, looking at the items now on the counter. There was fresh ham, cheese, grapes, apples, bread, cans of soup, and packets of noodles, milk and yoghurt.

'There's enough here to feed us for a week,' Jolie said and then realised what she had said when Rona looked at her. 'We could be here for a week,' Jolie added.

'A week?' Gable parroted and Jolie made a mental note to watch what she said. Somehow, she had to sugar-coat this whole experience so that when they left and got home, it wouldn't be a traumatic memory for them. Idris would want to go skiing again, and she couldn't let them develop a fear of coming to a mountain or even leaving the country again.

'I'm going to need you to get a message to Idris,' Jolie said again quietly as she took a chopping board and a knife and began slicing bread and cheese to give the children once they were settled at the end of the kitchen island.

'I'll need to take your phone,' Rona said.

'Oh, I was hoping you could do it from your phone.'

'Wouldn't he worry, a message from you coming from a stranger's phone?'

Jolie thought for a moment and agreed, yes, Idris would think it odd. But the idea of handing her phone over was terrifying, even though she had no reception and wasn't receiving or sending any messages.

'If you type the message, I'll take the phone back down to the village and hit send once I'm in range of some Wi-Fi.'

Jolie gulped and tried to look confident with the idea. 'That's really kind, Rona. Don't you have some work to do? I must be keeping you from your duties.'

'Yes, it is busy in the village,' Rona said flatly. She seemed distracted by her thoughts.

'Of course, sure. It's not like I can do anything with my phone anyway.' Jolie attempted to laugh, but it turned out weak and hollow.

Rona gave a half smile.

'Can you have a cup of tea first? You just drove here.'

'Yes, that would be great.'

Jolie let out a sigh of relief. Rona was hard work, and Jolie found it difficult to know where she stood with her. Here she was, doing this gallant act, and yet she seemed so distant, as though she were preoccupied with something.

'I've just realised, I haven't paid anything for the lodge yet. You must send me a link so when I have Wi-Fi again I can settle up.'

Rona nodded and waved her hand 'We'll worry about that later.'

Jolie looked at her and wondered in all the chaos of the cancelled flights if Rona hadn't checked her in officially.

Jolie went to the kettle and filled it with water. She organised cups and milk.

'I've no sugar,' Jolie noted.

'I can bring some back with me.'

'Thanks,' Jolie said.

'I can manage without. I don't have much of a sweet tooth.' Rona put teabags in the cups.

Jolie took two yoghurts to the children and Rona finished making the tea.

The two women sat at the seats next to the fire.

'Such an odd situation,' Jolie said, sipping her tea.

'It is. I don't think I've ever heard of anything like this.'

'It's has me pretty shaken up; I can't deny it.'

Rona nodded.

Jolie took another sip of tea. Her mind was whirring with images of Martina. It felt as though she were everywhere, yet nowhere. She wanted to speak her name, to mention her to Rona.

Rona looked down at her teacup.

'Does her mother come here every year to look for her?' Jolie asked.

Rona looked up and their eyes locked.

'Do you mean Martina Acosta?' Rona said, and Jolie felt her heart squeeze at the mention of her name. A vice was clutching at her heart again as she remembered the last days with Martina and what else she could have done.

Jolie nodded.

'To look for her, yes, I suppose. But then, I suppose it's just habit.'

Jolie focused on Rona, who was still looking down into her lap.

'Why do you say that?'

Rona's head shot up, her eyes a little wider than before. She looked up at Jolie for a few seconds.

'Well, because, you know, it's been so long.'

Jolie nodded. 'Yes, I guess.'

The air felt suddenly thick, the unsaid words floating between them, neither of them daring to grasp for them.

Jolie was intrigued, she wanted to know what Rona thought. But it had been a long time; memories were hazy. But the way Rona spoke, it was as though she was saying that everything Martina's mum was doing was a waste of time and that it was already too late.

Jolie shifted in her seat; the tea had taken on a bitter after-taste in her mouth.

Rona pulled her mouth downwards. 'I mean, I barely knew her.'

Jolie tried to remember the dynamics of all the relationships and who had spent time with whom, but it was all so fuzzy. There had been a lot of alcohol involved for most of the months that Jolie had lived here.

'You were pretty good friends, weren't you?' Rona placed her cup down on the table next to her.

Jolie gripped the side of the chair momentarily, jerked by the memory of how suddenly Martina was there one minute and not the next.

'Yes,' Jolie said sadly.

'And then you left if I remember rightly?' Rona asked.

Jolie gulped her tea. It was too hot; she burned her mouth and throat. She felt so exposed. That was what had happened. She had already said too much. If she talked any more about this there was every chance she would put herself in a precarious position. She couldn't let Rona know that she was one of the last people to see Martina. She had gone to Cil del món back then to make a new life for herself, to make new friends and build herself a good reputation. Instead, she had been a terrible friend. Again.

'There didn't seem to be much point staying around after she had gone,' Jolie said eventually. And there didn't. Once Martina had gone, it was if all the light had gone out of the sky. And besides, she had to get away, she had no choice.

'Right, well, I need to get going if I'm going to get back to the village and send that message for you. I have a couple more errands to run. I'll stay tonight once I get back, so you're not alone. You know what with the snowstorm on the way. I think we'll need to camp out here for a few days.'

Jolie stood up. 'Yes, of course.' She felt a wave of relief flood through her. She wouldn't be alone tonight. And the idea of a couple more days was just about manageable. She put her cup down, went to the kitchen island, and picked up her phone. She removed the passcode and then tapped out a message to send Idris.

> Hey, I'm fine, and the children are fine. My friend Rona gave us a lodge an hour's drive up the mountain – you remember the ones you looked at and we decided they were too rural. Well, that's where I am now. For a

> few days until the flights start again. There is no Wi-Fi in the lodge, again! I'm sure your network would be working flawlessly out here! This message was sent when Rona kindly took my phone, when she had to go to work. We must stay in the lodge as a snowstorm is coming and there is no accommodation in the village, which is miles away. I might not be able to message again soon. I will get another message to you in a few days once we're back down in the village and getting ready to board a flight. We miss you and love you xxx

Jolie handed over her phone to Rona, who took it without looking at her. It was just a stupid piece of plastic and metal, but Jolie suddenly felt a panic rise through her. She was about to have her only form of digital contact removed. But it was temporary and there was nothing she could do with it up here anyway. It was thoughtful of Rona to suggest she use her own phone, although to be honest with the way that Jolie's phone had been performing whilst they had been here, she didn't actually think Idris would be that shocked if a message came through for him on someone else's phone. But Rona was going to make once last dash to the village and Jolie was thankful for that. Finally, she could get a message to Idris and he would know where they were.

Yet still, as Rona headed out of the door and towards her car, Jolie couldn't stop the pulsating fear, because even though she had no reception, she had just handed over her only form of contact with the rest of the world.

17

RONA

Rona settled herself in her car and looked out at Jolie's pathetic face, like a dog pining for its owner. She knew Jolie had been reluctant to hand over her phone, but who wouldn't be when everyone's whole lives are on their phones? She put Jolie's phone in the glove compartment and started the engine. She could still feel Jolie staring at her, so she looked up and gave her a small wave before she drove off. Jolie waved back enthusiastically.

It wasn't ideal, but it was better than nothing. Jolie would be fine enough there with the kids. Of course there were things that could happen whilst she was gone; Rona only hoped it wouldn't come to that, that she could get this silly business wrapped up in the next few days, and no one ever needed to know that Jolie Holloway had been there.

Rona eventually arrived back in the village, around 3 p.m. She supposed that it was decent of Jolie to consider that she had work to do today and that coming back up and down the mountain was a slight inconvenience.

But now, after another hour of driving, Rona needed a coffee and something sweet. She also needed to check the lodges, that the guests were all checked into their accommodation and that there weren't any issues. Rona knew how easily a small inconvenience could escalate into a drama with a specific type of clientele. Rona was good at dealing with them; she had a way to defuse situations quickly and efficiently. She dropped her car at her flat and then walked into the village. She had to zip up her coat and dig out a hat. The temperature had dropped now the snow was here. Fat flakes fell on her nose as she walked the short distance to the cluster of lodges. Everything looked okay from the outside; the lodges were closed and inhabited with guests, from what she could see. Lights were on, fires burning in some of them. There were no staff running around carrying extra towels, extra linen or tissue boxes; just some of the many items that were requested as soon as guests arrived and inspected their surroundings. Rona felt a swell of pride. They had done well without her. Then she felt a stab of panic. They had done well, *without* her.

Her phone buzzed in her pocket. She pulled it out and took off her glove. She clicked into her messages.

Corrine: We need to talk. Meet me at the café in five.

Rona rolled her eyes. Just as she had been satisfied that there were no dramas, Corrine the operations manager for Tranquil Lodges was on her case. Well, it was fortunate for Corrine that she was on her way to the café anyway.

She took a seat on the opposite side of her usual spot; she wasn't feeling herself today. Plus, the café was busy again with stranded guests. She checked her WhatsApp messages. There was nothing else except the message from Corinne.

The door to the café swung open with force and Corrine spotted her and headed straight over. The waitress was upon her immediately. Corrine held a perfectly manicured hand up to decline. The niece of Estelle, her predecessor, Corrine was alike in every way. Perfectly pruned and turned out, always in a matching suit with extra-tight trousers. Today was a purple and green ensemble and Rona had to glance away as the pattern overwhelmed her senses.

'Hi, Rona,' Corinne said as she pulled her chair up closer to the table. It made a harsh scraping noise and Rona flinched.

'I know what you have been doing, Rona, and it has to stop.'

For a second the image of the lodge came into Rona's mind. She felt mild panic at what Corrine might do. Calling the police was not out the question.

'The girls are all tired of it, and so am I. Now we've been gracious and understanding, considering the years you have dedicated to Tranquil Lodges. My auntie always sang your praises, and it was she who asked me to go easy on you.'

Rona tried to hold Corrine's gaze, but her head moved too quickly; her lips were too red and glossy.

'It has been over a month now since you were asked to leave the business. There is no longer a role for you here, and whilst I understand that twenty years is a long time to give to one company—'

'Twenty-three years,' Rona interrupted.

Corrine looked thrown. 'Twenty-three years, right, yes. It's a long time, Rona, but due to the circumstances, we had no choice but to let you go.'

'I would hardly say you didn't have a choice,' Rona interjected. 'In fact, I'm pretty sure there was a choice. You could have chosen not to fire me.'

'You were discovered having a bath in lodge 23, Rona. The client came back and nearly had a heart attack. And that wasn't the only incident; things were said, about how much time you spent lingering after your shift had finished. Most people just go home; you were making the staff and some of the clients feel uncomfortable. Like you're doing now. And you don't even work for us anymore. I could report you and get a restraining order.'

'You can't do that. I live here. I can walk anywhere.'

Corrine cleared her throat, looking exasperated. She took a deep breath and placed her hands on the table.

'Rona, please.' She lowered her voice to a tone that was almost pleading. 'Stay away from the lodges and the girls and let it go. Move on with your life.'

Rona felt a pain her chest like a little stab. Move on! That was easy for Corrine to say, but Rona had spent a significant amount of her life here on the mountain and dedicated all that time to one company. The incident with the bath had been a misreading on Rona's part. She thought she had read the signs right. But it turned out she hadn't at all. Or perhaps it had been a cruel trick. She wasn't entirely sure. But there was no way she would have been able to recover from that, scrape her way back. She told them she would go back to being a host. But she was cast out.

Rona had never really warmed to Corinne and she knew the feeling was mutual. Corinne had swooped in and taken the job Rona was supposed to have. After management, Rona wanted to apply to operations. But of course, family came before experience or integrity. She had given the best part of her life to the same company to have the very job she had been aiming for and planning for and perfecting herself for, snatched away from under her feet; and then she was sacked weeks later.

Rona had always been a good employee – an exceptional one. She stood in for every host who called in sick; there had been hundreds over the years. She'd taken two weeks off when she needed to have an operation on her leg three years ago, and that was the only time she had been off sick. She rarely used up her holidays, allowing weeks to go unused. And she did her job to perfection. No one ever complained about the lodges she had prepared. But where had all that got her? Well, Rona had had enough of being treated this way. It had been Jolie showing up here that had made her listen to her inner voice more, the voice she had been ignoring for years. Just the very sight of her, looking exceptionally turned out, and the kids with their ruddy faces and impeccable manners. How did Jolie end up getting it so good? When she lived in Cil del món twenty years ago, she was a shambles. She had shown up here without a clue about work or life and fallen straight in with Martina. She had barely noticed Rona. But that was Rona's fault; she was always good at keeping within the shadows. It had served her well. In the end.

Rona felt the familiar surge of rage creeping through her and so when she saw Mercy arrive at the café, she was thankful that she didn't have to deal with those emotions or with Corrine any longer.

'So do we have a deal, Rona?' Corrine said, standing up. When Rona ignored her, she walked out of the café.

Mercy had come at the right time. Rona ordered a coffee for herself and sparkling water for Mercy. Just as the waitress was walking away, Rona ordered a piece of chocolate cake. She looked at Mercy and grinned. Mercy agreed it was the right time of day for cake, so Rona didn't feel so bad for ordering it.

The cake arrived, and she devoured it. Mercy asked how it was, and she told her it was amazing. Thank goodness Mercy wasn't into sweet things, as Rona hadn't wanted to share.

Mercy didn't have much to say today, which was helpful for Rona, as she really did need to get on. There was much to do. With the rage from her interaction with Corrine still simmering, and thoughts of how selfish Jolie had been and still was, she took Jolie's phone from her bag where she had stashed it when she got out of the car. She glanced again at the message that Jolie had written for Idris and then she hit delete.

She began to type.

> All is well. A few more days here is exactly what we need. We have some accommodation. The kids are happy. No Wi-Fi so will message in a few days.
> x

That was better. What Jolie had written contained far too much information. Where was she staying? Who had put her there? No, Rona didn't need that. Her message was much better. It contained only what Jolie's husband needed to hear and nothing more.

Next, still in Jolie's phone, she turned her attention to the Facebook page where Jolie had posted her message asking for help. She found the delete button and the post was gone.

Rona put Jolie's phone back in her bag.

She said goodbye to Mercy and hurried back to her apartment; the weather was turning fast.

Once inside her apartment, she worked quickly. She looked around the small space and thought about what she would need. Inside the small kitchenette, she took some packets of biscuits and chocolate bars and stuffed them into the side pocket of her holdall. Then she went to the bedroom and packed warm jumpers, leggings and thermal underwear, a toiletry bag, a toothbrush and toothpaste.

She looked at her tidy desk and put a wad of A4 paper plus some Sharpie pens into the holdall.

Next, she went to the cupboard beside the kitchen. She slowly opened the door and looked at the two objects. She didn't think it would come to this, but it had. She took a deep breath and without further hesitation, she put them in the other side compartment of the holdall, zipped everything up, and got back into the car.

About fifteen minutes into the drive back to the lodge, the snow began to come down fast, great chunks settling on the road around her. She had spent too long in the café; now she would pay for it with a difficult drive. She wasn't even sure if she would get to the lodge at the rate the snow was coming down. She pulled over at a favourite spot where, when it was good weather, she liked to stop and enjoy the view. She took out Jolie's phone, turned it off and threw it as hard and as far as she could down the side of the mountain.

18

JOLIE
TWENTY YEARS AGO

A few days later and Jolie still hadn't said anything to Martina about leaving the bar with Duncan. She wanted to see if Martina might come and say anything to her; they had only known one another for a few days, and Jolie had a deep, growing desire to be friends with her. She didn't want to press Martina and ask her what was going on. It could push her away. But when Jolie did see her the day after she had left Mak's bar with Duncan, she had a bright blue bruise on her left cheek. Martina had said she didn't wish to talk about it.

Jolie could see trouble ahead. Martina could not continue relationships with two men in such a small village.

However, it was obvious to Jolie now that something was going on between Martina and Duncan. And surely by now Adam must know. How could she hide that from him? The fact that Duncan came here four times a year, three of those without his family, clearly indicated that he wanted to get up to things that didn't involve his wife but did involve young women like Martina. It didn't surprise Jolie that Martina had fallen for a man like Duncan. She could have been having a relationship with him for some time. Duncan looked as though he were in his late thirties, possibly forty, so a young girl like Martina, in her early twenties would be enticing.

Duncan, Rebecca, Mark, Alison, and all the children left straight after breakfast to go up the mountain; Jolie prepared dinner, made the beds, and did a general tidy. She had seen Martina arrive at her lodge this morning. She didn't look too bad, considering she might not have returned until late last night. All the hosts lived in the same apartment block, and Martina and Adam lived two floors above her. Jolie had gone home just before midnight after Paul and Sabrina showed up, and she hung with them for a bit. Then, she woke around 3 a.m. to the sound of a taxi pulling up and the door slamming. Jolie had peered out of her bathroom window and saw Martina thanking the taxi driver and walking along the path to the apartment's front door.

Jolie couldn't help but think about Adam. They had seemed like a perfectly normal albeit bickering couple when she had met them a few days ago, and now it seemed Martina was cheating on him with Duncan. The thought of speaking to Adam bothered Jolie. Would she be able to look him in the eye while knowing what his girlfriend had been up to behind his back? She was sure she wasn't about to get into any deep and meaningful conversations with him anytime soon, but Jolie could only hope that Martina would open up and tell her everything. That would surely cement their friendship.

Jolie began the arduous task of making a beef bourguignon for the family's evening meal. She had never attempted one before and regretted it when she looked at the ingredients the local grocery store and butcher had delivered her this morning.

She had just spread everything across the counter and was consulting the handwritten recipe from the menu suggestion folder – a book full of tried-and-tested recipes popular with guests – when there was a light knock on the door. It would probably be Martina, and Jolie braced herself to quiz her subtly.

'Come in,' Jolie called, hoping Martina was ready to advise on the quickest way to get this bourguignon going. The door opened slowly, and a large pair of glasses peered around the edge of the door.

'Hello, can I come in?' said the woman in a strong Midlands accent.

'Oh, hi.' Jolie wiped her hands on her apron and walked around the island to meet her guest. 'Please come in.'

The woman came fully into the lodge, clutching a pile of towels. She wore red corduroy trousers and a beige jumper under her snow jacket.

'I've brought towels,' she said, the laundry pile towering right up to her chin. 'Estelle gave me your message. She said you were up to your eyeballs in it.'

'Oh my God, you're a lifesaver. I forgot to put their towels in the tumble dryer before I left after dinner last night, and they're down to the last ones this morning. And then I got so swamped with everything, I didn't know if I'd have time to nip back down to the laundry shack.'

The woman paused and peered at her over her glasses, the way a particularly condescending teacher used to look at her.

'Well, we're all busy here,' the woman said, putting the towels on a chair. Jolie felt herself tense up. 'But you know what they say: "If you want something done, ask a busy person." You're Jolie, right?' the woman asked.

'Does my reputation precede me already?' Jolie laughed.

The woman narrowed her eyes. Jolie laughed again to make her joke more obvious.

'We do get a few characters here, but you've only been here a few days.'

'That's enough time for me,' Jolie replied, wondering why she was saying these things that must sound so ridiculous to this woman who looked way more conservative than anyone she had met here so far.

'Thanks again for bringing the towels.'

'I'm Rona,' the woman said.

'Nice to meet you,' Jolie replied, her mind fully on the task in front of her as she scrutinised the recipe, trying to decipher some of the words amongst the appalling handwriting.

'How are you settling in?' Rona asked.

'Good, I think. The families I'm hosting are nice enough.'

'You have the Jenkins Reids and the Prowses.'

'That's right.'

'Duncan Jenkins Reid,' Rona said quietly, as if she were speaking to herself and had forgotten that Jolie was standing beside her.

'That's right,' Jolie repeated.

Rona looked up as though she had suddenly realised Jolie was there.

'And Martina, you and her get on okay?'

This woman asked a lot of questions. They were firing out of her like bullets. 'Yes, she's great. I think we'll be good friends.'

'Good friends?' Rona quizzed. 'I didn't realise Martina had any good friends.'

Jolie felt the sudden animosity from this woman, and she was curious to ask why she had that opinion. She had only just met Martina, and aside from her choices of getting it on with married men, she really couldn't see anything she disliked about her new friend. If anything, she was excited to get to know her and spend more time with her. She hoped that would happen this week, as Jolie was just a bundle of energy, having just arrived and being excited to know everyone and settle in fast.

Out of the corner of her eye, Jolie could see Rona peering around the lodge.

'How long have you worked for Estelle?' She decided to turn the questions back on the stranger.

'This is my third season. So I know everyone pretty well. I know the ins and outs of everything, so if you need any help, you know, you can come to me, cos I'll be able to help you.'

'Okay, thanks for that,' Jolie said, trying to work this woman out. She seemed a bit all over the place, as though she wasn't sure how to interact with people. Jolie would be sure to ask Martina about her and get some more inside information. Jolie wanted to be friends with everyone; she was here, after all, to make some wonderful memories after the mess she'd left behind in England. She was so focused on the dinner and this woman had brought an air of unease into the lodge. Jolie wasn't entirely comfortable with the conversation and Jolie could usually talk to anyone.

'You know there is a great spa here, right down in the valley,' she continued, and Jolie looked blankly at her. She wasn't sure why she had just told her that.

'We could go if you want to?'

Jolie felt a slither of horror; she couldn't imagine spending any time with this woman. It was a hard solid no. 'I'm a bit busy here right now.' Jolie gestured to the mess in front of her on the counter.

'Oh, I didn't mean now . . . I meant . . .' Rona sounded as though she wanted to say more. Jolie could have helped her out, done the right social thing, and told her that she would love to any other day, but she left her sentence hanging in the air, not wanting to commit to anything with this woman. Jolie knew when she had made an instant connection with someone.

Rona looked down, cleared her throat and then her eyes rested on the mess all over the counter. 'Do you need some help?'

Jolie looked up with glee. Whilst she may not be friend material, Jolie was sure she could use the woman to her advantage. She had been here three seasons already after all. 'I would love some help.'

Two hours later, a beef bourguignon was slow cooking in the oven, and Rona was in the bathroom putting the fresh towels out. Jolie had just finished making Duncan and Rebecca's bed and the two women met in the hallway.

'All done?' Jolie asked.

'Spic and span,' Rona said.

'Thanks, you're a lifesaver. I should probably think about getting up the mountain. I've a lesson booked. Do you ski?'

'Not really,' Rona said. 'I prefer the other activities: shopping, lunch.'

'They sound fun too. Après-ski? Do you like to party?' Jolie did a little dance on the spot.

'I like to, occasionally. I don't like having a sore head for work the next day. I'm trying for a promotion.'

'Really?' The women walked into the communal area and Jolie did a quick mental check, making sure everything was as it should be for when the family got back later.

'Yes, I hope to make manager next season.'

'That's really exciting. Well, I cannot ski to save my life so I should get going.'

Rona was standing right in front of Jolie, and as Jolie did a sidestep, so did Rona, and then they both stepped the other way, and Jolie laughed. Rona pushed her glasses up the ridge of her nose and cleared her throat.

'Have a nice time at your lesson.' Rona walked towards the door. 'It was nice to meet you, Jolie. I'll be seeing you around.'

'And thanks for the towels again,' Jolie called. She had already forgotten the woman's name.

'Okay.' Rona waved and left the lodge.

Jolie stood for a moment, shaking her head. What a strange person. Jolie was thankful for the help, but she was pretty sure she wouldn't be spending much time with her again.

'You just have to relax and feel the flow,' Paul said, grabbing her as she almost fell over for the umpteenth time. Every inch of Jolie's body ached. But it had been nice to spend some time with Paul alone. That moment between them in the bar had felt like something, a connection. Even if it wasn't romantic, she was glad of it.

'I don't think I'm cut out for it.'

'Nonsense. I was like a baby deer my first time. You've shown plenty of potential.' Paul flopped down in the snow, shielding his eyes with his hand, his goggles hanging around his neck. Jolie fell next to him. 'So you have Duncan and his family in your lodge?'

Jolie looked at him.

'All I will say is . . .' Paul paused.

'What?'

'I just heard some stuff about him, that's all.'

'Like?' Jolie prompted.

'Just that he's . . .' Paul stopped himself again. 'I just don't want you getting hurt, that's all.' Paul slapped her on the back as though he were trying to make light of it.

'The only one hurting me is you with that slap,' Jolie said with a small laugh, but she was thrust back to last year at university and all those awful feelings that had come with her last few days there. Of course she didn't want to get hurt, but to Jolie this felt like a classic male-ego thing. Paul was trying to warn Jolie off Duncan so that he could make his move on her. She felt a warm glow inside. It felt nice to be cared for.

Paul's hand was on her shoulder again. 'You're a nice person. I'm just looking out for you, that's all. The way I would look out for anyone.'

He looked at her and Jolie felt the weight of his words. He was being genuine; she was sure.

'Right, well, thanks for all your hard work today, kid.' Paul stood up, looked away and busied himself with unclipping his skis. 'You know where I am if you need me.'

Jolie's lesson had been a disaster. Her last interaction with Paul had been a disaster. She left the mountain disappointed and confused. She couldn't connect any of her turns and spent more time on the ground than she did standing. Her coccyx was aching from the falls.

She came straight back down the mountain. She didn't fancy meeting Sabrina or Arnie, even though they had all said they would meet her for a legendary hot chocolate with brandy in the café at the top of the mountain.

It was almost 4 p.m., and Mak's was just opening. She headed straight to the bar and ordered herself a beer.

'That kind of day?' a voice said, and Jolie looked up. Duncan was sitting on a stool a few feet away. She hadn't even noticed him there in her hurry to get a drink down her neck. She felt a rush of shame and embarrassment; she would be serving them all dinner in an hour, and here she was getting a drink in before work.

'I can't ski,' Jolie admitted, taking a long drink of her beer.

'Don't worry, it's only your first week. You'll be flying down the mountain before you know it.'

'But not of my own accord,' Jolie said, and Duncan laughed.

'You're funny,' he said.

'Well, I can't ski. I had a ski lesson; it was terrible. So I need to be able to laugh, or I will cry.'

'Why don't you try snowboarding?' Duncan stood up and walked to the stool next to Jolie. Jolie eyed the stool as he sat. He didn't even ask if she minded.

'I can't manage to balance on two skis, I doubt if I could manage one board.' Jolie took a swig of her beer.

'I reckon you just have the wrong teacher. I'll show you the basics. A few hours with me, and you won't know yourself,' Duncan said, and Jolie looked at him. Did he actually just say that? It was a double entendre of some sort. She felt the line between staff and client blurring. Duncan had certainly been the friendliest and most forward out of everyone so far. An image of Martina and Duncan leaving here together the other night flashed through Jolie's mind. Was this who Duncan was: a man who seduced all the staff? Jolie didn't want to be that kind of girl. She wasn't that kind of girl. She was here to make friends. She needed everyone to like her.

But she also needed to fit in, and skiing or snowboarding was part of the experience. She needed to be able to do one or the other. And maybe snowboarding was an easier experience. She had hung out with skateboarders in her teens and they always made it look easy. She had to accept that she was going to be bruised and aching for a long time.

'This is your family holiday; you don't want to be babysitting me on the nursery slopes. Besides, wouldn't Rebecca mind?' Jolie looked at Duncan. He looked down at his Adidas shell toes, and a small smile appeared on his lips.

'I'm a big boy now, Jolie. Rebecca is going into the valley to the spa tomorrow with Alison. We've hired a nanny for the day for the kids. Mark is going on an off-piste trek with some old school friends.'

'So, all on your lonesome,' Jolie said, and she heard the playful tone to her voice, and she knew Duncan had noticed it too.

'Well, I won't be if you're with me. I think we could have fun.'

If there was one thing Jolie was sure of: Duncan was absolutely right; they would, of course, have fun. The fact that every inch of her body was on high alert and reacting to his very presence was testimony to that.

An image of Martina in her mind stalled her for a moment. What would her new friend think about her spending time with Duncan? Even though a part of her brain was trying to warn her off and tell her that heading up the mountain with Duncan tomorrow would only bring trouble, she ignored it, smiled at Duncan, and said she would love to join him.

19

JOLIE

NOW

Jolie stoked the fire and put water in a pan to boil for the noodles. Thank goodness her children had grown up eating Japanese cuisine and quick noodles were always a staple in her house.

Jolie had been looking out of the window every few minutes for the last hour as the light faded from the sky. There was no sun today because of the snow clouds. Outside was a blur of grey and white, with only a faint outline visible through the falling snow, which was coming down so heavily that Jolie couldn't see beyond a few feet in front of her from where she stood at the window. While Rona was away, Jolie had been trying to find some perspective in the madness, to stop herself from feeling as if everything was spiralling. But it was impossible. She couldn't relax; she was panicking that things were going to get infinitely worse. Because of course things could take a sudden, unexpected turn and Jolie had been in such a situation, where one minute she had felt safe with someone she cared about and the next she'd had to make a decision. One that had haunted her ever since.

She began to make a mental list of what she did have to counteract the negatives. Her children were here and they were, so far, unaffected and seemingly happy.

They had food, water, space, and warmth.

All of these were good things. But Jolie had just handed her phone over to Rona and watched her drive away, and now the big dump was coming. What if Rona didn't come back? What if she had an accident? What if her car rolled off the cliff? Jolie had lived here, and she remembered how difficult it was to walk in snow boots just to get up and down the road from her flat, let alone trying to walk to the lodge to work. She would be in it up to her waist out here. She would freeze to death before she got anywhere. She wished she were back in the village to access Wi-Fi when needed and check the flights. And she would be close to people. She had only been here one night but was already missing human contact. It was nuts. Jolie often found London busy and craved the open space of the countryside.

Jolie wished she had slept better last night; everything would seem clear and less hazy.

She recited the positives to herself again: health, happy children, food, water, warmth.

But it wasn't enough. Jolie needed to know what was going to happen. She needed to see into the future and know with absolute certainty that she and the children were going to be okay.

'It's enough,' she said to herself, trying the words out to see how they made her feel.

'What's enough?' Gable asked as he came into the room without Jolie noticing.

'Oh, just looking at the noodles; I think that's enough for you, don't you?'

Gable looked at the bowls on the counter. 'I'll have that bowl.' He pointed to the medium-sized one.

'Good choice,' Jolie said and ruffled his hair.

She served the noodles and placed them on the dining table. The children hurried to their seats and hunched over the steaming bowls.

Jolie managed to rile herself up into such a panic that she could only focus on the sensation of her heart pounding. So she didn't hear the car pull up and the door open; she was only aware that Rona was back when she turned and saw her standing in the doorway.

'Thank God.' Jolie hurried to the door. In the few steps it had taken Rona to get from the car to the door, she had accumulated a lot of snow on her hat and the shoulders of her coat.

'You look like the abominable snowman.' Jolie laughed, feeling a rush of happiness that she was no longer the only adult in the lodge. And also that Rona had managed to get here just in time – she could see how heavy the snow was. Any longer and her car wouldn't have made it back up.

Jolie looked past her into the darkening sky. 'It's going to be a big dump.'

'Yes, it is,' Rona said, squeezing past her. 'I'm lucky I made it back at all.'

Jolie heard the resentment in Rona's tone. The slice of happiness she had just experienced dissolved instantly. Jolie was an inconvenience. Of course, she was.

'Hi,' Gable said, looking up from his noodles. 'You're back,' he noted.

Rona stared at him as if in shock for a moment, then she glanced back at Jolie as if she wasn't sure what she was supposed to do.

Jolie tried to smile. She wanted to say that he was only saying hello. How difficult was it to say hi back? He was just a child. It was terrifying how close Jolie was to saying this, to letting all the anger spill out of her; it was all bubbling so close to the surface. But it wouldn't do any good, she realised, if she fell out with Rona. They had to exist in the same space for who knew how long, and Rona was the one with the car, bringing the food. So, Jolie bit her tongue, stayed quiet, let it simmer down, even though there was something about Rona that got under Jolie's skin. She realised she knew it back then, and she knew it now. Having remembered who Rona was back then, she realised she had always been fine with saying hello to her, but having her close for long enough, Jolie had always begun to feel as if her skin was itching. And Jolie could feel that sensation again. She had completely forgotten about it, the way Rona had made her feel whenever she was close by.

Rona stared at Gable. 'I'm going to need to stay here the night. There's no saying how long the snow will come down for, and as you can see, I only just made it; half an hour later, and I wouldn't have got up here. The snow trucks won't make it out for at least a few days.' She spoke to him as though he were an adult and under normal circumstances, this would have thrilled Jolie; she hated it when people patronised her children. But now was not the time for such intricate details. Especially when Rona was dropping bombshells like this.

Jolie gulped back the terror. 'A few days?'

'Yes.'

'Wow, how do they manage when the guests come and stay up here?' Jolie tried to sound as though this was an interesting fact rather than a life-or-death situation. She had said a week, but at the rate the children were getting through the food, would it even last that long?

'I guess they wouldn't come, or they get snowed in. It's all part of the experience. What they pay extra money for.'

Jolie closed the door and shivered amongst the flurry of cold air that had been brought in.

'I'll take the back bedroom,' Rona called as she walked through the lodge, and Jolie breathed out. At least Rona was here, Jolie supposed.

My phone, Jolie suddenly thought and followed Rona. She stood in the doorway to her bedroom; Rona had just unzipped her bag on the bed and was leaning over it. She paused when she sensed Jolie.

'Hi, I was just wondering if you managed to get that message sent to Idris?'

'I did.' Rona didn't turn around.

'Great,' Jolie said, expecting Rona to return her phone. She waited a few more seconds and when Rona didn't say anything or move to fetch the phone, she retreated from the doorway.

'I'll leave you to get settled,' Jolie said as she walked down the hallway, feeling like a naughty child. She would leave Rona to unpack her bag and change her clothes.

'I'll make some more noodles,' Jolie called back over her shoulder again, feeling her appetite returning now that the message had been sent to Idris. Even though the snow was coming down thick, she felt she would be able to relax more tonight. She just hoped that Rona would not be up for a rehash of the past. As much as she was intrigued to know what Rona knew, she was more focused on keeping her own secrets safe.

Jolie would need to be clever with what she said to Rona. She couldn't let on about anything she knew from the time when Martina went missing.

Rona had been good to her before and she was being good to her now. That was all Jolie needed to remember: that Rona was on her side and what had happened back then when Martina disappeared would remain a secret.

A few minutes later, Rona joined them at the table. She hadn't changed, but she had dried her hair and taken off her coat.

Jolie looked at Rona's empty hands. She hadn't brought her phone with her.

She took a seat at the dining table. The children glanced at her and then at Jolie. Jolie smiled and placed two more bowls of food on the table.

'Good old noodles,' Jolie said and picked up her fork. 'You can't beat them.'

'I love noodles,' Vita said, slurping a forkful into her mouth. Rona looked at her, and an expression of confusion flashed across her face.

'Do you have nieces or nephews?' Jolie asked Rona.

'I do, but I rarely see them. My life is very much here, and they are all still in England.'

'That's a shame,' Jolie said.

'Is it?' Rona said, and Jolie laughed because it sounded like a joke.

When she could see Rona wasn't laughing, she said, 'Oh, I see. You don't get on with your family?'

'Families can be . . . difficult. Not all families are perfect.'

'Oh, well, I get that.' Jolie understood but wasn't prepared to share her own tales of family woe. 'The job kind of took over your life?'

'I guess so.' Rona stabbed some noodles with her fork.

'Oh, wine!' Jolie stood up and went to the kitchen counter where she had placed the two bottles of wine earlier. She didn't know if she would have the appetite to drink them, but now she almost felt there was a call for a celebration. Well, not quite that, but things didn't seem quite so bleak.

Jolie took the wine and two glasses to the table. She filled them both and handed one to Rona.

'I shouldn't,' Rona said.

'Come on.' Jolie grinned. 'Let's have a glass of wine.'

Rona seemed to loosen then and accepted the glass of wine. 'Sure.' She lifted the glass and Jolie reciprocated.

'To old times,' Jolie said, knowing that was the most she would say with reference to the time they had both spent here before.

'To old times,' Rona repeated, and the two women held each other's gaze before taking a sip.

20
RONA

Once Jolie had put the children to bed, she returned to the lounge area and topped up Rona's wine glass. The room was warm and the skin on Rona's cheeks was hot and dry where she had been in and out of the cold all afternoon, and the long drive with the heating on. She knew Jolie would have a bag full of skin care at her disposal. That was the one thing Rona had forgotten to pack; it didn't feel relevant then. But no one wanted dry skin no matter what was happening.

Rona was tired. She had wanted to eat and go straight to bed. But here was Jolie wanting to spend time with her, have a 'girly chat'. She just hoped that it didn't veer into past territory. Rona was not ready to have that conversation with anyone. But she couldn't help but feel lifted by something more than just pleasantries even though she knew that was not why she was here. It was Jolie's past mistakes that she was concerned about and she could not let the desire to be liked by the popular girl cloud that. However much Rona still craved to be liked. Rona had always felt invisible around Jolie; she had never wanted to know her. Rona remembered the first time she met Jolie. She had asked her if she had wanted to go to the spa, and Jolie had practically recoiled, said she was busy and didn't bring it up again. Ever.

But Rona needed to remind herself that this wasn't just a social visit, as much as Jolie might believe it to be. Jolie had not contacted her when she arrived. Rona knew that she had obviously not been in Jolie's mind once after she left. Whereas Jolie had featured many times in Rona's thoughts over the years. The same way Martina had. Rona had remembered; why had Jolie not? The frustration simmered as she fixed a smile on her face.

Rona could tell Jolie had relaxed; the wine had helped with that. It always did. Yes, Rona knew that was the point, but sometimes people got themselves into trouble when they drank too much. Rona had witnessed it too many times over the twenty or so seasons she had worked at Cil del món.

'It is cosy in here, isn't it?' Jolie sat down in an armchair and cradled her wine.

'They are the most luxurious cabins. People pay a lot of money to be up here, alone with no other guests around. This is one of the most remote ones though. It's the furthest from all the neighbours.' Rona took a swig of her wine and watched that fact settle in with Jolie. A warm glow spread through her as she watched Jolie's face contort a little.

'I can see why that would appeal, and in any other circumstances, I would relish a trip like this.' Jolie's voice was wobbling. 'Why isn't this lodge booked out? It's the busiest time of year after all.'

Rona watched her for a moment, saw how the wine was taking effect. 'They don't tend to get that busy; you have to be a certain type of person to stay up here alone.'

Again, Rona watched as her words pinched and Jolie absorbed the fact that this was indeed a remote lodge.

'Oh, I just realised, I didn't get my phone back from you earlier.' Jolie leaned in towards Rona.

Rona stared at Jolie. 'I . . . lost it.'

'What?' Jolie sat up, leaned forward and put her wine down on the coffee table. 'You lost it?'

'That's right. The snow began coming down hard and I was hurrying to get a bag packed. I knew you wouldn't want to be alone another night and then I needed to set off before the snow got so bad that I couldn't drive. When I got here, I realised I didn't have your phone. I must have dropped it somewhere.'

'Shit,' Jolie gasped. Rona watched the horror and realisation flood Jolie's face. 'My life is on that phone. Are you sure? Did you check everywhere? The car?'

'Of course I did,' Rona snapped. She saw the way Jolie looked at her. Shock etched across her brow. 'Listen, it's not as if we can do anything up here. We have to wait until the snow stops, the snowploughs come, and we can drive back to the village. Hopefully by that time, the flights will be back up and running.'

'And I can get home,' Jolie said absently and picked her wine glass up again.

'I was just focusing on getting back to you and the kids.'

Jolie let out a snort.

'What?' Rona asked.

'It's just that word. Kids. I hate it.'

'Hate it?' Rona quizzed.

'Yes, it makes me think of goats. I never call them that; it's always children. Idris takes the piss out of me, calls me a snob, but he sees my point.'

Rona stared at Jolie for a long time as Jolie seemed to find comfort in her anecdote. But Rona wasn't thinking about the story; she was recalling the text message that Jolie had written out. She had used the word 'children'. Rona was from Birmingham. She had grown up on an estate where the word 'kids' was hollered and echoed around the buildings a hundred times a day. When Rona had retyped the message, she would have automatically used the word 'kids'. She was sure.

Rona imagined that message would already have raised the alarm in Idris's mind. But even if it had, there was little he could do when the flights were still cancelled and would be for several more days. He had no idea where his wife and children were. Everything could still happen as she had planned.

'Well, anyway, I did it for you. And for the *children*.' Rona put an emphasis on the word 'children', but Jolie didn't seem to notice. She was almost at the end of that first bottle of red wine and Rona was still on her first glass.

'And I appreciate it.' Jolie was slurring her words now. She had told Rona earlier that she had barely slept last night. The wine on a stomach of just noodles added to the party.

Jolie stretched out and put her feet up on a foot stool. She looked pretty comfortable and Rona wouldn't have been surprised if she fell asleep right there.

'It's been a long day. I think I'm going to turn in.' Rona stood up.

Jolie rolled onto her side. 'I had no idea how exhausted I was. I didn't enjoy being alone last night.' Jolie's voice was small and far away now.

Rona picked up a blanket and laid it over her.

'Goodnight,' Rona said.

As Rona turned to walk to her bedroom, Jolie's arm reached out and grabbed Rona's wrist. Rona flinched at the shock of the move. Jolie's movements had been slowing down a moment ago; she had taken Rona by surprise.

Jolie looked at Rona; her eyes were half closed but she was focused on her.

'I missed her so much when she left.'

Rona looked down at her wrist; Jolie followed her gaze and then let go. Rona knew she was talking about Martina.

'People walked back then. You have to be strong to withstand even one season.'

'Is that what you think?' Jolie asked. 'That she walked?'

Rona paused for a moment. She took a deep breath. Then she saw Jolie had closed her eyes and her mouth was open slightly.

'We'll talk more in the morning,' Rona said, going to the hallway.

But Rona knew that they were way past the point of talking now.

21

JOLIE

TWENTY YEARS AGO

Jolie downed the rest of her hot chocolate with a large shot of brandy and looked at Duncan. He had a huge smile on his face, having just finished his booze-fuelled drink.

'And you say this will help with the skiing?'

'Snowboarding. We're snowboarding,' Duncan said.

'Oh yes, that's it. I was rubbish on two legs; now I'll be rubbish on one.'

'You said this before, but I know you have a lot more going for you. And you know that too, so you can just drop the pretence now. We've had a hot chocolate and brandy together now; that makes us friends. You can just be yourself.'

Jolie raised an eyebrow at Duncan, a warmth trickling through her gut at his declaration of their friendship. 'Are you always this perceptive?'

'I have to be. It's my job.'

'What do you do?' Jolie asked, putting her feet up on the chair in front of her and lowering her sunglasses. The mountain bar was busy with people enjoying a late lunch. She looked out across the snow-covered plain and the slopes surrounding it. There were hundreds of people scattered around the mountain, all on skis and snowboards, and all wearing the brightest salopettes and snow jackets. The site in front of her was a sea of colour. Some people were a lot higher up and were almost dots on the edge of the mountain, ready to take a drop down a black slope and then seamlessly slide past the nursery slopes and either back to the gondola to get another run in or to take a break and end up here at one of the many cafés and bars.

'I have a very good job, which allows me to come to luxurious places like this several times a year.'

'You just told me I am much cleverer than I make out, so please don't insult my intelligence now.' Jolie looked at Duncan. And it was his turn to raise an eyebrow.

He turned his head, looked across the plain, and then looked back at Jolie.

'I like you, Jolie. I liked you from the first moment I saw you. You and I, we're similar. In lots of ways.'

'That's not an answer,' Jolie scoffed.

'I know.' Duncan laughed. He leaned over to Jolie. 'I'll tell you more. I promise.' He stood up. 'Let's snowboard.'

'You have potential,' Duncan said as they both fell to the snow, their boards perched upright.

'But I'll need more practice?'

'You will. I'm leaving soon; I'll be back, but I recommend getting yourself a tutor today. The more you practise, the easier it will be. I want to see you flying down those slopes when I get back. And once you nail it, I promise you will enjoy it.'

'You can assure me of that, can you?'

'I'm never wrong, Jolie. That you can guarantee.'

There was an intensity in his eyes that unnerved Jolie and not for the first time since she had met him. It was unreadable. Was he that confident or was it something else? Jolie could not tell.

Then the look was gone as suddenly as it had appeared. 'Besides, you seem like the sort of person who enjoys trying new things.' Duncan looked at Jolie.

'I'm an only child. I had to forge confidence. There was no one else to speak up for me.'

'Not your parents?' Duncan said softly, not looking at her.

Jolie looked out across the mountain.

'I'll take your silence as a no.' Duncan unclipped his board from his boots and stood up. 'I'll go and get us another brandy.'

Jolie had unclipped her board by the time Duncan had returned and had managed to get them seats just at the entrance to the bar. She took the glass of brandy he was offering her. No hot chocolate this time. But she pretended that she was fine with it, and in a way she was. When the second neat brandy arrived, Jolie began to worry.

'Promise you'll be gentle with me tonight? Please don't be annoyed if my work is a bit sloppy,' Jolie slurred.

'I promise. Now, tell me all your problems.'

Jolie took a sip of the second brandy and felt its warmth circle her veins. She felt a sudden sense of relaxation.

'My parents dealt with most issues with money. In a way, that's why I'm here, I guess.' Jolie looked at Duncan, and his face clouded with intrigue. 'I'm not going to give you my poor little rich girl sob story.'

'I didn't expect one. Just because parents have money, does not mean they can give us the things we need, what we truly desire.'

Jolie watched Duncan's brow. Did he have parents who had treated him similarly to hers? Perhaps she wasn't the only person who felt this way, even though she had been cradling these emotions for months now, trying to make sense of them. Constantly feeling as though she needed to suppress them because no one was willing to discuss things with her. Yet here was Duncan, the first person to show interest in what she had to say. The only person who had been perceptive enough to realise that she was holding on to such deep-seated emotions and needed to expel some of that before she turned in on herself.

A loud clattering startled Jolie and suddenly there was a raised voice. It took Jolie a moment to realise it was Duncan's.

'Oi mate, watch where you're going!' Duncan stood up and made a show of wiping his T-shirt, which looked perfectly dry from where Jolie was sitting. The man who had been carrying a tray of drinks had dropped a bottle of lager, which smashed on the floor. A staff member was already there cleaning it up. The man briefly looked at Duncan, his face a wash of unease. He edged past, trying not to meet his gaze, but still wary of him.

'We're the same, you and I, Jolie. You don't need to tell me your story; I get it,' Duncan said. His demeanour had shifted; he was speaking exactly as he had before the man had dropped his drink. The shock of Duncan's response to the spilt drink was still reverberating around her so she remained quiet for a moment until Duncan touched her arm. 'But it might help if you did. Look around you. We're literally at the top of the world. We're as far away from it all as possible. Many people come here to get away from something or hide from someone; it's not unusual, and it's not frowned upon, it's just the way of life. For some.' Duncan spoke steadily. 'We've all made mistakes; we've all done things we regret.'

Jolie let out a loud sigh, thoughts of Duncan's sudden behaviour change already dispersing as the brandy continued to inch its way through her body.

'It feels like such a long time ago, but it was only a few months ago.'

Jolie felt all the air coming out of her as though she had been holding her breath for months. Just the notion that she would let some of this story out was a relief, to say the least.

'Okay,' Duncan said calmly, letting the air settle between them before saying, 'Go on.'

'I was at uni. Living in halls and having the time of my bloody life actually. And there was this girl; she was obsessed with this guy, and I mean obsessed, she wouldn't leave him alone. But he was kind of into me.'

'Okay, I can see how that might be.'

Jolie heard the compliment but didn't respond.

'So one night, she went to his room. Uninvited. I was there, but he wasn't. She was a bit drunk and came waltzing in, asking where he was. She had this cigarette behind her ear. I told her she needed to get out, that she wasn't welcome, and she was drunk. Eventually, after a bit of a ruckus, I managed to get her out of the room. But when I looked down on the floor, I saw she had dropped her cigarette. It was a no-smoking building, obviously, as it was halls. I was so stressed that I took the cigarette, opened the window and smoked it there and then. I used a plate as an ashtray. I received a text saying someone wanted to meet me at the student bar. I left the room, with the window open.'

Jolie felt Duncan tense next to her.

'Go on,' he whispered.

'The next thing I heard was the fire brigade.' Jolie paused, took a deep breath and swallowed hard. 'The room had caught fire, the wind had blown the cigarette onto the carpet. The entire room went up, everything. And the rooms on either side. The entire halls were evacuated and no one could use that floor for months.'

Duncan cleared his throat. 'And who got the blame?'

'Well, the girl who was obsessed with my boyfriend obviously. She had been seen by three people entering his room just before the fire. No one knew I was already in there. She was so drunk, she didn't remember lighting the cigarette, but then she didn't remember a lot else.'

'So she took the flak.'

'She did.'

Duncan bent towards Jolie a little. Jolie continued. 'I left university the next week. My parents sort of haven't spoken to me since. I can understand. I didn't complete the course. They were livid. I just lay about all day, every day until eventually my father put some money into my bank account and that was that. I haven't spoken to any of my friends since. They called in the beginning until I ignored them enough they stopped calling.'

Duncan let out a sigh. 'I'm sorry, Jolie. That's rough.'

'Yeah, but I deserved it. I started the fire and didn't admit to it.'

'It sounds as though you're good at keeping secrets.'

Jolie frowned. 'You make it sound so good.'

'It's a skill, Jolie. Not everyone can do that. It shows strength. The way you didn't falter. You just walked away. No one connected you to the fire; they just presumed you were being aloof.'

'Do I seem aloof?'

Duncan assessed her for a moment. 'I think you are pretty much perfect.' He grinned.

Jolie felt a swell of happiness rise from her gut to her chest.

'Do you want to help me with something? It's a little project I'm working on; I just think, well, everything about you means you would be perfect for the role.'

Jolie scoffed. 'Is it paid?'

Duncan smiled broadly. 'Oh, it pays. And the good thing is, you don't have to work outside of your job. Everything you do for me will happen during your normal working hours. You don't even have to leave the complex to do it.'

Jolie furrowed her brow.

'It's simply moving things. From one lodge to another.'

'Things?' Jolie was intrigued yet confused.

'Goods.'

'Goods?'

Duncan nodded.

'Is it legal?'

He smiled. 'Of course not, Jolie. But all the best things aren't.'

Jolie smiled knowingly. She had sensed something when she had met Duncan – that there was more to him than just a quiet family man holidaying with his wife and children.

Duncan spoke calmly and quietly and gave Jolie the information she needed to know. Three times a week on a Monday, Wednesday and Saturday, she was to go to the laundry shack – a small building where all the clean laundry was dropped off – take a set of bound towels with a red label, and deliver it to lodge 23. This was to be done at 8 a.m. before she began cooking breakfast for her guests. On Saturday, an envelope taped to the bottom of the bound towel pile would contain cash for Jolie.

'It sounds easy.'

'It is easy. You have the easiest job.'

'Can I ask what I'll be delivering?'

'Do you need to know? Wouldn't you be happier if you didn't know? See no evil, hear no evil.'

Jolie pondered for a moment.

'Okay, well, I can imagine what it is.' Jolie flicked her hair over her shoulders nonchalantly. She had to move some towels and in return, she would receive five hundred euros a week. On top of her host wage, she would do well out of this.

Jolie looked at Duncan and squinted her eyes against the sun. She thought of her parents and the sad little send-off she was given, if it could even have been classed as that. She thought of the mobile phone in her luggage, still boxed, uncharged and empty of contacts.

Jolie knew that what Duncan was offering was not what she had expected when she had come here, but wasn't that how people made something of themselves: by taking risks and going against the grain? Martina had an edginess to her and that was how Jolie wanted to be seen. Not a goody-two-shoes newbie.

'Okay, I'll do it.' Jolie spoke fast.

Duncan, who had been examining his salopettes, looked up at Jolie. He nodded and smiled. 'You won't regret it.'

Jolie smiled, but then it felt like hard work. There was a sensation in her body, trying to push through the alcohol, desperate not to be dulled, trying to tell her something; she wasn't sure what. But she pushed it back, sank into the feeling of inebriation on a bright sunny day in the Pyrenees mountains, and clinked glasses with her new employer.

22

JOLIE

NOW

Jolie sat upright, her breath quick and ragged. It took her a moment to realise it was still dark, and another to work out where she was. She looked to her left, where the embers of the fire were crackling. She had fallen asleep by the fire. There was a blanket on her knees, and she was shivering. Jolie tried to figure out the time by looking out the window. She could still see the moon. She automatically reached for her mobile phone, but then she remembered she didn't have one. She had a watch somewhere in her jewellery bag, a pretty one Idris had bought her for her fortieth birthday, which didn't go with all her outfits, but she liked to wear it with some of her more feminine clothes.

She flicked the light switch next to the coffee table, and a warm glow surrounded her. She stepped into her bedroom next door and searched through the suitcase until she found the watch. It was just after 3.30 a.m.

It was not unusual for Jolie to wake at this hour at home, even if she hadn't been half lying in an armchair. She had been experiencing some stress symptoms recently, and waking up very early in the morning was one of them. She had been on edge all day, so it was hardly surprising that her body would not let her sleep peacefully through the night. Now she knew the time, her mind immediately turned to the children, and she hurried to their room. In the hallway between hers and the children's room, her foot made contact with something. She bent down and felt around her feet. She picked up something soft and realised she was holding Pooky the bear. Jolie's stomach lurched. She dashed into the children's room; she could just about make out two figures under blankets in the beds. Damn it, why did Rona have to lose her phone? It still had its uses as a torch. She went to Vita first and hovered over her, pressing her ear to her daughter's mouth to listen for breath, a routine she had been doing since both her children were babies. She heard the gentle in-and-out sounds. She stood up and exhaled, finally releasing the breath she had been holding, then pulled the duvet up to Vita's shoulders. The temperature had dropped, and she shivered in her thin top and trousers.

Next, she went to Gable's bed and repeated the process: listened to his breath and then touched his forehead. Gable had always been prone to fevers as a baby and as a young boy, and touching his head was a habit. Jolie's eyes had adjusted to the darkness in the room, and she looked down at the bear she was holding – Vita's favourite since she was a year old. She had lost it too many times for Jolie's liking.

In all those years, Vita had never been without him, never slept without him. Jolie had never found him carelessly discarded on the floor. Pooky bear was like a brother to Vita. So why had Jolie found him in the hallway, far away from her bed? Jolie went back to Vita and tucked Pooky bear under her arm.

A slight scuffle made Jolie spin around and walk out of the room. A light was on in Rona's room, and Jolie saw a shadow on the floor by the door at the end of the corridor. Then the light went off. Jolie tiptoed to the end of the corridor until she was standing outside Rona's room. She tried to calm her breath so that if Rona was on the other side of the door she wouldn't hear her. But Rona had to be there, to have turned off the main light.

She balled her hand into a fist as though to knock, her mouth open, her lips poised to speak, to ask Rona if she was there, if she was okay. Her hand remained there for a few more seconds before she dropped it to her side and she walked back along the corridor and back into the main living area. She picked up two large sofa cushions, took them into the children's room and laid them on the floor. Next she went back to her bedroom, took the duvet and a pillow from the bed and went back to the children's room. She spread the duvet on the cushions and laid the pillow at the top. She crawled under the makeshift bed and wriggled around for a few moments until she felt semi-comfortable. There was a slight indent between the two cushions where they didn't quite meet.

Jolie couldn't say precisely what it was that had made her want to camp down next to her children. Maybe it was waking up next to the fire, or Pooky bear lying disowned on the floor, or maybe it was the light under Rona's door that plunged to darkness just before she approached it. Or maybe it was just being so far out and so high up, and Idris not knowing where they were, not being able to hold her phone at least so she could see what time it was or look at old family photos to comfort herself.

As Jolie lay there, drifting in and out of sleep, she began to form a thought. Rona had done a kind thing; here she was, somewhere safe with her children, but the truth that lay beneath it was simple. She really didn't know Rona at all.

Jolie woke to the soft tones of her daughter's voice and the feel of a fluffy teddy on her cheek.

'Mummy, Mummy, Mummy,' Vita chanted. 'Why. Are. You. Here?'

Jolie opened one eye and saw Vita hanging out of her bed, holding Pooky bear by his arm. The bear's other arm was grazing Jolie's cheek.

'I missed you both; I wanted to be near you.' Jolie's voice was crackly. Her head was pounding from little sleep. She was certain it was still early and she hadn't settled properly on her nest of cushions. She was desperate for a cup of tea but the UHT milk was terrible and the high altitude meant the water would never boil properly. But it was just one more thing to look forward to when she got home.

Jolie felt her stomach flutter, a symptom of her morning anxiety, which had increased over the past two mornings. Yesterday she was climbing the walls waiting for Rona. Today she was . . . what was she thinking about Rona? Had she been awake last night? Had she been near the children when Jolie had fallen asleep by the fire? Had she moved Pooky bear from

Vita's bed? These questions started to form as she was drifting off last night and were now at the forefront of her mind.

She tried to push past the thought. She was sure she was just tired and anxious, and maybe a smattering of cabin fever was setting in. Allowing her mind to focus on anything other than looking after the children and getting them safely back to London was fruitless.

Gable was still asleep, so Jolie put her finger to her lips and took Vita's hand. She led her to the living area. She shivered and looked at the dead log fire. She put Vita in the chair she had fallen asleep in last night, took the metal dustpan and brush, and began to empty the ash into the silver bucket. She looked in the log basket and saw a few measly scraps of wood and no kindling.

'I'll empty this outside and get some more wood. Stay cosy under that blanket.' Jolie dropped a throw into her daughter's lap and picked up the ash bucket.

She went to the back door and turned on the outside light as the sun had not yet risen. She slid her feet into her boots, pulled on her thick ski jacket, and stepped outside. The snow had stopped, at least for now. It was still too dark to see how much snow there was, but Jolie could feel it; it was already up past her boots, and she was lifting her legs to walk through the pure mounds that had piled up. It felt like she was crunching through polystyrene and a part of her wished to wake Gable, put him in his boots and make giant footsteps together.

She walked around the corner to the log hut, where there were enough logs stacked to last weeks. This was a comforting thought, but Jolie had no intention of staying here for weeks. Today she wanted to make a plan with Rona about returning to the village and organising transport to the airport. She would stay at a hotel nearby for as long as necessary, but she didn't want to stay in the resort much longer. As idyllic and peaceful as it was, the children would soon become restless.

Jolie's feet were held steady by the snow. She began to remember how easily the weather could turn up the mountain, how the snow could hold you steadfast in its grip. Jolie shuddered, and she took a moment to look around in the dark. She couldn't see much, but she could sense the energy of the snow; it made everything around her feel dense and flat. The sound was muffled and less echoed. The silence was eerie. Jolie wished to get the logs and go back inside as quickly as possible, but her eyes were drawn to the snow around her feet. She bent down, and even with just the light bulb on the lodge wall, she could see footprints all around her. She dropped the ash bucket and followed them, her legs aching with the strain of every lift, snow seeping through the tops of her boots.

The footprints went around the corner to the front of the house. She carried on walking, crouching down as far as she could, and lifting her legs higher and higher each time to wade through the white powder. She could just make out the outline of the footprints and kept following them until she reached Rona's car. She stood for a minute, feeling the cold inch through her clothes. She looked down again and saw the footprints went all the way back to the lodge. She followed them back to the log pile.

Jolie thought back to Pooky bear in the hallway and Rona's light on after 3.30 a.m. Had she been outside last night before Jolie had woken? Was that why Jolie had jolted awake so abruptly? Perhaps she had been startled awake by a noise.

Jolie emptied the ash into the large bin. Luckily, there were some pieces of kindling in a box out here, which she put into the bucket. She topped up the basket to the brim with logs, hoping that would get them through the day, and went back inside. Next to the back door were Rona's boots. Jolie put down the basket and bucket and bent over, and as she had suspected, there was a small pool of water around each boot. Rona must have been outside; that was why her light was on. However, it didn't explain why Pooky was on the floor. Jolie wished she had knocked on Rona's door and asked if everything was okay. Had she heard something outside? Was that why she had gone out there alone at such an hour?

Jolie shuffled out of her boots and carried the kindling and logs back to the fireplace. Vita was still under her blanket so Jolie worked quickly to get the fire going. She prided herself on building a good fire and within minutes, it was well on its way.

She stepped back, still in her jacket, as it was cold. As she stood there waiting for the fire to heat up, she looked at the space around her. She hadn't paid much attention before, but now she noticed the room had three radiators, pure white, so they matched the walls and so blended in. She must have seen them before but her brain hadn't registered. She went into the hallway and saw a thermostat on the wall. It was set to twenty degrees. Jolie moved it back and forth a few times. The radiators had not come on. Where was the boiler? There was hot water coming from the taps, as she and the children had showered last night.

Jolie looked in the pantry and then remembered a cupboard in the hallway that contained a vacuum cleaner. She went back to it and opened it. Inside was the boiler. There was a large red illuminated switch. That must be the immersion. That was why they had hot water but no heating. Surely keeping the heat going in a lodge was crucial in this weather; it needed proper heating to stop mould growing in between guests. Jolie filed her concern to the back of her mind, where she was putting all the other things that were niggling at her. She was truly someone who benefited from being busy and having distractions. And when she didn't have major focus points in front of her, like shopping, cleaning, cooking, children's homework, school runs and so on, she realised her brain could go off in all sorts of directions, clinging on to incidentals like the heating or the footprints.

Jolie closed the door to the cupboard, but then her ears pricked up to a sound; it was a low murmuring as though someone was whispering. She edged towards Rona's door, and for the second time in hours, she stood very still and listened. She could hear it more prominently this time. It was hard to make out the words, as though Rona were having a hushed conversation with someone. Jolie leaned forward even more, so that her head almost touched the door. She strained to listen, stopping her breath altogether so she could try to make out any words, hearing the sounds but not being able to decipher them.

'Mummy.' Vita's voice from the end of the hallway made Jolie lose her balance. She hit her head on the door, which cracked loudly, and she stepped back in shock.

'What are you doing?' Vita asked as she stood wrapped in the blanket. 'I'm hungry.'

'Yes, right,' Jolie said and as she turned to walk towards Vita, the door to Rona's room flew open and there stood Rona in blue and white striped pyjamas. She was wearing her glasses. Suddenly an image of the woman she had met twenty years ago, was standing right in front of her. Thoughts of her and Martina together flooded her mind. The way they had referred to Rona as Dowdy. Jolie hated herself for thinking it, but that was exactly how she still looked. She had done well to disguise herself when she had met Jolie in the café to offer her sanctuary. Now Jolie wondered why she hadn't arrived wearing the glasses. Clearly she'd been lying about having laser surgery.

'Your glasses,' Jolie said.

Rona touched them.

'You said you had them lasered?'

Rona stared at Jolie.

'You must have misheard. Contacts.'

'You wear contacts in the day?'

'Yes,' Rona agreed, her voice croaky.

Jolie tried to rewind to the conversation when they had first arrived, when Rona had revealed who she was, but the words they had spoken to one another were already fading, being pushed aside by the worry of being stranded.

'Sorry about that bang, I tripped, I was er . . . I was looking in the cupboard there; I was thinking about the heating, and why it wasn't working?'

'Are you cold, Jolie?' Rona asked, a quizzical expression on her face.

'No, I've got the log fire going; I was just wondering why the boiler didn't pump out heat.'

'I guess it's waiting on maintenance; this cabin has been vacant for a few weeks, which you knew. Is everything okay, Jolie? I know this isn't the standard you're used to but—'

'Oh God, no, Rona, please, that's not what I was suggesting. I was simply curious as the cabin has hot water from the boiler, but not heat.'

'I'm not a plumber.'

'Oh yes I know, sorry, sorry to disturb you.' Jolie could feel the awkwardness between them growing and was beginning to wonder why she had agreed to help them in the first place.

'Mummy, I'm hungry,' Vita said in a voice that Jolie thought was a little too whiny, as her nerves began to fray even further.

'I'm coming, Vita,' Jolie said sharply, and she smiled awkwardly at Rona and went to her daughter. Just before she reached the end of the hallway, she stopped and turned back around, but Rona had closed her door. Jolie was sure she wouldn't have asked this question out loud, but she was curious; Rona had arrived at the door quickly, wearing her glasses. Which meant that Jolie hadn't woken her. So what was all the muttering if it wasn't sleep talking? Either Rona was conversing with herself or doing some sort of meditation.

Jolie went to the kitchen and opened the cupboard; she looked at the rations, as she was referring to them now. Whilst the food that Rona had brought both times initially looked like a lot, it wouldn't satisfy the children's hunger for much longer. They were used to having at least one hot meal a day: meat and vegetables. As kind as it was for Rona to bring this food, she found it difficult to fathom how someone who had catered for children as a host would think that some dried and canned goods and a bit of bread and cheese would suffice.

Jolie didn't want to seem ungrateful; she just felt the panic setting in. She had tried to push it to the back of her mind, but it was no use; the story she had heard when she'd worked here would not leave her. A family were staying in one of these lodges far up in the mountains and got snowed in for a week. A huge snowstorm had hit, and no one could get in or out. When the snow subsided enough for the plough to reach the top of the mountain, they found the family safe and well, if a little shaken. As Jolie recalled that story, she vaguely remembered that they had stopped children coming up this high, and the lodges up here were reserved purely for adults. The slopes up here were for the more advanced skiers, so it made sense. But Jolie wished that she hadn't remembered that part of the story because she was in that same situation, except no one knew her children were here.

However, Jolie had given enough details to Idris; she had mentioned that they were moving further up the mountain and stated they were with Rona.

Jolie began buttering a brioche and adding jam. She noticed that her hands were shaking. She stopped and took a few deep breaths. She slowly cut up an apple and put it on the plate with the brioche. She put it on the table where Vita was sat hunched over, the blanket swaddling her.

'There you go,' she said to Vita, and her daughter looked up. She looked tired. Had one day's lack of sunlight already done that to her? Jolie was beginning to worry that the children would have rickets and a vitamin D deficiency if they didn't get outside soon. Yesterday, it had been snowing too much, and she didn't want them out of her sight. She knew how easy it was for accidents to happen in the snow and to lose someone right before your eyes.

The lodge began to warm up, so Jolie slipped her jacket off and hung it over the chair. As Jolie made her coffee, taking her time, she wondered what Idris must be thinking, receiving that last message and then not hearing from her again. She wondered if he was feeling anxious. They had never been out of contact like this before. It felt strange, and she was always ready to pick up her phone, even though it was nowhere near her person. Jolie then started thinking about how Rona had told her she had lost her phone. It seemed plausible and the sort of thing that could have happened in the rush of things, but she wouldn't have done that with someone else's phone. She would have been much more aware if she was carrying someone else's property.

Jolie noted that Rona didn't carry a handbag, which Jolie thought was strange. She didn't know a woman who didn't stuff everything they would need for every scenario into an over-the-shoulder bag. Where did she put all her paraphernalia? Jolie was sure Rona would not have lost her phone if there had been a handbag in the equation. The phone may have got lost within the depths of it, but certainly not lost in the middle of a ski village.

Jolie's stomach lurched as she had the sudden realisation that the lock was off her phone and that if anyone found it, they would be able to look through everything. Jolie shuddered at the thought of the semi-naked images of her that she had sent to Idris and the petty arguments they'd had by text, not to mention so many photos of her children. Maybe Rona had already seen everything. Maybe she'd had a good look at it all before she lost it. Jolie couldn't bear thinking about it and hit herself on the side of her head to try and dislodge the film of mortification that was playing through her mind.

'Are you okay?'

Jolie looked up from the coffee cup to Rona, who was standing in the doorway. She was dressed in jeans and a grey sweatshirt.

'Quite well,' Jolie lied. She would keep lying to Rona, to her children, until this ordeal was over. 'Would you like a shit cup of coffee?'

Rona raised an eyebrow.

'The milk,' Jolie confirmed.

'I don't mind it. My taste buds are used to it.' Rona sat down at the table next to Vita. Vita looked up from her plate of brioche and apple and smiled a goofy-tooth grin at Rona. Rona looked away and back at Jolie. Jolie was preparing herself for a smart-arse remark from Rona about how the coffee wasn't to the standard that Jolie was used to in London, but she didn't speak. She just sat, looking uncomfortable next to Vita.

Christ, Jolie thought, Rona really didn't know how to interact with children; it was official. Luckily, her children were at the age where they didn't get too affected by other people's lack of social etiquette.

'Right, then one not so shit coffee coming up.'

'Mummy,' Vita hissed. 'Stop saying shit.'

'Sorry.' Jolie pulled her mouth down and widened her eyes at Rona, to get a reaction to her telling-off, but Rona just remained poker-faced.

'Sugar, please, if there is any. There might be a stray sachet knocking about in the back of a cupboard.'

Jolie reached her hand to the back of the cupboard in front of her. There was nothing. She bent down and rustled around in the cupboards below. Then she turned her attention to a drawer on the far side of the kitchen that she hadn't looked in yet; she bent down and saw it was empty except for a piece of paper wrapped in cellophane. It looked like a fine that a traffic warden would slap on your windscreen; it had bold red letters around the top: ADVERTENCIA, which, Jolie knew from her short time here as a host, meant 'warning'. She thought there must be some English within the text somewhere, perhaps on the other side, so she tucked it into her trousers and pulled her sweatshirt down over the top.

She turned back to Rona, who was gazing out of the window, watching the sky get a little brighter. Jolie followed her gaze and could see that the snow was coming down again, in thick clumps.

She swallowed hard and tried not to think about how it was settling upon the already great mounds of powder and how there was no chance of getting any vehicles up or down the mountain. Asking Rona to get her back to the village was pointless. There was no way she would risk driving in this weather. It would be too dangerous.

What was Rona thinking of when she had suggested they come here? It couldn't have been the only option surely, but Jolie had been so stressed and tired and desperate when Rona contacted her, she would have said yes to anything. Now she was here, and she could see the snow encasing the lodge one flake at a time, she was beginning to truly understand the meaning of cabin fever.

'No sugar, I'm afraid.' Jolie smiled, but the act felt unnatural, and her hands began to tingle as panic rose through her body. She somehow knew that the warning paper she had found in the drawer was going to be something awful, but she would take it to her bedroom and examine it carefully away from the children and Rona.

She made the sugarless coffee for Rona and put it down in front of her.

'Just going to check on Gable.' She smiled again; this time, it didn't feel as painful. She was going to have to get used to looking as though everything was okay.

Inside her room, Jolie ripped open the cellophane wrapper and unfolded the paper to reveal a photograph of the very lodge they were in.

She saw a jumble of words in Spanish and turned the sheet over, looking for an English translation. But there was nothing. She turned the paper back over and scanned the words below the warning, to see if she might recognise any. And there it was. One word staring at her as though it had been waiting for her to see it all this time. It was an easy word to recognise because it was so similar to the English version.

She blinked and stared at the solitary word that made fear shoot straight through her.

Avalancha.

23

RONA

Jolie was acting strange. She was becoming skittish; her face was a permanent pained expression masked as a smile. Rona had seen this on people many times. She knew the signs. Rosa was sure she had a few suspicions. When the mind is freed from distractions, it will tap into your intuition. Jolie had no distractions here. No phone, no TV, no computers or blaring music. She just had her children to think about and weren't they just so bloody angelic? She would be thinking about their welfare. Rona thought about how she had referred to Jolie's children as 'kids' in the text message and her whole body became tense when she replayed it in her mind. Why hadn't she thought harder before she sent the text? Why didn't she read what Jolie had written and noticed she had written children instead of kids?

It was late morning, and so far, Jolie had been wittering on about the heating. Now, she was in her bedroom. The other child, the boy, had got up and he and his sister were bickering over something. Honestly, she could knock their skulls together. Rona decided to bang on Jolie's bedroom door and check that she was okay.

Jolie swung the door open; she was holding a piece of paper in her hand. Rona tried to focus on it.

'Everything all right?' she asked.

'No, Rona, everything is not okay.' Jolie pulled Rona into the bedroom. She could still hear the sounds of the children playing and fighting, which only became muffled as she closed the door, and her nerves only partially settled.

Jolie held out the piece of paper to Rona. 'What is this?'

Rona took the paper and examined it briefly; she recognised it as the notice that had been put out about this lodge.

'I presume what this says is that this lodge is at risk of an avalanche. Is that why this lodge is closed, why the heating has been cut off and you had to use the immersion for the water? Is that why no one has been in it, for how long, Rona?'

Rona was quiet for a moment. There was no denying what Jolie had already seen and been able to work out with the little Catalan she understood. It would be pointless trying to lie to her now.

'Yes,' Rona said, and Jolie turned her whole body as though recoiling.

'Why, Rona?'

'It says "at risk"; it doesn't mean it will happen.'

'But it might, which is why they have condemned the lodge in the first place. God damn it, Rona, I have children. I cannot protect them here.'

'Calm down, Jolie.'

'Don't you tell me to calm down! You barely know me, you don't know my family or my children, you . . . you've lost my phone and now I'm stuck here in a lodge that could be buried in snow in the next few days if the weather continues the way it is.'

Jolie sounded hysterical, and Rona felt her skin prickle, her mind awash with ways to deal with this kind of emotion, but her brain was not tapping into anything.

'I did what I thought was best for you, for your family.'

This time, Jolie didn't speak; she just threw her arms in the air. As they came back down, the paper made a crackling noise as it hit her leg. Rona winced at the sound, which was so loud in the small room.

'I was the only option you had,' Rona reminded Jolie. Her voice had an edge to it this time, which caught Jolie's attention. She stood still and looked at Rona, intently.

'You had no one. You put out a plea on Facebook, and no one could help you. Except me,' Rona said, this time almost through gritted teeth.

Jolie looked stunned; her anger seemed to disappear in front of Rona's eyes. 'I know. And I am very grateful for that, Rona . . . I just—'

'You just thought you'd get it all off your chest? Try and blame me for everything that has gone wrong, because surely someone has to be made accountable?' There was a deepness to her own voice that scared Rona yet spurred her on all at once.

'I am here for you. I am trapped in this godforsaken lodge too and now all you want to do is rant at me!' Rona's voice went up again, and this time, she felt a hand on her arm. She looked down and then at Jolie.

'Rona, I'm sorry,' Jolie said. 'Of course, I'm sorry. I just got scared. And, well, look at us?' She gestured to the room but was referring to the entire lodge. 'We're stuck,' she whispered, but her voice broke. 'I'm scared and I took it out on you. I apologise. Profusely.'

Rona felt the rush of adrenaline slowly start to disappear. Her tense body began to relax. She mustn't allow herself to get like this, she reminded herself. It would be stupid at this stage. She had to make sure she did what she had set out to do. She would regret it so much if she let herself slip now, if she let her own emotions get the better of her, the way Jolie's were getting the better of her.

Jolie had been a class-A bitch back in the day, when they worked here. She had just admitted to her now, that she thought Rona barely knew her. But that just went to show how blind Jolie could be. How blind she was back then, and how she always thought of herself before anyone else.

She could hardly believe it when she saw Jolie's message, pleading for help; the Jolie who was always so sure of herself, so cocky, the Jolie who, within a few weeks of working for the lodges, thought she owned the bloody place.

No matter what happened, Rona had Jolie exactly where she needed her, and she would go ahead with her plan if it was the last thing she ever did. Finally, it was time for Jolie to take responsibility for her actions.

24

JOLIE

TWENTY YEARS AGO

That Wednesday, Jolie was given her first assignment. She had woken with a tingling in her tummy. How was this happening? She had been here four days and already had a second job earning twice as much. By the end of her time here, she would have thousands saved. She could go anywhere and do anything. She didn't need to worry that her parents would let her room out and would probably not be putting the welcome-home banners out for her.

The instructions were so simple it was ridiculous. Jolie had approached Duncan when the others were in the lounge area or in their bedrooms at the lodge that night after he had offered her the work. She wanted to check that she wasn't missing anything because moving towels just felt too simple for the money he was offering her.

'Don't speak to me when my family are around,' he had said, barely looking at her, and walked away. Jolie had felt bereft, and also as though she had been punched in the gut. When she had left the lodge that night, she heard the door open and footsteps catch up with her.

'You'll do great. I know you won't let me down.'

She had been given her instructions, and she didn't want to seem incompetent or needy. Duncan had put his faith in her. Someone she had only just met. She was going to prove she was worthy of this task. She needed to feel worthy. She was looking forward to the sense of accomplishment that she'd managed to do something right and that someone was pleased and proud of her. She wasn't sure she would get that from Estelle, from what Martina had mentioned and also from Jolie's own observation; she seemed fairly into herself and not the type of employer to give regular appraisals.

Jolie woke up before 6 a.m. and couldn't get back to sleep, so she got up, showered, made coffee, and sat by the window watching the street below as it began to get busy.

It was still dark, but people were making their way to work. She'd heard the front door slam an hour or so ago and presumed it was Adam off to his early morning chef shift at the hotel. She didn't envy him that job. Up at the crack of dawn to work in a hot busy kitchen for probably less money than she got. At least he had his gigs, which seemed to make him happy and hopefully paid well. But it would never be as much as Jolie was making. Jolie wasn't thinking about what it was that she was doing either. Duncan had insinuated something illegal, but as he had said, see no evil, hear no evil. Jolie wasn't going to ask any more questions. Her tummy tingled as she thought about what she might do when she left, where she might go, and all the possibilities. She could buy herself a little flat; she could get a brand-new car, which would show her parents.

By 7.30 a.m., Jolie was dressed and ready to leave the apartment. She made her way up the hill. She was early. She stood in front of the laundry shack. It was dark inside and still locked. Jolie didn't wish to appear over-keen on her first assignment, so she ducked behind the Tranquil Lodges HQ offices. That was never open until at least 10 a.m. when Estelle decided to show up.

She lurked there, peering her head out now and again to see who would be the one to deliver the towels. Jolie began to panic about the etiquette. What would she say if she crossed paths with the person who had dropped them off? Jolie pondered this for a moment, thinking of the films she had seen and how the men or women would walk past one another, not even making eye contact, as they dropped a suitcase next to the foot of one person, who would immediately pick it up and carry on walking. Was there some seamless routine she was supposed to know, or would that come with time? In the end, Jolie decided to wait until the towels were in the shack, and then she would go in once the person had left.

She caught movement from the corner of her eye and jerked her body to the left.

It was the woman who had come into her lodge the other day and helped her with the tidying. Ronda or something, wasn't it? She was ambling along the path. Was there someone else there? Jolie strained to see who else might be there with her, but she couldn't quite see far enough without revealing herself. And no one had arrived at the laundry shack yet. She looked down at her watch. It was still five to eight. If anyone who worked for Tranquil Lodges walked past and saw her here, they would chat, and she wanted to be in the laundry at eight. If she was there on time, the towels couldn't get mixed up or taken by someone else. Jolie was intrigued to see how it would work.

A van pulled up no sooner than she'd begun to mull this over again. It had a square logo that looked like a washing machine; it was the laundry company.

Jolie watched and waited. The van driver hopped down, hauled the side door open and pulled out a huge blue bag. He was a sturdy, muscular man, and he could carry the bag quite quickly, whereas Jolie thought she would have crumpled under the weight.

He entered the shack, and Jolie held her breath. Eventually, she breathed out. A minute or so later, the man left the shack, empty-handed. He got into the van and drove away. Jolie looked at her watch. It was 8 a.m. exactly. She stepped out from her hidey-hole and glanced to her left. Rona was seated on a bench a few hundred metres away. Either way, she was distracted and not looking at Jolie.

Jolie strode quickly to the shack. Inside, she could see the shelf with the arrivals on it. Later, whoever was working here would move the towels to the back of the room, rotating the stock so the clean laundry went to the back. It was a bit of a cushy number, minding bed sheets and towels all day, but these were luxury towels and luxury bed sheets. The staff member's shift began at 8.30 a.m., giving Jolie a window to get the towels and transfer them to lodge 23.

Lodge 23 was situated on the corner of the village. It served as somewhere to train the hosts to make beds. If you wanted to practise a recipe, you could do it here, and if you wanted somewhere to chill between shifts, this was where you came. But at eight in the morning, it was empty.

Jolie eyed the shelf, located the towels and lifted the bundles one at a time until she saw it: a red sticker. Her heart leapt.

'Oh my God,' she whispered and then looked around to make sure she was still alone. She picked up the towel bundle and assessed its weight. It felt a little heavier than she had anticipated a bundle of towels to feel, and Jolie began imagining what product was sitting in the middle.

She found the lodge unlocked, as it was for most of the day. Jolie stood in the entrance, suddenly aware that she couldn't remember where she was supposed to leave the towels.

Fighting her rising panic, her early morning brain fog evaporated, and she looked at the cupboard in the corner of the room. That was where she was supposed to leave them. She strode over to it. All the shelves were empty. She put them on the middle shelf. She stepped back and let out a long breath. She had completed the task. And she felt completely normal.

Duncan glanced at her when he entered the living area and sat at the dining table. Rebecca, his three sons, and Ali and Mark, along with their two children, were also there, so there was no possibility of a conversation about what Jolie had just done, no matter how hushed. Duncan carried on as normal, taking breakfast with his family. Jolie went about her duties, clearing away the dishes for nine, wiping down the sides. She gave the fridge a quick wipe-out, swept the floor and eventually put on the dishwasher. All the while, she was acutely aware of Duncan's presence, and she felt that he wanted to say something as much as she did. Jolie listened to the conversation between Ali and Rebecca and felt herself cringe more than once as they swapped tips on hair removal and reducing cellulite.

Finally, the boys went outside to play with Mark and the women went to finish up beautifying themselves in the bathroom, although Jolie was always baffled by how much make-up went on when they were about to sweat it all off up the slopes, but Jolie had a feeling Ali and Rebecca didn't do a hell of a lot of skiing and the make-up was for lunch and après-ski.

Jolie and Duncan were alone in the kitchenette.

'How was it?' Duncan asked, his voice low and tight.

'It was fine. I did it exactly as I was supposed to.'

As Duncan moved past her, he gently touched her arm.

'Good girl,' he whispered. And Jolie shuddered. The way he had softly grazed her skin as he had walked past, as though he had barely done anything at all, the feather-light way he had delivered 'good girl', whilst still maintaining a deep tone in his voice. But most of all, Jolie was moved because finally someone was telling her that she had done something right. She wasn't bad, she wasn't incapable, she wasn't lazy. She was good.

Jolie's shudder moved through her body until she felt every inch of herself tingle with a warmth that came with the kind of praise she had not only been craving for the last few months but also for the majority of her life.

25

JOLIE

NOW

'Rona, I need to go to the village. You have to take me, now,' Jolie said to Rona when she was finally up and dressed. Jolie felt as though she hadn't slept, and she hadn't really. Not when she'd woken halfway through the night by the cooling fire and then been woken again by Vita a few hours later. She could feel the nervous energy, the way she used to feel when both the children were babies and she hadn't got nearly enough sleep.

'I'm afraid that's not possible,' Rona replied in a monotonous voice.

Jolie wanted to slap her. It was like being on hold to an AI assistant.

'What do you mean?' Jolie wrenched her hands through her hair.

'Because of the snow, Jolie! Can't you see what's going on out there? Besides, the car isn't working. The battery is dead. I saw a light on last night, and went to check but of course it was too late. I had drained the battery.'

Jolie thought about the light on at 3.30 a.m. in Rona's room and the footsteps to the car she had seen early that morning.

'Right,' she said.

'Sorry.' Jolie didn't think she sounded sorry. She sounded a little bit smug. Jolie turned and went to the bathroom to take a shower. Just so she didn't have to look at Rona's face a second longer.

Jolie thought she was well and truly going mad. She was surprised she had allowed it to happen so quickly. She assured herself she was going to hold herself together for the sake of the children. Everything had to be for the sake of the children. Yet she had allowed herself to get focused on menial things, things that she would never have usually noticed or thought about. But everything was so amplified here. Losing her phone in the UK, she could have had a new one delivered by now. Here, it felt like an impossibility; she felt so helpless. It felt as though she might never be connected to anyone again. But she had to keep on smiling for the children, even though it pained her to do so. Even though terror spiked through her. And now Rona had admitted that she had brought them to a lodge that was condemned. The thought of being buried by snow was constantly whirring away in her mind.

Yet Rona had stayed here, with Jolie. She knew the snow was coming down hard, she knew the big dump was coming, and she knew the lodge was condemned, yet still, here she was. It was a good thing to do, yet Jolie had a stirring in her gut that was trying to tell her something else, the very opposite of goodness. Why did she feel that there was something odd about Rona? Well, it was why she had never interacted with her when she had lived here twenty years ago. But now her instincts had changed; call it becoming a mother, general life experience, she wasn't sure, but something felt off. She was supposed to put her trust in a woman she hadn't seen for two decades, and she felt anything but safe right now.

Rona was in the kitchen rifling through the cupboards. It was dinner time, and even though the children had barely moved all day, they still somehow needed more fuel.

'I seem to have underestimated how much food we might need,' Rona said to the wall as Jolie walked in; somehow, she sensed Jolie was there. Rona's tone was emotionless. It alarmed Jolie because running out of food would be one of the worst things that could happen right now, with the snow building up around them and at least half an hour's drive to another human or anywhere they might find food, and the car would not get them there – it was kaput.

Jolie tried not to tune in to her desire to throw Rona against the wall. Then she reminded herself that she was not a violent person and that such a thought was a million miles away from who she was. Under normal circumstances. But these were not normal circumstances, and people behaved very differently when faced with threat, danger, or imminent starvation.

Jolie wished she had some music to listen to because that would soothe her thoughts, but there was nothing vaguely suitable on the children's devices. They were already rewatching the films they had downloaded. Jolie felt her stomach lurch again as she realised how out of control everything was.

'How long realistically do you think we'll be here? Especially now the car isn't working?' Jolie asked and Rona turned around, a can of soup in her hand.

'Do your . . .' she paused '. . . children . . . do your children eat soup?'

Jolie eyed the can and thought of the fresh chicken noodle soup Vita and Gable would eat at the local Chinese restaurant. The soup Rona was holding had been canned about two years ago, and was most likely gloopy and tasted artificial. The children would absolutely hate it.

'I guess they will have to give it a go,' Jolie replied.

The fact that Rona hadn't replied to her question about when the hell they were getting out of here was not lost on her. But she could see that Rona was trying to do something – something good, maybe? She was trying to feed them; surely that was a decent thing that decent people do.

'Soup okay for you too? There's plenty of that bread left.'

Jolie muttered, 'Yes that's fine,' and went to find the children. They were in the bedroom, surprisingly not on a device. They were both sitting on the floor opposite each other, their feet either side of one another's bodies, holding hands.

'What are you doing?'

'Pull-ups, making ourselves strong,' Vita announced.

'I'd rather you didn't use up too much energy.'

'Why not?' Gable asked, laughing as his weaker sister tried to haul herself back up.

Jolie wanted to scream '*because we are running out of food!*' Not at the children, but at Rona, who would hear it and realise she had been a complete idiot over the supplies.

'Just because it's a nice time to relax,' Jolie said, knowing it was a half-hearted answer. She was surprised when neither Vita nor Gable asked 'why' again; instead, they seemed quite content with their game, and usually, Jolie would be revelling in this beautiful display of sibling harmony. She would usually be dragging them away from their screens at home, but here, she wished for nothing more than them immersing themselves in the games and TV shows they had downloaded so she could go back to worrying about them and everything else in peace.

'This *is* relaxing.' Vita laughed as Gable pulled her forcefully. Jolie couldn't bear the idea of one of them dislocating a shoulder. What would she do? She thought of all the time she'd had in London whilst the children were at school. Why hadn't she made better use of all that freedom? Why hadn't she booked herself on a first-aid course? Good grief, Jolie knew that when they got out of here, she was going to be a new woman. She was going to grab life by the horns, expand her knowledge. Get some therapy, stop allowing the past to haunt her.

'Go carefully, Gable,' Jolie said, knowing she sounded ridiculous and that she needed just to let them be and get on with what little enjoyment they could find. She should, she realised, be satisfied that they were getting on with it, that they, unlike her, hadn't picked up that anything was off or out of place, or on Jolie's unsettled mood, which under the microscopic circumstances they all found themselves in, was a miracle. She wondered how long that would last; she wondered when one of them would look at her and ask, 'What's wrong, Mummy?'

Rona was opening cans of soup and pouring them into the pan. Jolie felt her heart sink at the sloppy sound as the congealed mass hit the pan.

'I think two will be fine,' Jolie intercepted, knowing Vita and Gable would manage a few mouthfuls of the lumpy gloop before looking at each other, pushing their bowls aside and filling up on bread and butter.

Rona looked around in acknowledgement. Jolie found two smaller bowls in the cupboard and placed them beside Rona. 'You can use these for the children,' she said softly. She didn't want to seem as though she was interfering.

As expected, the children looked at each other throughout dinner, raising the spoons to their mouths and then dropping them again, barely eating anything. Then, they devoured the rest of the fresh bread and butter.

Jolie finished her soup, needing some energy. Energy to think. She would soon be going into her third day here in the lodge, and the snow was making no sign of subsiding. Regret lay heavy on her chest. Why had she allowed Rona to bring her and the children here, so far away from everyone and everything else? Her thoughts often turned to Idris and what he must be thinking. Was he going out of his mind with worry?

'I brought paper and pens,' Rona said after dinner, and Jolie looked at her with surprise.

'I didn't know why I thought we might need them, but we could play hangman.'

'Hangman, hangman,' Vita chanted, and Jolie always wondered how the game still managed to retain its gruesome name after so many years and how the PC world had not managed to change that into something more benign.

'Hangman, it is, then,' Jolie said as she cleared the table while Rona went to her bedroom. The children seemed to get another burst of energy after their bread and began chasing one another around the table. Jolie tensed at the screams and reached for the second bottle of red wine. Rona's room was too far to shout to ask if she wanted a glass, so she walked into the hallway to call to her, still clutching the bottle of red. As she stood at the end of the corridor, she heard a murmuring. *Rona?* she wondered. Was that her speaking again? She began to walk softly towards Rona's room.

The door was open, and the murmuring grew louder with every step. Jolie could hear the rise and fall of her voice, as though she was conversing with someone. She held her breath to try and decipher a word or two. What if Rona had a mobile phone? What if she was talking to someone outside and this was all a sick joke? Had Jolie been that dreadful to Rona when they lived here in their twenties? If she had, then this must be some sort of revenge. Why else would she have conveniently lost her mobile phone?

Jolie took two more steps; her heart was hammering in her chest, and she wasn't able to hear much above the sound, which seemed to reverberate through her entire body.

She was standing just by the open door to Rona's room as the murmuring came to a sudden halt and then there was Rona in the doorway.

Jolie yelped, fear pelting through her body at the sudden sight of her, the bottle of wine slipping from her grip. The sound of the glass smashing on the floor beneath her brought the children's playing to a halt, and then they were running towards her.

'Stop!' Jolie screamed. She turned to look at Vita and Gable. They both had expressions of shock and intrigue on their little faces. Why did children become so interested in smashed items and want to get closer to inspect them?

'Don't walk over here,' Jolie said quietly. She felt a sob rise in her throat from the shock of the smash, but also, she knew, because she had just lost the last bit of alcohol in the lodge, and she had needed a drink to get her through this evening. The children turned and walked away. Rona was still standing in the doorway, holding paper and pens and looking down at the mass of red liquid and shards of glass at her feet. Jolie followed her gaze and felt the red wine seeping through her socks and the bottoms of her trousers.

'Damn it,' Jolie muttered.

'Stay there, I'll get something to clear it up.' Rona looked back to the doorway and stepped over the mess. She heard a whoop of joy from the children as Rona must have deposited the pens and paper on the dining table. Jolie stood fixed to the spot, as though the wine had glued her there. Rona's door was open and Jolie tried to strain to see through it; she could just about see the edge of a holdall on the bed.

'This should do it.' Rona's voice made her draw her neck back. She felt like a helpless child. She stepped back from the mess and removed her socks. Rona had a bucket and a wad of paper towels. She began to scoop up the glass and deposit it into the bucket. Then she soaked up as much red wine as she could with the remaining towel. Why did Jolie feel so incapable? Why did she keep thinking that something was up with Rona? The woman was probably just muttering away to herself the way Jolie did at home sometimes. It was perfectly normal.

'Thank you, Rona. I'm sorry about the mess. I was coming to ask you if you wanted a glass of red wine.'

'That would have been nice,' Rona said, and Jolie thought she almost cracked a smile.

'I'll go and get a mop and bucket for the rest.' Rona walked away. 'You might want to change your nice trousers.'

Jolie looked down at the red wine splattered across her cream loungewear. She padded back down the hall to her bedroom and closed the door. She sat down on the bed, and the tears began to fall. She let herself weep quietly, her shoulders shuddering, and she gulped and softly gasped as she cried. How was this her life right now: stuck in a condemned rural lodge in a snowstorm during an airline crisis? She had never felt so helpless. She went to the bathroom, pulled off her trousers and put them in the corner with the rest of her dirty laundry that she hoped she wouldn't need to start washing soon. She was living off her spare clothes, which she always brought on holiday, just in case. *Just in case*, she thought. This was finally a reason to turn to the spare underwear and clothes she religiously packed every holiday.

She turned the tap on and splashed her face with water. She hadn't bothered with make-up today, but her skin was tanned from the mountain sun. She dabbed her face with a towel, went to her suitcase, pulled out another similar pair of loungewear trousers in a darker shade and pulled them on.

The kitchen was a hive of activity. The children were immersed in a game of hangman, the kettle was on, and Rona was putting out mugs.

'Coffee is the next best substitute,' she said, and Jolie smiled. It was no substitute for wine; it wouldn't help to tether her fraying nerves, but it was a kind gesture, and Jolie felt herself well up again. Her mind was twisting this way and that way with all that was going on, and she was so confused about why she felt so paranoid. Why she continued to look at Rona as though she were anything else other than someone who was here by her own willingness to help her and her children.

But watching Rona standing there making the coffee, Jolie realised why she was flooded with such contradictions from one minute to the next. Rona was calm and collected. *Too* calm and collected, and Jolie realised that was what was gnawing away at her.

Rona was showing very few signs of emotion. And that, for Jolie, was a big red flag. She had watched enough true crime documentaries to know that someone who displayed so very little concern for their current situation was someone who could potentially have psychopathic tendencies. Jolie took the coffee from Rona and smiled, calmed her thoughts and tried to put everything that had happened in the last couple of days into perspective.

Rona had not mentioned to Jolie that she knew her in their first message. Yet she did know her; she had remembered her. Why had Rona not made that obvious? She had now lost her phone and brought them to a lodge that was condemned. But here she was making them soup and suggesting she play hangman with her children.

Nothing made sense, and Jolie was going out of her mind with the yo-yoing thoughts. She wished more than anything she could speak with Idris to ask his advice. He would tell her exactly what she needed to hear. For now, she had to keep trying to tap into her instincts. But nothing was normal here and what good were her instincts now that she was trapped in this lodge at the top of the mountain, with no way to escape? She needed to get into Rona's room and maybe find out exactly what she was hiding from her.

26

RONA

Rona went to her room to fetch the paper for Jolie. She wasn't exactly sure why she had brought it with her, but she was sure there would be a reason and she was right. It had finally presented itself. Jolie's children were distracted. They had something to entertain themselves. Jolie only had damn devices for them. What parent didn't bring a notepad and pens for kids to play with? It was Rona's go-to activity. There were always children in the many lodges she had worked with over the years, and she had lost count of the times she had walked into a lodge in the morning to complete chaos. Children running riot, not listening to a word their parents were saying. Rona had only to take out the paper and pens from her bag and slide them across the table in the direction of the children, and then there was silence. It would usually take the parents a good few minutes to realise that their little ones were suitably entertained, but they never thanked Rona; they just presumed the paper and pens had arrived magically.

Rona could gauge that this was a very different situation for them; these children were no different to the hundreds of other privileged kids she had come across. They were probably used to a life that was busy, bustling with activities and play dates, but it just goes to show that when things were stripped back, kids could survive without all the distractions. They both seemed to be taking it in their stride. Kids . . . children, were resilient like that.

Rona had always known Jolie was fragile. She had seen it in her back then, and although she seemed to have grown – Rona had heard motherhood could do that to a woman – she could still see the tiny cracks where Jolie had tried to mend herself. She was still that vulnerable little girl underneath all of this. Rona thought about the other items she had packed. The side pocket of her holdall remained zipped up, but she could see those two items she had packed in her mind's eye. She knew it wouldn't be long until she would need to use them.

Rona suddenly felt hot, so she opened the window.

Abruptly a voice that sounded like Mercy's was there.

'This is another fine situation you've got yourself into, Rona. This keeps happening. Why can't you leave well alone? You know you're only making things worse. You had a choice, didn't you? You could have walked away; you could have just left it as it was. The past is the past. It's been twenty years, for goodness' sake. Why do you want to involve yourself in all of that nonsense again now? Jolie is not the same person. You see her vulnerabilities, but she has those kids to protect. And women will do anything to protect their children.'

Rona froze and she spun around to the door that was open a crack. Footsteps, heavy breathing. She leapt up and was at the doorway in a second; there was Jolie, creeping up on her again. There was a smash and Rona looked down. Jolie had dropped the bottle of wine.

Rona felt nothing. She didn't need wine; she was running on pure adrenaline right now. Although she knew she disguised it well. She knew that about herself, the way she presented herself. She knew what people thought about her, the way they saw her. What they thought they knew about her.

Jolie looked as though she were about to cry.

The kids were there, they were trying to look at what was happening.

Jolie screamed at them, shocked at her own response.

Rona looked back into her room. She closed the door.

'Stay there. I'll get something to clear it up.' Rona stepped over the mess and went to the kitchen. What had Jolie heard? What did she think she knew? Rona knew Jolie was constantly checking in, trying to ascertain if she was real or fake, if she was here to help or not. Rona thought she had done a pretty good job of showing Jolie that she was here to protect her, but a mother's instinct was stronger.

A little while later, Rona handed Jolie a cup of coffee. She needed to calm her down; she could see the way her eyes had begun to flicker back and forth, the way she pulled at her clothes and looked around at the children. Rona knew she had to remain calm, she couldn't let Jolie become hysterical. She needed to stay alert, stick to the plan, and it would all be over very soon.

27

JOLIE

TWENTY YEARS AGO

The end of the week arrived, and the families began packing up to go home. Jolie was in the kitchen on Saturday morning, having just moved her final towel bundle of the week. She had taken a sneaky look at the envelope attached to the bottom of the pile and as she had been told, there was indeed five hundred euros there. Jolie's heart had sped up, and she had to calm herself down with some deep breaths. A part of her had thought that she might not get anything, that she might have to have an awkward conversation with Duncan. But this was the easiest, most uncomplicated job she had ever done in her life. There had been no awkwardness, and she had been paid on time as promised. She'd done jobs in the past where she'd had to speak to her boss when her wage was late. But this set-up was seamless, and she couldn't believe she had managed to become a part of it.

Jolie was busy getting breakfast ready as usual when Ali sidled up to the kitchen counter.

'Could you possibly pop all those bags by the door? That would be great,' and she walked away without even looking at Jolie.

Duncan heard the exchange, and a smirk appeared on his face.

'Does she think I'm a porter?' Jolie joked.

'Better just do it,' he said and Jolie waited for the smile, the little joke they might share about it, but there was none.

Duncan walked over to Rebecca and pulled her into him for a long kiss. *He knew I was watching that*, she thought. Then she remembered Martina and the way she had seen them leave the bar together. Duncan really did think he could have anything. And he did – the wife, the mistress, the dealings that were making him a fortune on the side.

'The coach arrives in thirty minutes. Any chance we can get the breakfast on the table for the children?' Rebecca pulled herself away from Duncan.

Jolie didn't look up and began placing the pancakes and fruit on the table.

She flicked the kettle ready for coffee and thought about how she had a day off tomorrow. The new chalet guests always arrived on a Sunday night and were given a meal at the local restaurant or helped themselves to the prestige items in the gift hamper. Either way, it meant that she could party tonight, and the best bit was that she had a pocketful of euros. She had intentions for the money she was making from the towels – which sounded funny even in her head, but as far as she was concerned, she was working for a bundle of towels – but tonight she was going to celebrate. She looked at Duncan, wondered if they might have an opportunity to speak again. He had been pleased with her work and she wanted to hear him say something positive again before he left. But the opportunity hadn't arrived.

'I'll be back in a few weeks,' Duncan muttered as he passed her on the way to the door. 'Any issues, text me on that number I gave you.'

'Okay,' Jolie whispered just as Rebecca came back from the bedroom. She noted the food on the table and the children tucking in and couldn't possibly have anything to say, but she was looking at Duncan, and Jolie wondered what she knew about his 'job', if she had anything to do with it, if she condoned it or if it irritated her. But if it was what funded her annual two-week trip to Marbella with the girls, plus all the plush outfits she had been modelling all week, she really had nothing to complain about.

It was Duncan who moved the bags in the end and then the skidoo arrived to take their luggage to the road. Then there was a lot of commotion as they all tried to leave the lodge, still collecting their belongings and forgetting things. Finally, they were all at the door, except for Mark who stopped by the kitchenette and placed a twenty-euro note on the counter.

'Thanks for all your help this week; we couldn't have done it without you.'

Jolie looked down at the money between the two of them and then looked up at Mark. He had kept himself to himself all week and had been pretty quiet in between meals. Jolie imagined he had a job in an office, maybe accounting. She looked at the note again. It was a kind gesture, and a few days ago Jolie would have been thrilled with a twenty-euro tip.

Times that by twenty weeks, if every family was as generous, which she had heard they were, then that could be four hundred euros by the end of the season.

Jolie did the math in her head and felt her mouth twitch as though she wanted to laugh, then she remembered herself and thanked Mark profusely. He left looking pleased with himself.

Jolie now had to turn the whole lodge around ready for the next guests arriving tomorrow. But then she was free. The challenge was to see how quickly she could do it. The average time was three hours, but Jolie had heard someone had done it in ninety minutes before.

She waved the family off, waiting for one last look from Duncan, which came once he was on the last skidoo. He did a quick tap to his head, which looked like a salute, and Jolie waved. Then she closed the door, walked over to the sofa, and collapsed into it.

In the end, Jolie tidied the lodge in just over two hours. She was pretty pleased with herself, and when Estelle arrived just before she left to check everything, as this was the end of her first week, she struggled to find anything to quibble with. She had forgotten to restock the tissues next to the bed and she hadn't turned down the toilet roll at the edge the way Estelle had shown her, but other than that, everything was as it should be and Estelle swept out of the lodge with barely a goodbye.

Jolie locked up and headed back to her apartment.

She was walking through the door to the foyer when she almost collided with Adam, who was heading out.

'Oh, hey,' Jolie said. Adam looked at her as though he wasn't sure who she was. He looked tired. His eyes had black rings under them.

'Jolie,' Jolie said.

'Right,' Adam replied.

'Good day at work?' she asked.

Adam looked vacant, as though her question had barely penetrated him.

'Errr, work, yeah. Well, yeah I suppose.' He scratched his head and then began rubbing his arm.

'Okay, well, I'll see you in Mak's tonight? You're gigging there, right?'

'Er, yeah, that's right,' Adam said, barely able to make eye contact with her.

'Okay then.' Jolie pushed past him and made her way to the stairwell.

'It's Jolie right?' Adam called after her and Jolie turned and nodded.

'Yep.'

Adam nodded and walked outside. Jolie snorted out a laugh and shook her head. She'd had a few interactions with Adam since she had been here, barely enough to cement a relationship, but that one was particularly odd. He looked terrible.

Jolie had arranged to meet Paul and Sabrina and Arnie in the bar tonight. After her lesson with Duncan, she felt a little more confident about going up the mountain, but it wasn't calling her or inspiring her.

She had just got into her apartment and collapsed onto the tiny sofa when there was knock at the door.

Jolie stood up, letting out a loud sigh, and opened the door. It was Martina. Jolie felt her stomach do a tiny somersault. She had been disappointed with the way Duncan had left, and she was glad to see her friend.

'Mountain?' she said with a broad grin on her face. 'We'll do green slopes?' Martina cocked her head to one side; she knew Jolie was a beginner and hadn't yet caught the bug.

'Sure.' Jolie sighed, thinking she could nap after a few runs before going out that night.

Jolie and Martina sat next to one another on the chairlift. Jolie took in her surroundings – the mountain ahead of her and the huge drop beneath her, where tiny skiers were hurtling down the slope. She looked ahead as a cold breeze whipped at her face. It was pretty cold today, and the sun was stubborn, refusing to come out from behind the clouds.

Jolie was far away in her own thoughts, thinking of the first week she'd had and how unexpected it had been. She felt a pull in her gut that Duncan was suddenly gone. But she had his number. She could text him or call him, even. But then she thought of Rebecca's pursed face, and Martina and Duncan leaving the bar together. She would be silly to try and get any more involved in any other way than just colleagues. He was her employer now.

It took Jolie a while, as she was so far away with her thoughts, to realise that they had been on the gondola for quite a long time. She turned to Martina and then looked down beneath them. She recognised the green slope she had been used to going on, but they had just passed it and were getting higher.

'Where are we going?' Jolie asked.

Martina was quiet. After a few seconds, she turned lazily to Jolie.

'To the black slope.'

'You said green,' Jolie said quietly. She didn't want to give Martina the satisfaction of seeing her anxious.

'I think you'll be good on black.'

'Martina, I can barely snowboard as it is. I need to stay on the greens.' It was too late; the stress was already in Jolie's voice, and Martina could hear it. Jolie was sure she could see a smile forming at the edge of Martina's lips.

Finally, the gondola stopped and Martina hopped confidently off, thrusting herself forward on her snowboard and making a show of turning and slicing up the snow to stop.

'Come on, Jolie!' she said and Jolie thought she was going to be sick. There was no way she was making it down this mountain on a black.

Jolie stood and glanced at the other ski lift a few feet away that was headed back down the mountain.

'Martina, you know I can't.' Jolie's voice broke. She was suddenly so cold. The temperature was so much lower up here. She shivered. But she didn't move. She could try it, but she would be on her backside the whole way down. Why had Martina brought her up here when she knew she could barely get around on a snowboard yet?

Martina sliced up the snow a bit more, snapped her goggles down over her eyes, and launched herself down the mountain.

The word 'pussy' rang out loud.

Jolie felt her stomach twist and tears prickled her eyes as she edged her way to the lift, released herself from her snowboard, slotted it outside the cart, and took a seat inside, ready for the slow descent down the mountain.

28

JOLIE

NOW

Jolie stood at the window. The wind was definitely much stronger. She had been standing listening to it for a while now. Hoping it would subside, but knowing that this was the beginning of the storm Rona had mentioned. As if a huge dump of snow was not enough, now Jolie had the worry of the wind bringing down the snow from the mountain above them and potentially burying them. Jolie had an overwhelming desire to run. Her body was in fight or flight, and she had nowhere to escape to, nowhere to expel the fear that was raging through her body.

She turned and marched to her room, pulled out her suitcase, and rifled through until she found her leggings and a sports bra. She had intended to use the gym when she was here but had spent all her time with the children on the nursery slopes. Now, she needed to exercise, to do a hard workout to expel all that anxiety. There was no way she was going to get through the evening otherwise.

She pulled on her gym gear and returned to the living area. She began to imagine a high-impact track in her mind. She could see herself in her gym class in her mind's eye, surrounded by others, the instructor hollering directions from the front of the room, as she began running on the spot. The children raised their heads from their game.

'Can I do it too, Mummy?' Vita scraped her chair back and ran over to her mother. Jolie ignored her and focused on running on the spot. Vita began to copy her, mimicking her speed and trying to fall in time with her. Her little legs were flaying about like a new-born lamb, and she was grinning and panting and laughing all at once. Jolie stared at the space in front of her, not thinking about the snow or the threat of an avalanche or the grounded flights or her lost phone or her husband safe at home in England; she just focused on the lactic acid surging through her thighs and occasionally the sounds of her daughter trying to keep up next to her.

Suddenly, running on the spot didn't seem to be giving her the satisfaction she was craving, so she put her foot out to begin moving side to side, just at the same time Vita, who was all over the place, landed in front of her. Jolie stood on Vita's foot and tripped simultaneously, landing on top of Vita, and her knee made harsh contact with the wooden floorboards beneath.

'Vita! For goodness' sake!' Jolie screamed, falling to her side and cradling her knee into her chest. Out of the corner of her eye, she saw her daughter jump up and run out of the room.

Jolie was flooded with every emotion: anger, frustration, and then slowly, little by little, guilt. The guilt was always there, ready to jump in at any given moment. And now, it was flooding through her system as though she had been injected with it through a needle.

She lay on the floor for a moment, listening to the deafening silence, knowing that both Gable and Rona would be looking at her, waiting to see what she would do next. Perhaps they were expecting her to combust spontaneously. It wouldn't surprise Jolie if she did, because she no longer knew what might come next in the torrent of emotions she was going through.

Hauling herself off the floor, she looked at the bewildered expressions on Gable and Rona's faces and headed into the bedroom that Vita was sharing with her brother. Jolie found her lying face down on the bed. Jolie lay beside her; Vita edged up to give her space, which was a good sign. Jolie wasn't a snappy mum. She didn't lose her crap with her children daily. She knew how to balance discipline well and when to let things slide, which was why she didn't allow herself to cling to the guilt too fiercely. It was an unprecedented circumstance. Jolie didn't imagine that she would ever find herself in a situation that would test her patience as much as this ever again.

'I'm sorry for shouting,' Jolie whispered and Vita let out a little sniff for good measure. Jolie edged in closer and Vita turned over rapidly and nuzzled her face into her mother's chest.

'I miss Daddy,' Vita murmured. And whilst usually this kind of comment would make Jolie feel perturbed, she thought of Idris back home in England and nodded.

'I miss him too,' she said.

After a few more cuddles and bogus sobs, Jolie and Vita left the bedroom and discovered Rona and Gable on the floor with the paper and pens.

'What's going on here then?' Jolie asked as Vita fell to her knees to get involved straight away.

'You throw this rolled-up piece of paper and see which piece of paper it lands on. See, this is a ten. It's the hardest number to get because it's right at the top, but if you hit it, you get ten points.'

'I want a go,' Vita demanded.

'Okay, Vita, wait because I haven't finished writing all the numbers out yet. Can you roll up some more paper into balls?' Gable asked his sister.

Vita happily obliged and Rona took a step back.

'They love a home-made game,' Jolie said hating that Rona was back doing something helpful and kind again. Why couldn't Jolie just work her out once and for all?

'Well I grew up in Birmingham in the nineties. We had to make our own fun.'

'Didn't we all,' Jolie said, knowing that Rona might not quite believe her. Now, she had adopted a soft plummy tone living in Kensington over the last decade, but she'd had to find her own way as a child. She didn't receive the guidance and love and care that she craved and she had been living independently ever since her parents had effectively thrown her out in her early twenties. But she didn't feel like telling her little sob story to Rona right now; every one of her emotions felt as though it had been dragged through the ringer today.

'You should have children, Rona,' Jolie said and walked over to the fridge to get some water. She knew she hadn't said it in a kindly manner, but she was done with this situation. It was all Rona's bloody fault. She was almost out of patience. Jolie knew her anxiety was now manifesting as anger and there was no one else but Rona to take it out on. In fact, it was because of Rona they were here in this unsafe lodge in the first place. Rona had lied. She had knowingly put them in a condemned building. But even Jolie knew at the time, there was little choice available to her. Perhaps Rona simply thought she was doing the right thing.

Rona shook her head. 'I'm too busy. I have a life that I like, and I just don't think ki . . . children,' Rona corrected herself again, 'would have a place in it. I don't think I could give them what you do.'

Jolie paused to consider Rona's words. While it was hard to see oneself from an outsider's view, she thought that others likely saw her as a mostly composed woman who loved her children deeply. She recognised that not every woman was cut out to cope with the demands of motherhood, which lasted many decades.

Jolie was not one to make other women feel pressured to do something she had consciously chosen to do. Rona had made her choices, to stay living in Cil del món all this time, when for Jolie it had been a fleeting moment, a place she had passed through. She would certainly never have imagined living there, but Rona had chosen to do this for a reason, surely? It wasn't just the job, because making it as far as manager in two decades was surely not reason enough to stay living somewhere as cut off as Cil del món. Jolie had soon become claustrophobic, longing for a savannah plain or a sea; a week was long enough.

Despite how frustrated Jolie was feeling at Rona, and the complicated mess she was now in as a result of her 'helping', the game was a huge success, and the children finally began to show signs of tiredness. Jolie breathed out a sigh of relief, but she wondered how she might fill the hours before her bedtime. There was now nothing to drink – she shuddered as she replayed the horrors of losing the wine and then her anger at Vita. She wondered if Rona would craft together some kind of evening activity for them to do. Netflix, a pizza and a bottle of wine was her preferred option but she would take anything now for the distraction.

Jolie got the children into bed. Gable wanted to read, which Jolie said was fine, but Vita was out after one story.

In the kitchen, Rona was boiling the kettle again.

'I found some mint teabags at the back of the cupboard,' she said.

'I thought you would tell me it was coffee again. I cannot take another cup of the stuff.' Jolie sighed.

'They're not famed for their ability to make a good coffee in Cil del món.'

'No, that I had noticed. I am craving a decent latte from our favourite haunt in London.'

Jolie watched on as Rona poured the boiling water over the teabags and realised she probably sounded spoilt and posh.

'I'd take a biscuit – I have an overwhelming craving for sugar. Must be the stress.' Jolie tried not to let Rona hear exactly how panicked she still was, as the tightness in her chest grew.

'Biscuits!' Rona exclaimed, and Jolie jumped.

Rona looked up at Jolie. 'I packed biscuits in my holdall. I didn't pack much else, but in the rush, I managed to get them in.'

'Well, hoorah for you. That's the best news I've heard all day.' Jolie felt a little relief at the prospect of something sweet hitting her system.

A loud beeping startled them both and they ran to the windows to look outside. Rona's car was flashing.

'Your car alarm,' Jolie said.

'Yes,' Rona said, her voice was light and airy.

'But the battery?' Jolie asked brightly. Did this mean the car could work? That they did in fact have a way back down the mountain once the snow stopped?

'Yes,' Rona said robotically.

'It was dead?'

'Car alarms often go off when batteries are dead. More so in fact.'

'Right. Well. Where are your keys?' Jolie asked, happy to trek the few metres to the car to disable the alarm.

'I'll go.' Rona went to the back door, collected her snow boots and slid them on and went outside. Jolie lifted the teabags out of the cups and put them in the bin bag.

'Biscuits,' Jolie said to herself, and as she did, she realised she had a good excuse to nip to Rona's room. She could quickly scout around, see if anything looked out of place. She padded down the corridor to Rona's room and opened the door. The bed was perfectly made. She opened the wardrobe. It was empty. The only item on the bedside table was a torch. Jolie quickly opened the bedside drawer. Empty. She fell to her belly and looked under the bed. Nothing. She walked over to the holdall in the corner. *Now where would Rona stash biscuits?* she wondered and went instinctively to the side pocket and unzipped it.

'Oh God.' Jolie's hand went to her mouth. Her body suddenly felt heavy, and a thickening sensation arose in her throat. Of course the car was not dead. Rona had been playing her all this time. She had been brought here for a reason. And she was now staring at it. In the side pocket of Rona's holdall was silver tape and rope. Jolie could only think of one reason why Rona would bring those two things all the way out here, and she knew it – what she had been fearing all this time but had been trying to suppress. She and her children were not safe here with Rona.

29

RONA

Rona came back in the front door, smacked her boots on the thick mat and pulled them off. There was a possibility that the snow or a blast of wind had set off the car alarm, but Rona had lived in Cil del món a long time. It would usually take a lot more than that to set it off. She was wary. She was sure she had done enough to ensure that no one knew where she was. The lodge was condemned. She had taken a real chance bringing Jolie and her children here. Rona had to be clever. She had to make sure no one knew where they were. That was why she had erased the message Jolie had typed to send to her husband. Because all it would have taken was for him to call and communicate with someone in the village, and then someone would have worked out where she was. Jolie had put far too much information in her original text. But Rona knew she had made an error writing 'kids' instead of children. Would her husband have picked up on that and worked out that Jolie had not written the text? Would he have picked up the phone and called someone in Cil del món?

And then there was the Facebook post that Jolie had put out. Rona had been clever, she had replied to her inbox. And now that was erased as well. But Rona couldn't help worrying that she had been too late to get to it. That too many people had seen it.

'Tea is ready,' Jolie called. Rona knew Jolie was trying to put on a brave face. She had heard the tremble in her voice, and she could see how she was beginning to unravel, even more so than when she found her in the café a few days ago.

Rona began walking over to the kitchen counter and slowed when she saw what was on top of it – the biscuits from her bag that she had hurriedly packed before she got here.

Jolie was smiling. 'I found the biscuits in your bag. And chocolate too, you devil, Rona, hiding that from us.'

If Jolie had found the biscuits, what was the possibility that she had opened the side compartment to the holdall first? Had she seen the tape and rope? Rona tried to assess Jolie's behaviour, but she was all over the place at the moment. Rona couldn't decipher if she was skittish and if it was because of what she had just discovered. Rona went tentatively to the kitchen counter and picked up her mug of tea. She looked up at Jolie. Jolie was watching her.

'Car sorted?' Jolie asked.

'Yes, I think like I said, it was probably just a bit of wind or snow.'

'But the battery. It's dead?' Jolie said again and Rona felt her skin prickle.

'That's probably why it's going off,' Rona repeated. She had already had this conversation with Jolie. Why was she questioning it again?

'Right,' Jolie said. 'I didn't know that could happen.'

'It does.'

'Well that explains it then, doesn't it.'

'Yes.'

'Exactly. What else could it possibly be?'

'Exactly,' Rona said. The two women stood at the counter, the packet of chocolate biscuits between them, the inanimate object that seemed to be telling Rona that she knew, she had seen. Of course she had. The side pocket was the obvious place to look first. Only Rona had decided to put the tools she needed to restrain a person in there instead. She really hadn't thought any of this through. She had tripped up and made mistakes in getting Jolie up here. It had been a rushed decision. She hadn't known that Jolie would be here; it was a complete fluke, her being in Cil del món, the planes being grounded. The only thing that wasn't unusual was the snow. There were at least two major dumps throughout the season, and snowstorms were not uncommon. It was both a help and a hindrance, though. It meant that no one could get to them, but it would not prove easy getting out if it didn't ease up.

As much as Rona was used to this weather and being in a small village, she was not enjoying being trapped in this lodge any more than Jolie was. Only Rona had a better of way of managing her emotions, mainly because she tended not to have them. She felt things for sure, but feelings – sadness, happiness – didn't arrive when they should do, or at all. It didn't bother Rona. But it did bother other people. Rona had noted how it had unsettled Jolie. She could see it in how she looked at her, waiting for her to say or do something else to fill the void.

Rona was acutely aware of how much Jolie had changed. She was no longer the fly-by-the-seat-of-your-pants girl she had met in the lodge that day. She still seemed vulnerable, but she was much more together; she seemed as though she might be able to handle situations much better nowadays. But Jolie had never been in a situation like this before. Rona still had the upper hand. She was sure she was still in control here.

Jolie picked up her cup of tea and Rona watched her hand as though it were happening in slow motion. She was poised and ready in case that boiling water came at her face. But Jolie slowly lifted the cup to her lips and took the tiniest sip. She then placed her cup down on the counter. She took the chocolate biscuits and ripped them open. The cellophane wrapper crunched so loudly it hurt Rona's ears. Jolie carefully laid out some of the biscuits on a plate in a fan pattern.

She pushed the plate towards Rona.

'Have a biscuit, Rona,' Jolie said. 'After all, you did bring them.'

'Well, for emergencies, really.' Rona shuffled her feet and looked at her tea. Her mouth was dry. She could do with a drink.

Jolie looked around and scoffed. 'I'd say this was an emergency, wouldn't you? I can't remember the last time I was trapped in the Pyrenees mountains, staying in a condemned lodge in the middle of a snowstorm,' Jolie said, the sarcasm oozing from every syllable.

Rona took a biscuit and then lifted her tea and sipped it.

'Lucky you found those teabags.'

'It was,' Rona said. She was sure they were over a year out of date. But they tasted okay.

Jolie shifted behind the kitchen counter and Rona was suddenly aware that it looked unnatural, and that Jolie was staring at her just a little too hard.

Rona took a step back, her mind racing, wondering what she might be able to grab to protect herself. She was not prepared. She thought she would have to wait another day or two before she had to start using force. She had been working herself up to it slowly. It had been a long time coming, all of this, and now she had little choice. She would need to deviate slightly from her plan, but that was fine. Rona was okay with that.

But before she had time to think about what to do next, she realised Jolie was moving fast from behind the counter, and she was now at her side. Her hand was raised; there was something in it.

'No!' Rona shouted and raised her hand to protect herself.

Rona couldn't see what it was Jolie was holding, but then it came down hard on her head and everything went black.

30

JOLIE

TWENTY YEARS AGO

Jolie had been in Cil del món for three weeks when Duncan sent her a text and said he was due back next week. She realised she was excited to see him. She had just received her third payment – another five hundred euros. She got the same thrill when she saw the packet as she had the first time. She was sure this was never going to get old. She now had one thousand five hundred euros stashed under her mattress, plus her wage, which was going into a bank account here in the Pyrenees.

She was just about to finish up with her family for the week and then she wouldn't need to be back into work until Monday.

Martina burst into the lodge just after her family had all vacated.

'Oh my God, I am so done already.' She fell onto the sofa.

'Hey, do you mind? I just fluffed that,' Jolie said.

'Fluff this,' Martina said and raised her middle finger to Jolie. Jolie acted shocked. This was what Martina did; it was all a big show. But deep down Jolie knew there was a little girl who just wanted to be loved and cared for. That was why she was looking to Duncan to give her that. Jolie had managed to forget about the mountain episode. She had been tired, let her emotions get the better of her. Martina was an accomplished snowboarder and Jolie would be holding her back if she expected her to get on the green slopes with her.

Martina didn't really seem to care about anyone but herself, yet in a way, Jolie thought it was refreshing to see someone who didn't try so hard all the time, the way all her friends at uni had.

'Duncan is back tomorrow,' Jolie began and Martina shuffled down into the sofa.

'And?' she said childishly.

'And, you know. You two.'

Martina let out a loud, short laugh. 'Us two?'

'Yeah, you know.' Jolie felt more comfortable now with Martina, so she decided to mention what she had seen that first week. 'You left Mak's together, that night. I saw you.'

Martina frowned. 'I can't remember.'

'Well, I'm telling you. You did.'

'Oh, I'm sure I did. I just can't remember the night.'

'So, what's the crack with you two?'

'There is no crack.'

'But I thought you liked him.'

'Have you ever heard of unrequited love? Don't you English write about it all the time?'

'Ahh, so you like him, but he . . .'

'He's married,' Martina said. 'Besides, we are more business acquaintances. The two cannot blur.'

Jolie stopped folding the towels on the pristine kitchen work surface.

'What did you say?'

'I do a little work for him from time to time. Help him out.'

Jolie rushed around to the sofa. 'What sort of work?'

Martina rolled her eyes and laughed. 'Oh, come on, Jolie. We don't need to pretend here. We both know what Duncan does, why he comes here so often without his wife.' Then she turned and pointed at Jolie. 'And we both know what it is you're doing to help him out.'

Jolie felt her face flush, but she couldn't deny that Martina's voice was tainted with resentment. Martina was already in with Duncan from what she had just said. Was Jolie now stepping on her toes? She wouldn't like to think what Martina's reaction would be if she knew Duncan had given her private snowboarding lessons. She wasn't even sure if she was supposed to admit to Martina what she was doing for Duncan. He had taken her on for her discretion; her ability to lie easily. Whilst she regretted what had happened at uni, she was grateful for what she had here with Duncan.

'I . . . I don't know what to say.' Jolie tried to be as vague as possible.

'Towels!' Martina pointed to the pile on the counter.

Jolie looked at Martina, and they both started laughing.

'Are we supposed to be talking about this?' Jolie asked her friend.

'I've worked here for two years; this is my third year. I know everything that goes on. It's a small place; if you open your eyes you can see. I see you in that laundry shack first thing in the morning. I didn't need Duncan to tell me that he had employed you to do the job I was doing last year.'

'You did that?' Jolie whispered even though there was no one in the lodge but them.

'Easiest job in the world.'

'Tell me about it,' Jolie said excitedly, thrilled she could finally talk about it with someone, even if they were still not saying it exactly. 'So you still help him out?' she asked.

'We're business partners,' Martina said. Her voice was high and showy.

'Oh, right,' Jolie said.

'Why are you saying it like that?' Martina sounded offended. She sat up straighter on the sofa.

'Oh, sorry, I didn't realise I was; I just meant that . . .' Jolie paused. She wasn't sure what she meant exactly, except that maybe Duncan didn't seem like the partner type or that Martina was quite flaky and loud and self-absorbed. Was she the sort of person that Duncan would trust his business to when he was out of the country? She couldn't say any of these things of course. Martina settled back down into the sofa. Her feathers had been truly ruffled.

'So are you enjoying your little missions?' she asked, a little sarcasm in her voice this time.

'Of course I am. Like you said, it's the easiest job ever and the, well, you know the package on Saturday.'

'Oh, I know, that was a big bonus. I bought my mother a car the first year.'

'Did you?' Jolie had already thought of what she would spend the money on, and none of it would be going to her parents.

'Of course, my remuneration is a lot higher now.'

'Oh really?' Jolie was intrigued.

'Yes, because I am more involved. I have to take bigger risks.'

Jolie nodded. It made sense now why she'd left the bar late with Duncan that night.

'So you work—'

'Yes, directly with the big boss,' Martina interrupted her.

'Duncan is not the big boss?'

'No he is not.'

'Oh.' This was all brand new to Jolie. She had bought a bit of weed when she was in halls from the local dealer, but she had never been this close to the crooks of it before. She wanted to know more but at the same time, she didn't want to.

'I can't believe we've both been doing this and we didn't talk about it.'

'Well I knew of course, but I was waiting to see if you might say anything to me. It seems you're very good at your job and at not discussing it.'

'Thanks.' Jolie smiled, that happy glow creeping through her with the little bit of praise. 'You know, I'm kind of surprised there is a demand for what we do here.'

'Oh, don't be surprised, Jolie. I have realised that nothing can shock me now.'

'And Adam?' Jolie asked. The bruise had faded on Martina's cheek but there was a hollowness to Martina's eyes, as though she hadn't slept for a week.

Martina looked confused.

'What does he think? I presume he knows.'

'Oh he knows. He is very well looked after in that department; in fact, it is becoming a bit of a problem.'

Jolie thought back to a few weeks ago when she saw Adam in the foyer and he looked terrible. She had seen him a few times since then and he hadn't looked much better.

'What's the matter with him?' Jolie whispered.

'He has an addiction,' Martina said. 'But it's my fault. I brought it into his life.'

Jolie wasn't sure what to say. 'Should we try to get him help?'

Martina shrugged. 'I don't think he would take it. Maybe he should go home. I have tried to tell him this, but he doesn't listen to me.'

'So things are difficult for you two?'

'We rarely see each other; he works early mornings in the hotel and late nights in the bar. I think that's why he needed it so much: to help with that.'

'But surely he doesn't need to work in the hotel. You have enough money for both of you?'

Martina snorted. 'You think I will give all my money to an Englishman?'

'Oh.' Jolie wasn't sure if she was supposed to feel offended by that comment, so she let it slide.

'Well, I think we should go and ride up the mountain to celebrate.' Martina stood up and put her arm around Jolie. 'You can do your silly green slope,' she said and ruffled Jolie's head rather too fiercely. Then she took the towels off the kitchen counter and put them in the cupboard.

Jolie did her final check and then took her key, and they walked to the door.

As Jolie stepped outside, she almost fell on top of someone.

'Rona,' Martina said, and what was supposed to be a greeting was filled with contempt.

Rona's eyes shot between Jolie and Martina.

'Were you coming in here?' Martina asked.

'No,' Rona said and carried walking along the path.

'She was coming to check up on us.' Martina began to swagger as she walked. Jolie suppressed a smile. 'She is so annoying. She is always there, nosing about. I don't like her. I call her dowdy; she is so you know . . . ?'

'Dowdy?' Jolie finished her sentence and Martina laughed so loudly that Jolie couldn't help but laugh with her.

'I don't really know her,' Jolie said once they had stopped laughing.

'Well, if you and I are going to be friends, you need to agree.'

Martina linked her arm through Jolie's, and they began marching off down the road to their apartment block together. But something stirred inside of Jolie, and she couldn't resist a swift look over her shoulder. When she did, she saw that Rona was standing there, watching them.

31

JOLIE

NOW

Jolie had done a pretty shoddy job when she looked at it, but the rope tied around Rona seemed to do the trick. She was sitting up in the chair, her head slumped to one side. The rope was wrapped and tied around her whole body. She hadn't bothered with the gaffer tape, but she held it in her hand, ready to stick it over Rona's mouth at any moment when she woke up and decided to start screaming. She didn't want to wake the children and involve them in any of this. She had no idea what she was doing, what would happen next, or how long she would keep Rona there. She needed to leave this place, but she now knew that Rona was not here to help her.

Rona began to rouse, and Jolie picked up the rolling pin she had found in a drawer, ready to hit her again. Jolie's heart raced, her mouth was dry, and she needed to pee. What if she had done something terrible to Rona? Brain damage or she now had some internal bleeding? Was Jolie going to be in a lot of trouble? But she was defending herself and her children. Their lives were in danger. What choice did Jolie have?

Rona was coming round. She was going to open her eyes in a moment and realise where she was and what had happened. Then she was going to kick out and start trying to escape, and Jolie was not sure she would be able to restrain her. Rona was much bigger than Jolie.

Rona began to murmur. Jolie wasn't going to be fooled; she had seen enough jump-scare movies to know you don't lean forward to hear what the captured person was saying, so they could head butt you or something. The words 'it's the quiet ones you want to watch' felt very fitting.

Eventually, Jolie deciphered a word.

'Stop. You need to stop.'

Jolie scratched her head and paced back and forth across the room. Thoughts of brain damage came back at her again. Rona wasn't making much sense. What if Jolie had hurt her badly? But what if Rona had hurt her or her children? She paced harder and then stood back in front of the chair.

Rona had begun to open her eyes and was slouched, squinting at Jolie.

'Noooo,' she moaned. 'Not this.'

'Rona,' Jolie whispered in a hiss, clutching the rolling pin in her hands.

Rona focused her eyes on Jolie. 'What are you doing?' She pushed out the words breathlessly.

Jolie pointed the rolling pin at Rona. 'Keeping you away from me and the children.'

'You . . . don't understand,' Rona whispered.

'I think I understand pretty well. I found the tape and rope in your bag. What were you going to do? Tie me up, leave me here, and take my children? Kill me? Come on, Rona, speak up because I need to understand this sordid plan of yours.'

Rona murmured something.

'Speak up,' Jolie spat.

'I don't want you dead,' she said. 'But someone else does.'

32
RONA

Rona could tell that Jolie didn't believe her, and why should she? It all looked pretty bad, even from Rona's perspective. The lost phone, the building not safe to sleep in, the tape and rope. But somehow, she was going to have to try and convince Jolie that what she was saying was true.

'You and your children are in danger, Jolie.'

Jolie spat out a laugh. 'That is hilarious coming from you. I will never let anything happen to my children, do you understand? I will kill you if I have to,' Jolie said through gritted teeth and suddenly Rona saw there was no doubt. She may not have been a mother herself, but she had seen what mothers did for their children; she had been told about the bond, the fierce love that was planted when a baby was born and grew into something so impenetrable.

'All those years ago, the job you were doing for Duncan . . .' Rona began.

Jolie stopped pacing and stared at Rona.

'You think I didn't know?' Rona almost laughed. Here was poor Jolie again, so sweet and innocent and completely unaware of what had truly been going on.

But Rona knew the truth. She knew it all, because she had been there, and she had been watching.

33

JOLIE

TWENTY YEARS AGO

Jolie was startled by a loud knock on the lodge door. The lovely Danish family she had been looking after for a few days, a husband and wife and three children, looked confused but still stared at Jolie, waiting for her to deal with it as though she were the butler.

She went to the door and looked at the woman in the pink ski jacket with tight blonde curls.

'Oh hi,' she drawled in an American accent. 'Our maid hasn't turned up. Could you come and make our beds when you've finished here?'

Jolie was dumbstruck, firstly at the audacity of this woman, but also that Martina wasn't at work. They had been out last night in Mak's. Jolie had left with Sabrina and

Paul; she didn't see where Martina ended up. She felt a stab of worry; she should have made sure she got home okay. But then again, she wasn't her babysitter. Martina was a grown woman.

'Have you contacted our office?'

'I tried,' the woman said, but it sounded as though she hadn't tried at all. 'But we've seen you and her together; we figured you help each other out. We managed to make our own breakfast but we really won't have time to clean our own bathroom and make the beds and you know, do all the extra things you maids do.'

Jolie felt her skin crawl a little. Most of her guests were an absolute dream, but occasionally, she would come across guests like this woman, and it would make her want to get on a plane and fly back to the UK.

'I'll see what I can do. I'm on a—'

'Oh, thank you so much, you're an angel,' the woman said without letting Jolie finish saying that she had quite a lot to do here. Her family had requested afternoon tea instead of dinner as they were going out, and Jolie had arranged to meet Paul and Sabrina up the mountain. She was certain she wouldn't get a chance to make a cake and finger sandwiches before 3 p.m., clean her own lodge and the neighbours', and get up the mountain. She cursed Martina under her breath. She closed the door and returned to her duties. Her family were already seated, waiting for their breakfast.

Jolie made it next door two hours later and felt her body completely deflate at the sight of the place. Clothes strewn everywhere, plates and cups and cutlery left from last night and this morning. She didn't dare think what the bedrooms and bathrooms looked like, but she would be able to guess.

'Hi.'

Jolie spun around. It was Dowdy, the woman Martina disliked so much. Jolie had forgotten her real name and she was too embarrassed to ask. Too much time had passed. But this woman was always in the right place at the right time.

'Martina not turn up for work?'

How the hell did she know? How was this woman so busy with her own jobs and still able to get to know everyone else's business? Martina had called her nosy, but Jolie wasn't sure that there was something to gain from someone like Dowdy, who was always willing to help.

It would still be hard going with two of them, if Dowdy were to help, which she was sure she would, but there would be no going up the mountain today for her. She would get the place looking immaculate and be praised for her efforts and for helping out her friend, even though Martina didn't deserve it and was probably at home sleeping off a hangover. But Martina had never not turned up for work before, no matter how out of it she had been the night before.

'Yeah.'

Dowdy shook her head and was already inside the lodge assessing the damage.

'I have some spare time, if you need help.'

She was already removing debris from the kitchen counters.

'Thanks but I . . . I think I can manage,' Jolie said and flashed Dowdy her best smile. The beginning of her name was coming to her . . . She felt rude not being able to remember it.

'If you're sure,' she said.

'Absolutely,' Jolie confirmed. She knew that Martina would not want this woman helping her out. She smiled weakly and waited for her to leave, which she did eventually.

Jolie looked around the lodge an hour later. It was as immaculate as any lodge on the first day before the guests arrived.

'That was a job well done,' she said to herself. She hoped that Martina would be grateful.

'Hey!' came a shout through the door and Jolie looked round to see Paul there.

'Oh hi!' She felt a wave of relief because as grateful as she was, she needed to get out of here.

'Are we off up the mountain?' Paul asked, placing an arm around Jolie's shoulder once she had locked the lodge and they were walking back down the hill.

'I'm off to see Martina. I just had to clean her lodge.'

Paul tutted loudly.

'What?'

'You know what. She isn't a good friend to you. Why do you waste your time with her? You have us.'

Jolie let out a sigh. 'I like her.'

'Hmmm. It's frustrating, isn't it, when you like someone, but they don't like you back as much.'

Jolie looked at Paul and then laughed. He laughed too as she rested her head on his shoulder and they walked down the hill together. She felt that this was a safe place, with her head on the shoulder of a man who clearly had feelings for her. She was sad she couldn't summon the same back.

Jolie needed to be back at her lodge to serve afternoon tea. That didn't leave her enough time to get up the mountain. She wasn't a fast snowboarder; she still hadn't really got the hang of it or got the buzz for it. She usually took her time and went very slowly. Rushing up and then booting it down a couple of slopes wasn't her idea of fun. She would relish the rest instead, but first, she needed to check in on Martina.

Paul had left her outside her apartment block and Jolie went straight to Martina's room. She knocked on the door, and there wasn't a reply. She knocked again, and this time, she heard the shuffling of feet approaching. The door was flung open, but Martina was already walking away. Jolie stepped in, closed the door, and watched as Martina, who was wrapped in a duvet, slowly made her way to the sofa, where Jolie imagined she had been for most of the day.

She went to the kitchenette, which was covered in dirty plates and coffee cups.

'Are you going to tell me what happened?' Jolie asked. She liked Martina a lot, but she didn't fall for these attention-seeking displays. Jolie had spent two years at university and witnessed many students who acted the same way. It was either due to being spoilt or not getting enough attention. Jolie fell into the latter, but she rarely sought it through acting out and not turning up to work. 'I had to clean your lodge. I missed my mountain meet with Sabrina and Paul.'

'You shouldn't have cleaned the lodge.' Martina's voice was small and hollow.

'Well, the woman from your lodge just came in and started ranting at me,' Jolie said, moving a few plates and cups into the washing-up bowl and turning on the tap.

'It will do her good to clean up her shit for once.'

Jolie added washing liquid to the hot running water.

'Why are you doing my dishes now?' Martina asked in a muffled voice.

'I'm just giving them a soak.' Jolie turned off the tap and sat down on the hard chair at the small dining table. 'She was pretty full on.' Jolie moved a few books and magazines away so she could rest her arm on the table.

'She's a class-A bitch.'

'Well, Dowdy popped in and wanted to help. I turned her away,' Jolie said absently.

'Dowdy!' Martina roared and sat up. The sad meek person Jolie had arrived to had gone and been replaced by a wild animal.

'Martina!' Jolie wailed. 'Your eye!'

Martina lifted her hand to her eye and grazed her hand across the big purple bruise.

'What happened?' Jolie rushed to her side.

Martina turned her head. 'Does not matter. What matters is why did you let that madwoman near my lodge?'

'I sent her on her way. I knew you wouldn't want her to help me. Even though I could have done with the help.'

'Just keep that woman away from my lodge,' Martina said.

'The American woman from the lodge, is she why you didn't go to work today?' Jolie moved Martina's hair to get a better look at her face.

'Of course not. I do not get affected by those people. I've been doing this job for a long time.'

She looked around the room; it was particularly unkempt today.

'Adam's left,' Martina said softly and Jolie almost felt sorry for her.

'Gone home? To the UK? Is he the one who hit you?'

'So many questions.' Martina waved her hand.

Jolie looked at her.

'He didn't say. He just got on a bus this morning and left. Took all his clothes and his snowboard.'

'Shit. How do you feel?'

'How do you think I feel?' Martina snapped.

It was impossible to tell. Martina was a medley of emotions all the time. Jolie would have imagined she was glad not to have Adam drugged up to the eyeballs lounging around the apartment all day. But she didn't say so.

'I guess that was a stupid question. I just meant . . . I don't know what I meant.'

'I'll get over it. Things were pretty shit between us anyway.'

'Sure.' Jolie nodded in agreement with Martina, as she knew how Martina felt about Duncan.

'Did he leave because of Duncan?'

'He hated me working for him.'

'And Duncan?'

Martina turned away from Jolie. 'He cares nothing for me. He sacked me.' Martina's voice broke.

This was why Martina was here, alone, bruised, and depressed. Because of Duncan.

Martina sat up and flung the duvet off herself.

'I've had enough, Jolie. You know he is taking me for a ride. Us both. You may think he's paying you well, but do you know how much he makes from all of this? We put ourselves at risk; we could go to prison. Did you ever think about that?'

Jolie had thought about it, but then she considered where they were and felt protected here for some reason. She was far away from real society. This wasn't real life; it was just people having fun, all the time.

'We have to do something. Look at me, Jolie!' Martina opened her arms in exasperation. 'He cannot keep getting away with it.'

So many questions were running through Jolie's mind – was it Duncan who had hurt Martina? Jolie thought back to the moment in the bar when she had witnessed Duncan snap over a spilt drink. His entire demeanour had shifted in an instant and then back again. She knew he could be cold sometimes too. But most of the time she saw his good side: fun, considerate. And he paid her very well. Martina was prone to these outbursts, and she was obviously emotionally involved with Duncan, which meant she may not have been thinking straight.

Martina stood up and began pacing the room. For the first time, Jolie was able to get a good look at her. She was dishevelled, obviously having been in bed all day.

Martina had lost control. Jolie could see it in her eyes. She looked like a wild animal caught in the headlights of a car.

'And you, Jolie, you must help me.' Martina jabbed her finger at Jolie.

'Me?' Jolie almost laughed. This was ridiculous; she was happy. She had a job that was okay; she wished it had slightly fewer hours, but she got just enough downtime, and she had been making a nice, tidy extra income from Duncan. She didn't want to rock the boat. She had a few months left here and then she could forget all about her time here. Martina could too. They just needed to get their heads down for a few more months.

Martina was about to mess that all up for her own frustrations and need for revenge. Besides, Jolie could not be sure of the full story. She was only hearing Martina's grievances.

'Jolie!' Martina snapped. 'You will help me, or I will contact the police and tell them exactly what you've been doing.'

'What the hell!' Jolie stood up and faced Martina. 'Why would you do that? You're still earning enough money; once we have enough saved up, we can leave, together. Don't make it like this, Martina. You'll regret it, you really will.'

'I have no choice, Jolie. In my country, people are not allowed to treat others in this manner. Duncan has crossed the line. He cannot get away with it.'

'Did he hurt you?' Jolie asked. 'Did give you that black eye?'

Martina softly touched her chest where her heart lay. 'Here. He hurt me here.' And she began to sob, falling into Jolie's arms and crying on her shoulder.

'Please, you must help me,' Martina said softly. And Jolie felt sick at the sudden conundrum she had found herself in. She was happy with her side job, but Martina was unpredictable. She was going to put herself in a position that was not only going to damage the project, but put her in danger as well.

34

JOLIE

TWENTY YEARS AGO

'Hey.'

Jolie spun around to see Duncan standing behind her at the bar. She had been spending less and less time up the mountain, choosing to enjoy a nice glass of wine in the afternoon or the occasional shopping spree in the valley, where everything was tax-free.

'Fancy seeing you here.' Jolie looked at the seat next to her and Duncan sat down without her offering it. It was Sunday, her day off. Jolie was about to enter her fourth week in the resort. Duncan was back for his second visit of the season.

'Busy today?'

'Yep. Same for Martina.'

Duncan made a sound as though he were sucking his teeth.

Jolie breathed out. She wanted to say something. She felt she owed it to Martina, to ask Duncan what he had done to make Martina so sad. So angry.

But Duncan began talking about something else. 'I get to come here and relax. When I'm not here, I'm busy in one way or another.' Duncan's smile consumed his face and Jolie tried to associate Martina's accusations with the man she was looking at. It was difficult trying to see the monster Martina perceived.

'Business all good?'

'You know I don't discuss my extracurricular projects, Jolie.' Duncan looked around. The bar was practically empty; it was a stunning day, and everyone was enjoying the warm weather up the mountain.

'Rebecca must be getting psyched for her Marbella trip.' Jolie couldn't keep the laughter out of her voice.

'Hey!' Duncan playfully slapped her arm. 'She loves it. Anyway, guess who you have staying with you?'

'What? You?' Jolie had no idea Duncan was her guest for the following week.

'Don't worry, I won't make you work on your day off. I'll be eating out. It's just me and a mate – Jim.'

Jolie had seen the booking sheet for Sunday to Saturday and it was definitely not Duncan's name on the sheet.

'But I was sure I had a German family.'

'*Es is sehr warm*,' Duncan said in a German accent. 'I can be German if you like?'

Jolie laughed. 'Don't be a dork. I saw their names; they were German. Did you get it swapped?'

'I might have pulled a few strings to get my favourite host.' Duncan put his hand up to the bartender.

Jolie felt a fizzle in her gut. Martina would not be happy that Jolie was hosting Duncan and his friend. She was sure of it. Jolie would be in close proximity to Duncan every day for seven nights. She could see the scowl on Martina's face now.

The young barman approached them.

'Two beers please.'

'Erm, wine please.' Jolie pointed to her glass.

Duncan looked at her glass. 'Oh, very sophisticated for an afternoon tipple. Another wine for the lady.'

'Seriously, though, Jolie,' Duncan said as the barman moved away to prepare the drinks. 'I really appreciate your discretion and continuity. I have had zero complaints.'

Jolie smirked. 'Well, it's not that hard, Duncan.'

'You'd be surprised how some people didn't quite adapt to the uniformity of it.'

For the last month, she had been on time every day to pick up the towels from the laundry shack and deliver them to lodge 23. She hadn't found it difficult, but she could see how others might begin to slack after a while, not getting there at precisely the right time, which was imperative to the system. Everyone had their part to play, even though Jolie had yet to meet anyone she was working alongside on this project. She hadn't even seen Martina in that capacity. Duncan had done well to keep them apart for discretion.

'Well here's to us.' Duncan lifted the beer bottle the barman had just set in front of him and Jolie lifted her glass of wine.

'Here's to us,' Jolie said back and they clinked the glasses together.

'Well isn't this just a cosy little scene.' Jolie swung around to see Martina standing behind her. Her normally olive skin was ashen, and her hair was ruffled.

Jolie felt herself shrink, and Duncan puffed out a long breath.

'Hey, Martina,' he said slowly.

Martina pushed herself in between Duncan and Jolie.

'You have some nerve showing your face in here.' Martina's accent was becoming more Spanish like by the second, something that seemed to happen when she was talking passionately or when she was angry.

'I come here when I want, Martina, always have done, always will do.'

'Oh, yes, that's right; because you have your little business, you think you can do what you want,' Martina said loudly and Duncan shot her a stern look. 'What would you do without all your customers? Your pretty wife would not have any clothes, and you would not have a fancy car.'

'Be quiet, Martina, you're just embarrassing yourself,' Duncan said through gritted teeth and Jolie tried to shoot Martina a warning look, but her eyes were set hard on Duncan.

'Oh sorry, did you not want me to say it out loud, what you do here, why you keep coming back?'

'This is exactly why you don't work for me anymore,' Duncan spat.

Jolie tried to catch a look from Martina but her eyes were locked on Duncan.

Martina recoiled slightly but she wasn't completely deterred.

Duncan turned in his chair. 'I got rid of you a long time ago, yet you still keep hanging around? Why is that? Do you not understand English?'

Martina went to lunge for him but Duncan grabbed her arm.

Duncan's chair shot back so hard and fast that Jolie jumped out of her own seat. Without looking at her, he marched her out of the bar. Jolie watched them leave and noted how Martina didn't flinch, or protest or try and shove Duncan off her. Jolie looked at the barman and smiled awkwardly. She thought of those bruises and wondered if after all it was Duncan who had given them to her.

'Think she's had too much to drink,' Jolie said but she felt her gut tighten as she said it.

Jolie sat back down and finished her second glass of wine just as Duncan came back.

'Sorry about that,' he said to her and then nodded to the barman, who appeared seconds later with a fresh cold beer. Jolie felt a stirring in her gut.

'Hopefully, that's her told,' Duncan said, and Jolie shifted in her seat, but Duncan's expression was hard and he focused on the beer he was handed. Jolie looked away out of the window and tried not to allow the seed of doubt and fear betray her.

Jolie arrived early at the laundry shack again on Monday morning; she watched as the van arrived and towels, duvets, covers, and pillowcases were delivered. Then she went in. It amazed her how prompt the van was every time, but then it wasn't as though it had to deal with the kind of traffic that she had seen in many parts of the UK. It seemed to sail in and out every time.

Jolie went into the shack and made a beeline for the towels. But just as she approached them, she heard a shuffle. It was darker in the back of the shack, and she rarely turned the lights on, allowing the light from the front door to illuminate the area she needed to see. But the sound brought Jolie to a halt. She felt a prickly sensation along her back. Surely, she was alone. No one ever came in here this early; most of the hosts were in here at midday, picking up supplies to replenish. It was most likely a small animal. But still, Jolie felt a slight tremor of fear pelt through her when she lifted the towels, as though the police might jump out and arrest her. Martina's erratic behaviour had got to her; she needed to put it behind her.

She scurried from the shack and went to lodge 23. She placed the towels down in the cupboard the way she always did, and this time, she didn't rush out. She wanted to see who might appear and take over the next part of the job. She had always been curious, but never had she been brave enough to wait around. Part of her didn't want to know because it kept things the way she needed them to be, as though she were playing her small part in this, and she didn't need to know any more. But today, perhaps it was the unrest Martina had caused or the sound in the shack just now, but she felt like stepping outside her comfort zone.

Standing in the corner next to the window in lodge 23, Jolie looked along the path. It was quiet; the laundry van had left, and there were just a few people she didn't recognise milling around. She looked at her watch; it was past 8 a.m., but she only had Duncan and his friend to cater for this week. She doubted they would even be up yet and once they were, they would be low maintenance.

So she waited another five minutes to see if anyone would come, and when they didn't, she walked out onto the path and looked up and down. No one was headed this way. She turned and walked back up the hill towards her lodge, ready to greet Duncan.

Just as Jolie turned away, a figure slipped out from behind the laundry shack. Rona took a few long strides until she was at the door of lodge 23. When she was sure that no one was watching her, she walked in.

Jolie wasn't long into making their requested simple breakfast of eggs and bacon, when Duncan came through, dressed in joggers and a T-shirt. He looked tired and his hair was ruffled.

'Wow, good night was it?' Jolie said knowing she sounded like a cliché, but also aware that this light banter was the right level for her and Duncan. She had left him shortly after the Martina incident. It had felt too uncomfortable to stay.

'You shot off pretty quickly?' Duncan said and Jolie thought she heard an edge to his voice.

'I was tired. And I needed to be up early to be here.'

'You know I don't care about that.' Duncan moved closer to the island. 'I would have liked to have spent more time with you.'

Jolie felt her throat go dry. She reached for a bottle of water and took a sip. 'Maybe another time.'

'I hope so,' Duncan said authoritatively. Jolie's heart pounded in her chest. Her mind was questioning her body's reaction to this man she had put her trust in. But Jolie knew she was uncomfortable with the way he had removed Martina from the bar and there was the unresolved issue of where her bruises had come from.

'We ended up playing poker until nearly 1 a.m. I left in the end, with slightly lighter pockets than when I arrived.' Duncan chatted animatedly.

'Oh dear, well, I have your breakfast nearly ready, and it's a great day to be up on the mountain, so I'm sure that will clear your head.' Jolie realised she sounded robotic. She no longer felt as free and easy around Duncan, and the look he gave her suggested he understood that.

The arrival of a man in the doorway took both of their attention away from one another.

'Ahhh, Jolie, this is my good friend Jim.'

'Nice to meet you, Jim.'

'Hi, Jolie, I've heard great things about you.' Jim shook her hand forcefully. Jolie smiled weakly.

Just before the men went to leave to go up the mountain, Jolie found a moment to grab Duncan aside. Maybe if she spoke to Duncan about Martina, they might be able to find a way to help her.

'I'm worried about Martina,' she said meekly.

'Don't worry about Martina. She's a tiny problem. She'll get bored soon, move on to someone else.'

'She's only mad because you sacked her,' Jolie reminded him in case it had slipped his mind.

Duncan spat out a laugh. 'Is that what she told you?'

Jolie felt stupid. Duncan sounded so sure, and Jolie had only heard Martina's side of the story, which she had automatically believed.

'So you didn't sack her?' Jolie asked.

'She worked for me very briefly. But it was obvious from the beginning she was not up to the job. Not like you.' Duncan smiled and his eyes twinkled despite how tired he looked.

Jolie began to replay all the conversations she'd had with Martina on full speed in her mind, reminding herself that Martina had insisted that she worked for Duncan, in a higher-paid job.

'Once I told her it wasn't working, Martina tried to set up on her own, maybe to get one over on me, I don't know, but what she was selling was garbage. Look at her boyfriend, look at her, the pair of them are in a state. She tried to use my name to get ahead, to make people buy her shit. I can't have people doing that to me, Jolie, do you understand?' He had edged closer to her. His words had become hard.

'I . . . I guess not,' Jolie said meekly. 'It's just she told me that—'

'I couldn't give a flying fuck what she told you.' Duncan's face was suddenly very close to Jolie's, his face red and his lips brimming with spittle. Jolie stepped backwards. Duncan stood up straight, moved his shoulders up and down.

'She seems to have got under my skin,' Duncan said quietly. And Jolie wondered if that was an apology for his outburst?

Jolie noticed her heart was pounding. She felt a growing unease, that she was stuck between two quite angry people, and she wasn't sure which one to trust. She guessed it would be futile to ask Duncan if there had been anything romantic going on between him and Martina. She was certain he would deny that too and possibly become even angrier.

'Could we maybe try and calm her down between us? She really is very upset. Whatever has gone on—' Jolie held up her hands '—she is raging about it. I just think it's important to keep the peace. I'm just thinking of you and your business.' Jolie looked around even though it was just her and Duncan in the lodge now.

'I've been doing this a while, okay, and there's always a Martina. Someone who wants so desperately to be a part of it they'll do whatever they can to bury their way through. But I can't have someone like Martina a part of things. Martina was one of my best clients.' Duncan almost sounded sorry when he said it. Jolie thought of Martina the last time she had seen her, the way her eyes had looked just like Adam's.

Jolie felt something cold surge through her body as the darker side of this mountain became clearer.

'She's so angry,' Jolie said, and she knew she sounded desperate. 'I don't know what to do.'

'There isn't anything we can do. The same way I've seen many go before her, Martina will end up on the same slippery slope as all the others.' Duncan's tone lacked any empathy. 'I get you're trying to be a mate.' Duncan patted her on the shoulder before he walked outside. 'But some people just are too far from saving.'

'But,' Jolie added, and Duncan turned around. 'Are you not worried?' Jolie whispered. 'About what she might do?'

Duncan just laughed and carried on walking up the hill, his snow boots crunching loudly in the morning air, as though Jolie had just said the funniest thing ever.

Jolie needed to think smart. Duncan had walked away and left her with an unpleasant feeling. He didn't care; it was all about the money. Martina was right. Duncan didn't care what happened to them. But her main problem was that Martina was going on a rampage. She was going to try to do something to ruin Duncan, and Jolie was sure she would suffer as a result. She needed to step in and do something, and fast, before it began to fall apart around her.

Jolie could sense Martina's rage building; and so was Duncan's. She just wondered who would blow first.

35

RONA

TWENTY YEARS AGO

Rona went into the laundry shack and walked to the back of the room.

'Right you, out,' she said firmly. Martina looked up at her with wide eyes like a deer.

'And you can give me that as well.' Rona snatched the camera from Martina's hand.

'Give me that back, bitch,' Martina spat; her face was red and blotchy. She looked like she had been crying in the laundry shack for a while.

Rona stuffed the camera down the back of her trousers. She was stronger and taller than Martina.

'I told you, this is not the way to go about things. You need to act smart. This is dumb, taking photos. Who are you going to share them with?'

'The police?'

Rona spat out a laugh. 'Do you not think that Duncan already has an in with the police? He'll no doubt be paying off the chief. He'll be lining his back pockets to turn a blind eye up here. No one wants a fuss. There's a perfect rich little resort that brings in a lot of money for the area and pays their wages. Everyone just wants to keep their job and enjoy the quiet. You're riling everyone up, and it's not going to help anyone. Let alone yourself.'

'Why do you know so much about everything?' Martina asked.

Rona smirked. 'I'm the eyes and ears of this place. I know everything that goes on and no one questions me because I keep my mouth shut.'

'Why are you helping me?' Martina asked.

'Because I like justice. I like to see people get what they deserve. I think you deserve better and Duncan deserves to be eliminated.'

'What?'

'Do you think anyone would truly care if the local drug dealer suddenly disappeared?' Rona asked.

'But you just said—'

'I know I said he's in with the chief, but that doesn't mean to say the chief wouldn't be happier if he were gone. He might be a little lighter in the pockets, but he won't have the stress of a massive drug operation going on under his nose.'

Martina scratched her head and wrinkled her nose.

'I suppose. So what are we to do?'

'Start piping down for a start and then you do what I say. I think I can get Duncan to listen to me, to meet with you. We could all meet up at lodge 59.'

'The rural one?'

'Yes,' Rona said.

'But why?'

'Duncan knows me, he trusts me, and I know all he wants is peace between the two of you.'

Martina snorted.

'You can't keep this charade up, Martina. It's come to a head.'

'Duncan won't want to meet me. Look at my face, my arms.' Martina rolled her sleeves up, displayed her recent set of bruises. 'This is what he does to me. He got what he wanted from me and then disposed of me. I thought he . . . cared.' Martina's voice cracked.

'Do you not know men by now, Martina? Let's not dwell on that.' Rona spoke coldly 'Let's just focus on moving on. He might want to pay you off, for you to keep quiet.' Rona raised her eyebrows.

'How much?' Martina looked intrigued.

'I imagine in the region of ten thousand euros?'

Martina nodded. 'It sounds okay, but I think I deserve more.' Martina flicked her hair and examined a tatty nail.

'Don't push your luck, Martina. Ten thousand euros is a fine settlement and you could do a lot with it. Take off, have a nice holiday on the beach, buy a car. Just stop getting involved with this shit. It's over. It's time to move on. Next time Duncan comes to stay, I will arrange the meeting. We will get this sorted once and for all.'

Martina let out a loud sigh. 'Fine. Just don't try and talk to me again when other people are around, and stop following me.'

'It's a small resort, Martina. I can't help where I end up.'

'Well this doesn't make us friends,' Martina said, standing up and brushing her trousers down, 'even if you're trying to help me.'

'I worked out a long time ago that I don't need friends,' Rona said.

36

JOLIE

NOW

'Everyone knew what was going on,' Rona explained to Jolie. 'Martina ruined it all in the end for everyone. She was long gone; she was far from saving. She did what she wanted to do and didn't ever think of anyone else. I tried to help her.'

Jolie nodded. She knew how out of control Martina had got in the end. However, it had never been acceptable for someone to hurt her the way they were. 'I tried to speak to Duncan to ask him to help, but he was . . .' There was a tremor in Jolie's voice. 'Well, he wasn't very nice in the end.'

'What did you expect, Joli? He was a class-A drug dealer. And you were his employee.'

'I wouldn't quite say I was—'

'Don't try and paint it any other way, Jolie. You worked for Duncan; you moved drugs around the resort for him.'

'From the shack to the lodge.' Jolie tried to justify what she had done all those years ago.

'It doesn't matter now, does it. What matters is that you were her friend. You know it all went under after you left? After Martina went missing.'

'I . . . I wouldn't know.'

'No, you wouldn't. You just disappeared. I don't even want to know why anymore. For a while, I did wonder. But now, it's not relevant. Listen, Jolie, if you want me to help you, you need to pay attention. First I need you to let me out of this rope. I need to be free to help you.'

Jolie ran a hand through her hair and fought back the angry tears. She had been flooded with days of frustration and had nowhere to expel it.

'I can see this is difficult for you, Jolie. Why don't we take it slowly? You untie me; I stay here. I give you full permission to wallop me again with that thing if I take one step near you.' Rona lowered her head to motion to the rolling pin that Jolie was still clutching.

Rona sounded completely together, considering she had received a blow to the head.

Jolie was running out of ideas. But first she needed to know who was coming for her. After all this time. Could it be . . . no, it couldn't be Martina.

Jolie stepped behind Rona and began to untie the rope. She was surprised at her strength and how well she had tied them, so loosening them took her a minute. She unravelled the rope around the back, keeping her eyes firmly on Rona, and then walked around the chair a few times until all the rope was off. Rona didn't move, just blinked slowly at Jolie.

'Thank you,' she said quietly. 'You did the right thing,' she added, still not moving.

'Well, like you said, one wrong move,' Jolie said. Fear pulsated around her, but she did not want to show that to Rona.

The snow was still coming down and, from what Jolie could now see, was turning into a blizzard, some snowstorm that might last the night into tomorrow. She had witnessed a small snowstorm that lasted forty-eight hours when she lived and worked here, and she'd hunkered down in her apartment. Looking back now, it was a beautiful time; she was within walking distance of cafés and other people. Here she was just so far away from everyone and everything.

Rona began to shift in her seat. She stretched her legs out a little and looked at Jolie.

'Now please tell me, who is coming for me and my children?' Jolie asked and braced herself, gripping the rolling pin again.

'Jolie, you won't need that for me, but it's good that you're ready. He's coming.'

Jolie almost slacked her arm as she asked, 'Who?'

'Duncan. And he wants you dead.'

37
JOLIE

'What?' Jolie felt her stomach tighten, a surge of panic that then turned into a rush of sickness. How was this happening? She clutched tighter to the rolling pin; she was ready to strike again at any moment.

But she needed to know more.

'When Martina left and then you left shortly afterwards, Duncan was livid. He swore if you ever came back he would . . .' Rona stopped.

'He would what, Rona?'

'I . . . wouldn't like to repeat exactly what he said, but the general gist was that they wanted you . . . dead.'

Jolie thought back to the Duncan she knew, the one she had confided in that day on top of the mountain, who had essentially taken her under his wing. She had come from a home where her parents had disowned her for her stupid mistakes.

Leaving university and making them ashamed of who she was, who she might become.

Jolie had then gone on to make further mistakes, getting involved with Duncan, being a little accomplice to his scheme, a scheme that had him making money from the locals and tourists for many years. He must have made an absolute fortune, and Jolie's few hundred a week was nothing compared to what he'd been raking in. She had looked back over her time there often, and with each passing year, she'd become more confident of how she had been taken advantage of. He had homed in on her insecurities, seen how she was weak, having just arrived alone and with no support from her parents, except the flight money and a little extra to get her the hell out of their lives. She thought of Martina, the way her personality shifted between managing her emotions and losing control. She was the perfect candidate for Duncan because she was malleable.

And Martina had let her down too; she had not been the friend she needed her to be. But she still loved her all the same. Because Jolie had been too young, insecure, and desperate to have others like her and to show people she was capable. But really, it was all deep-seated resentment towards her parents' abandonment of her. She might have been a young adult when she left, but their behaviour was no different to the myriad ways they had neglected her needs and emotions as a child, always making her believe what she felt wasn't valid.

Jolie had not recognised it at the time, but therapy had given her the knowledge and tools. She'd felt angry at times, when it had crept upon her unexpectedly. There hadn't been anything she could have done about it then. But now. Well, now . . . No, what was she thinking? She needed to get away from here. Rona had just told her that Duncan was here and that he was coming to kill her. She felt sick.

'How do you know, Rona, about Duncan? Have you seen him? You said his business went under and he left not long after me.'

'Jim told me.'

Jolie thought back to the time she'd met Jim. He'd seemed so quiet, kind, and placid – not someone who would be friends with a killer.

'This sounds preposterous.' Jolie stopped herself from pacing, watched where Rona was standing and made sure she didn't pull any fast moves.

'It isn't really. Between you and Martina, you messed up their business.'

'None of this is this my fault!' Jolie choked on her words.

'None of it is your fault? You just happened to have got involved with the wrong people. It might have all felt so innocent back then because you didn't have to see anyone or speak with anyone, but there was this whole other dirty world behind the scenes. And if someone like Martina decides to start messing around, then things are going to end badly, aren't they?' Rona spoke so pragmatically that it made Jolie sound pathetic.

'But it was so long ago!' Jolie hissed.

'I suppose so, but Jim went to prison; Duncan narrowly escaped it. They lost out big time.'

Jolie had heard enough. She knew what she had to do. She thought of her children sleeping in the room across the hallway; it was all about them now. They were innocent and she needed to protect them. Here was a woman she barely knew, hadn't seen in two decades, telling her that a man she'd had dealings with twenty years ago was pissed off and was potentially going to kill her.

'If Duncan is on his way–' Jolie emphasised the *if* – 'then can't I just talk to him? He and I were friends. We spoke a lot; we had drinks. I knew him.'

'Jolie, you did not know him. You knew a side to him, a very small side to him, and the other side was not so nice. I really think you need to get with it and start believing me because, come tomorrow, they will have exhausted all their options in the village. In another day or so, the roads will begin to get cleared, and we need to make a plan to get away, to get you and your children to safety, without dying in the freezing temperatures first.'

Rona delivered her speech in such a way that Jolie found it compelling.

Of course, these men were part of a drug chain, and that meant that no illegal activity was off the table, including murder.

'Is that why you brought the rope and tape?' Jolie asked.

'Yes, it's why I did everything. I wanted to keep you a secret. I didn't want to tell you. I hoped I could give you what you needed: a place to stay and keep you out of harm's way. But it seems that there's no way I could have kept you safe. It always had one ending.'

Jolie thought for a moment. 'So what's the plan?' she said eventually. She needed to get out of this lodge as soon as possible.

'The plan is we stay here for as long as we possibly can, tomorrow at the latest. We have to watch the weather. As soon as there's a slight sign of the storm subsiding, we run. There's a hut about a mile from here. It's used for off-piste skiers who need to shelter from a storm or a white-out.

'We need to head straight up the mountain, keep walking for ten to fifteen minutes, and when we hit a collection of eight trees, we take a left. Keep walking, and you pass an old fence, broken but still visible even in the storms. Pass that, and about two hundred feet on our right is the hut. It may be half hidden by snow, but that's good because we want to be hidden.'

Jolie was quiet as she took in the information Rona had just given her.

'And the children?' Jolie asked.

'We wrap them up. We can take it in turns to carry the little one.'

'Vita,' Jolie said, aware that Rona had still not said her children's names out loud. Jolie stayed looking at Rona. 'And Gable.'

'Right.' Rona averted her eyes. She couldn't look at Jolie.

'Say their names,' Jolie said.

Rona glanced at her, perplexed.

'Say their names, Rona. I need to hear you say their names. They aren't just a commodity; they are humans. These are my children. They have names; now say them.' Jolie needed to hear the names of her children spoken by Rona, who had been unable to utter them.

'Vita . . .' Rona said and paused. 'Gable.'

'Right. Good.' Jolie breathed out.

'Okay.' Rona held up her hands. 'She sleepwalked the first night here.'

'What?' Jolie asked.

'She came into my room; you were asleep by the fire. I don't think she quite knew where she was. I recognised it, because, well, I used to do that a lot as a child.'

'What did you do?' Jolie's voice rang with alarm.

'Well, I put her back to bed,' Rona said, with an edge to her voice that sounded like she might have done the wrong thing.

'Right, well, yes of course you did. Thank you.' Jolie thought about the bottle of wine she had sunk and how quickly she had fallen into a slumber by the fire, her worries melting away as the heat warmed her bones. She always had one ear on the children, but she had not been there for Vita that night. Jolie felt a stab of wretchedness. She remembered that night; she had found Pooky bear in the hallway between the rooms. Vita must have dropped it as she walked to Rona's room, but Rona wouldn't have thought to pick it up and wouldn't have understood it's value to Vita. 'And the tape, I presume that's for Duncan?' Jolie asked. She needed to get as much information from Rona as possible.

'That was the plan. I didn't have a weapon, but I figured we could use your baton.'

'It's a rolling pin.'

'Yes, a rolling pin. If we have to.'

'Let's just hunker down tonight, and we'll look at the weather in the morning. If we think we can make a run for it, we do.'

'But what about all our stuff and your car? They'll see it, surely. And know that we're not far away?'

'We'll put all the luggage, anything you brought, in the car. I'll roll it down the hill; there's a load of trees I can hide it behind. Make sure you keep your coats and boots. Anything else we won't need.'

Jolie closed her eyes and rubbed them.

'You should try and get some sleep. I can stay awake for a few hours.'

'I'll get our suitcases,' Jolie said, and went to the bedroom to fetch her case and then the children's. Both Vita and Gable were fast asleep, and she was anxious for their safety and envious they were able to sleep, not knowing or understanding what was really going on. The bedroom felt warm and cosy, and she thought she would sleep here again; she couldn't let them out of her sight.

She pulled the luggage to the front door where Rona was waiting in her snow jacket and boots.

'Clear all the cupboards, take the perishables in your rucksack.'

'Okay,' Jolie said feeling useless and stupid, yet also responsible for all of this. 'And Pooky bear.'

'Yes. The bear,' Rona repeated.

'Rona.'

'Yes?' Rona turned.

'You know I'll do anything I have to, to protect my children.'

Rona was silent for a moment. 'Good. That's the fighting spirit I like to hear.'

Rona left the lodge to pile the suitcases into the car. Jolie took herself to her children's room, with the sofa cushions and duvet and closed the door. Jolie knew every word that Rona had just spoken was a lie. But Rona would not have known that she knew this. For the first time since she had arrived at the lodge, she felt she had the upper hand. She locked the door to the bedroom. There was no way she was falling asleep tonight.

38

JOLIE

The light crept through the window at the crack of dawn. Jolie's stomach turned. Her head was light and airy, the way she used to feel when the children had temperatures and kept her up. She had thought long and hard all night. She had always thought Rona was a strange character, but she hadn't realised how involved she was with everything. Jolie knew she was always there, outside a doorway, listening, watching. But she didn't realise just how messed up the whole situation was. She stood and looked out of the window. The snow had stopped. Maybe the snowplough had started making its way up here by now. She couldn't risk waiting anymore – Jolie knew now was the time to leave the lodge and get to the shack Rona had talked of.

Jolie gently roused the children. It was early. She had only slept for an hour or so and it was early to get them up.

'What is it, Mummy?' Vita asked.

'We need to get up and have some breakfast, get some energy in us. We have to move, go to another lodge, a little shack. We're going to put on our snow boots and walk up the hill a little bit.'

'But why?' Gable asked. 'Why can't we just go down the mountain? I want to go home now.'

Gable had had enough. That was clear from the tone in his voice. There was no hiding it. Gable knew what he wanted and he didn't try and disguise his feelings about anything.

'Well, it's just a slight detour for now. I promise I'll explain it all to you afterwards. For now, we just need to get out of here.'

She got the children settled at the table. She waited anxiously for Rona to rise. All the while she was on high alert for anyone or anything.

After a while, there was still no sign of Rona. Maybe she had gone and left them. That wouldn't have bothered Jolie; in fact it would be ideal. She jumped at every small sound. As the children dressed, Jolie stuffed a rucksack with the last of the fruit and bread and crisps, chocolate milk and water, two of the blankets from the sitting area, a box of matches. She slipped the one small chef's knife from the drawer into the bag.

That would be okay, Jolie thought. She was going to be okay.

Once the children were ready, she made them brush their teeth and then pack their toothbrushes.

Jolie told the children to put on two jumpers and a coat, then put on their snow boots and gloves. She got them situated at the back door, Rona's directions on a reel in her mind. Jolie walked past the kitchenette and picked up one more item.

She found Rona pacing the sitting area, looking stressed. And she had every reason to be.

'You look worried, Rona,' Jolie said.

Rona's eyes gave her away. It was now written all over her face. None of what Rona had told her made any sense. Because it couldn't be true. Rona was a liar. She had been lying this whole time.

'You know I can't take you with me, Rona,' Jolie said and pulled the rolling pin out from behind her back.

Dashing across the room, she struck Rona once, across the head. Rona stumbled backwards, blood began seeping.

Jolie approached her and struck again. Twice, three times until Rona fell to the floor and was no longer moving.

Jolie turned and walked quickly to the back door where the children were already outside making giant steps in the snow.

'Quickly, children. Let's go. We must go now.'

39

JOLIE

TWENTY YEARS AGO

Jolie was angry that Martina hadn't turned up for work again.

It was now February and she had worked at Cil del món for over two months now and the number of times she'd had to save her arse was unbelievable. It had been getting worse and worse. In fact, she hadn't seen Martina for days now. She hadn't bothered to go round and check on her this time. Of course Jolie was worried about her, about the re-occurring bruises, about how she looked and seemed. But what could Jolie do? Martina was her own person and would not listen to anyone. Jolie told her to leave whatever grievances she had with Duncan well alone. But Jolie wasn't sure she could. She was a loose cannon. It was better if Jolie stayed away for a while until things calmed down.

Duncan was back for the third time, this time alone, and Jolie was his host again.

The time away had allowed her to reflect and with Martina in decline, her focus was more on her than what Duncan may or may not have done.

'I think we should try some off-piste today, me and you,' Duncan said. 'You've been here long enough; I know you can handle some fresh powder.'

Jolie tried to laugh, but she had a headache and knew she would be cleaning Martina's lodge as well. She didn't think she would have the energy to be up the mountain, let alone off-piste, which was notoriously harder work, especially for a beginner like Jolie.

'Oh, I don't know. It sounds difficult.'

'It might be, to start with, or it might not. Some find it hard the first time, but you seem to take to new things very well, so I don't doubt you'll be excellent at it right away.'

'With that kind of encouragement, how could I possibly say no?'

With Martina acting out, Jolie wondered if it was wiser to appease Duncan. She wasn't keen to go off-piste yet; she still hadn't spent a significant enough amount of time up the mountain. So far, Jolie didn't know what was blocking her. Confidence, lack of passion, it could be any number of things. She and the mountain just didn't click. It was always as if it was pushing her away, telling her no, get back, you don't belong here. But she knew if she were to see this season through, she needed to get better. Maybe throwing herself in at the deep end was the best way. Duncan was a good enough teacher, even if it did involve plenty of boozy hot chocolates.

She was no longer worried about what Martina might think of her spending time with Duncan. She was tired of picking up the slack for her.

Jolie cooked and cleared breakfast and was just tidying the sitting area when Duncan came through, salopettes on, ready to head up the mountain.

'I'll need to pop in and sort next door's lodge, just give it a once-over. Looks like Martina didn't make it to work today.'

A look passed across Duncan's face that Jolie found difficult to interpret. He didn't reply directly to that comment, and so Jolie interpreted it as he was sick and tired of hearing about Martina.

'I'll meet you at the mountain, by the café.'

Duncan nodded and tried to smile, but he looked distracted now.

Jolie nipped into the lodge next door, expecting it to look a mess and for there to be a whole load of work for her to do. She had said to Duncan she would give it a once-over, but Jolie knew there was no such thing in these lodges with the number of people they were hosting at once. But when she arrived, she was surprised to see it wasn't messy, and that Dowdy was standing behind the island counter, wiping it down.

'Oh, good morning, Jolie.'

'Er, hi.' Jolie looked around. 'You did this?'

'I did.'

'How did you know Martina wasn't here?'

'I was passing earlier, and the client was outside. He said the host hadn't turned up. So I cooked breakfast for my family, and then came here. I'll go back to my lodge later to clean it.'

Jolie couldn't help but think that she looked quite pleased with herself.

'Okay.' Jolie looked around again. She could see that it was all under control. 'Well, I'll leave you to it.' Jolie turned to leave.

'Shame Martina let everyone down.' Jolie heard right before she walked out of the door. Jolie thought for a second about how to respond but she ignored the comment, left the lodge, and walked the short distance back to the apartments.

She took the elevator to Martina's floor and banged on the door. This time she wouldn't be soaking her dishes or listening with a sympathetic ear. She was going to give her a piece of her mind.

'Martina, open the door,' Jolie said firmly.

She listened and then banged again.

'God damn it, Martina, you can't just keep doing this. I can't keep covering for you. Just so you know, your friend, Dowdy, is covering for you today. How does that make you feel?'

'She's not in,' came a voice.

Jolie spun around, and a woman she recognised was standing in the hallway.

'I have a key. She borrowed, like, eight of my tops last week and hasn't returned them yet. We swap clothes a lot.'

Jolie looked at her, blinking, waiting for the woman to say more.

'I went in there earlier to get them. She's not there.'

'Oh,' Jolie said.

'She has a key to my apartment, too. It's in case we lock ourselves out. Which we have done a lot.' The woman laughed, and Jolie noticed she looked stoned or drunk, so this didn't surprise Jolie, as this was precisely the sort of thing that Martina would do regularly.

'I didn't hear her come back last night either. I'm a night owl. I usually hear her come home or she knocks on my door and we have a smoke together before bed.'

This was interesting, Jolie thought. There were a few places she could be, a few friends' houses she might have crashed at last night.

But right now, Jolie was sick of worrying and caring. She didn't particularly want to get up the mountain, but she would do it, to keep Duncan sweet. They seemed to have an easy relationship and Jolie wanted to keep it that way.

Jolie got herself ready and put on a few layers so it would be easy to strip off if she got hot. She thought of Martina as she walked along the village path towards the mountain lift. She wanted her to be okay, but things had got so fragmented recently, she didn't know who Martina was. Maybe once she came back from wherever she was, she would make more of an effort to spend time with her and do things that mattered instead of drinking. Maybe they could go to that spa she had heard mentioned.

Jolie rode the enclosed lift; a couple were in there with her. Jolie didn't much like the lifts. As she looked down, she could see tiny specks of people on various slopes below her. She sipped her water and was glad when the lift stopped and she could get out and collect her snowboard.

She walked to the café and saw Duncan waiting there, his face pink from a morning's run, his teeth glittering white in the afternoon sun.

'Shall we?' he said, and they headed to the gondola to take them to the next point of the mountain.

'Have you been over here much?'

'Loads.' Duncan pulled his goggles down as they got on the chairlift. They clicked into their boards and Duncan helped Jolie on. The gondola wobbled as it set off and swung a little back and forth, but soon it was moving smoothly. Jolie's stomach was jittery though. She thought she was fine with it, but as it rose higher and she could see fewer people on the slopes around her, she felt a growing unease.

'It's so beautiful, and you'll love it, I promise. Oh look, there's Pedro. Do you know him? He's one of the snowboard instructors.' Duncan pointed beneath them but suddenly Jolie couldn't look. Images of Martina kept popping up in her head and she wanted to ask Duncan's advice, but he was so uninterested and had been angry with Martina for weeks.

'The weather has been great, hasn't it? I'm glad we've got this time up here to talk alone. There's always so many people around. This is a good place to have a business meeting, wouldn't you say?' Duncan asked.

'I guess it is.' Jolie looked around, wanting to feel as though she were on the top of the world yet wanting to be anywhere else. All she could see were the slopes, a blue sky and a few mountains in the far-off distance.

'Here we go.' The lift slowed and they both dropped off into the snow.

'Those are the standard slopes there, if we edge off this way.' Duncan began sliding forwards, bending his knees and letting the board take him where he wanted to go. Jolie followed behind, taking longer, as her board rarely did what she wanted it to do.

'Again, I am really not great at this.'

'Ah, come on, no one can see us up here.'

Jolie's boots didn't feel tight enough so she leaned against a tree and unclipped herself from the snowboard, tightening the boots.

A voice behind her startled Jolie. She turned and saw one of the mountain chaperones approaching Duncan. Jolie could see them from between two trees, but the chaperone couldn't see her. He was waving his hands in the air and pointing down the mountain where they were headed. Duncan said a few things back to him in Catalan and then the chaperone really raised his voice. She heard the word he was saying.

'*Perill, perill.*'

Perill. Jolie thought. Danger.

Eventually the chaperone threw his arms in the air and trudged back to his post by the lifts.

Duncan reappeared and looked down.

'Oh, there you are. I thought you'd gone off without me.'

'What was the chaperone saying?'

'Getting his knickers in a twist about nothing.'

'Are we allowed to go this way?'

'We can go anywhere we want.'

'He shouted *perill*?'

'There were some workers felling trees here, but they've gone now. It's safe. He's just being cautious. Come on, let's go!' Duncan edged himself away until he was cruising lightly across the snow.

Jolie pushed herself to standing and slowly began to move forward.

Eventually the ground changed and Jolie could finally feel herself moving down without any effort.

'Just stay close to me,' Duncan called as he began to speed up.

'That's easier said than done,' Jolie mumbled to herself, holding her arms out, managing just about to connect a turn as the incline began.

'Okay, I'm here,' Jolie said as she felt a surge of excitement shoot through her. Maybe she could do this after all. Jolie could see the horizon ahead – no sign of any recently felled trees. Duncan was going to be so disappointed. He would probably want to go much faster than this, and he would be able to.

'You're doing great,' Duncan called back as they moved along at a decent speed. Every now and again, Jolie connected a turn; other times, she just hung back on the edge of her board to slow herself.

She straightened up and took a long slow turn, making a snake pattern in the snow.

Suddenly, it felt different beneath her board.

'We're on powder now, right?'

'That's right,' Duncan called.

Jolie liked the feel of it; it was like she was gliding on a cloud.

'It's amazing,' she shouted, but she felt the ache in her legs as she realised how she needed to balance harder and concentrate more.

'I know, right.'

Jolie could sense how fast she was going. She didn't want to stop, yet she was scared that if she didn't she might topple at speed, or hit a tree.

Duncan turned around. 'See, I told you,' he shouted.

Jolie felt her upper body relax a little, but her legs felt tight and stiff.

They continued like this on a fairly even flat plain for a while and it felt good. Jolie was able to connect a few turns and it felt quite pleasant. Maybe she was finally getting the hang of this.

Suddenly she toppled, letting out a yelp as she fell into the snow. But it was like landing on a big cushion, not like the times she had fallen on her coccyx. Snow covered the left side of her face. Duncan had heard her cry, stopped and was now trying to bunny hop back up the snow towards her. Luckily, they hadn't been too far apart, so Duncan was next to her in no time.

'You okay?'

'Yes.' Jolie laughed.

'You were doing great; we were flying just then.'

'I know. I want to do it again.'

'Get your breath back first.'

'I was having a bad morning, and that just cleared all the thoughts out of my head.'

'What thoughts could you possibly be plagued with? Your life is so easy and simple.' Duncan snapped his goggles off and pushed his hair back out of his eyes.

For a moment, Jolie wasn't sure what to say, but she knew she needed to mention Martina.

'I was stressed about Martina.'

Duncan let out a tut and sighed. 'Why spoil a lovely afternoon mentioning her?'

'She didn't turn up for work this morning and didn't come home last night.'

'And?' Duncan said. 'Do you really care?'

'I do. Do you not?'

'Why would I care, Jolie? The girl was one big headache.'

Jolie went to reply, to defend Martina and say that she wasn't always like that and in fact they'd had some wonderful times together here and she hoped to have more. But she stopped herself. Duncan had just said 'was' – he had spoken about her in the past tense.

'What do you mean, *was*?' Jolie dared to ask but even as she said it, she felt the tingling sensation creep around her back and shoulders.

Duncan looked away and shook his head.

'Oh, Jolie, Jolie.' Duncan sounded almost patronising, as though he were addressing a small child. 'I thought you'd get it. Martina was someone who was always in the way from the beginning.'

He'd done it again. He'd said 'was'.

'So . . .' Jolie began tentatively. 'Do you know something? Has she left without telling me?'

Maybe she had done what Jolie had predicted, and just upped and left with whatever paraphernalia was in her handbag.

'Oh, Jolie, come on, you can't play the innocent with me. You're in it up to your eyeballs. Don't pretend that you don't understand what happens when people start mouthing off. They're a danger to the whole production. Martina was a danger.'

'I know; you said. But do you know where she's gone?' Jolie asked. A tremor arrived in her voice.

Duncan didn't speak. He looked out across the snowy plain. There was a large part of the mountain to the left, so high and so full of snow. Avalanche. The word popped into Jolie's head. It had snowed a lot here recently. Was that what the chaperone was trying to warn them about? Was there danger of an avalanche? Duncan had understood what he was saying, yet he'd still brought her here. Martina was missing, her neighbour who noted her comings and goings didn't know where she was and now Jolie was in a dangerous part of the mountain.

'Where is she?' Jolie dared to ask, even though her whole body was trembling. She felt the snow encasing her like a beanbag.

Duncan edged closer and whispered, as though anyone might hear, but they were totally alone out here.

'You don't need to worry about that, just know that she's gone, and she won't be coming back, which means my business is safe, as is your job,' Duncan said impatiently and snapped his goggles back on. 'Now, there's a nice spot down here to the left I think we should try.'

Jolie felt her stomach loosen, her throat tighten, and her palms become so sweaty inside her gloves that she ripped them off.

'What the . . .' Jolie said under her breath. She had wished for Duncan to carry on his business without Martina wrecking everything, and yes, she had been enjoying the extra income for having to do very little, but this? This was unbelievable. Jolie needed Duncan to say it: to tell her what had happened to Martina.

'What did you you do to her?' She finally eased the words out.

'Oh Jolie, You must have seen enough films; the blabbermouth always dies. Martina was a blabbermouth. She knew too much; she was talking too much. She had to go.'

'Oh my God.' Jolie bent her head to the side and retched. She heard Duncan sigh, and then she began to panic. But she couldn't control her body.

'Jolie,' Duncan said quietly, and Jolie noticed for the first time, Duncan was carrying a small bag across his chest. He normally brought his rucksack on his back with water and a few emergency essentials. She looked at the chest bag. The zip was slightly open, something silver inside reflected the sun and glimmered.

This cannot be happening, she said to herself but she knew it was.

'I . . . I don't know what to say, I feel . . . well, she was my friend.'

Duncan looked away into the distance. 'No she wasn't, Jolie. Get real, she was a snitch. She would have stopped production; you would have lost your income.'

Jolie didn't care about the income, she cared that someone had died. She cared that Martina had died.

'And besides, don't play the innocent with me. I hired you for your ability to deceive. You let that girl take the blame for your mistake at university. You caused the fire Jolie.' Duncan had taken his mobile phone from his pocket. He waved it at Jolie. 'I recorded our little conversation. For collateral.'

Jolie pushed her bare hands onto her face. They were freezing on her cheeks. She knew she had to get up, move down the mountain somehow and then deal with this when she was on solid ground. But what was that he was carrying? Was it a knife, a gun? What if she didn't make it back down? What if that was why she was here? Another part of Duncan's plan. Jolie didn't want to open her eyes, in case when she did, he was standing there with whatever was in the bag.

Jolie peeled her hands from her eyes. Duncan wasn't there. She looked down the slope in front of her, which seemed to stretch on for miles, covered in perfect, untouched powder. Then a tiny voice. Jolie clicked out of her snowboard and took a few steps forward in her boots. She observed where the snow had parted slightly, about the size of a body, and below that was a deep hole. Jolie had heard about these crevasses – holes that open up in the snow through which one could fall. She had forgotten about them, as they were quite rare and she never expected to go off-piste.

Peering in the hole, Jolie could just about make out a body; it was Duncan. But this was deep. Duncan's voice sounded far away, and he was being absorbed by the thick snow that encased him.

'Jolie,' Duncan's voice came at her like a tiny noise from far away. 'You need to get down the mountain and bring help. Do you think you can do that?'

Jolie couldn't speak. She thought about the venture, somehow getting down the mountain, somehow making her way back to this exact spot all in good time. She'd heard how these holes didn't hold out for long. She heard Duncan's last words to her ringing in her ears. Martina was dead. And he had a recording of their first conversation on the mountain that day, when she had told him everything about the fire at the university halls.

'Jolie,' Duncan called again. 'You need to go and get help. Right. Now.' But this time, his voice sounded even further away, as though he had slipped further down.

Even though his voice was small and sounded distant, Jolie could hear the urgency in it. Then her mind flickered back to Martina, and her last moments – wherever they happened, with whom, and what she might have been thinking and feeling.

Jolie didn't need to consider it for long to know that Martina would have been scared and probably died in pain somewhere all alone. She felt it now; she could sense Martina's passing, and Duncan had confirmed everything.

Jolie walked back to her snowboard, sat down, and clipped herself back in. She pulled down her goggles, slipped her gloves on again, and jumped onto her board. She took off slowly, knowing there was only one way – down. Then she glided across the snow, managing to stay upright, as if she were floating on clouds. Tears streamed down her cheeks as she thought of Martina – so frustrated and misunderstood. Jolie should have done better by her. But somehow, it had all balanced out; Duncan was exactly where he needed to be.

That chaperone hadn't seen her; she had been covered by the trees. He had only spoken to Duncan, warned him of the dangers and then watched as he snowboarded into a dangerous part of the slopes. Alone.

40

JOLIE

NOW

'How long must we walk for, Mum?' Gable asked.

'Until I say we're there.' Jolie looked ahead and could see only white. The rucksack was hard and tight against her back and shoulders where she had stuffed in the two blankets on top of all the food she was certain they would need.

Jolie wasn't sure how long they might need to stay at this shack but it might be a while.

She of course had no clue that this shack even existed. But she hoped it did. Rona wanted to move them from the lodge to somewhere even more remote and Jolie now knew why.

As soon as she mentioned Duncan's name, she knew Rona was lying.

Jolie knew Duncan was no longer involved in this, because he was gone. She had witnessed it with her own eyes. She'd had to clear his things out of the lodge when he didn't return from his venture up the mountain and she had to pack them into his suitcase so they could be flown back home to England to Rebecca.

There had never been a big fuss made about Duncan's disappearance because of what he did and his association with the place. There had been no big search party; he was allowed to disappear quietly. Everyone assumed the worst. An innocent ride up the mountain turned deadly. Besides, it was more than twenty-four hours before he was reported missing. Before Jolie told Estelle her guest had not been in the lodge for some time. Maybe he had checked out? Everyone, including Rona presumed he had simply disappeared for financial reasons, to protect himself from whatever damage Martina had caused.

Years later, Jolie looked him up on social media, found Rebecca, and saw a few sentimental posts that confirmed to Jolie that he'd never made it off that mountain. After that she too disappeared offline.

Jolie had forced herself not to think of Duncan again, but she would sometimes hear his voice calling her in her dreams, the way he had from that crevasse that afternoon. Instead of dealing with all the emotions that had hurled themselves into her system that day, she simply pushed them away and focused on being a mum. But she was still haunted by the voice, and that was the anxiety that she carried daily.

Jolie was left with little option; she needed to get her children away from Rona, and Rona had just given her the directions to the place they needed to go. Jolie was confident that Rona had been telling the truth about that at least. Rona had brought that rope and tape for Jolie; there was no doubt about it. She would lock herself in the lodge and fight for her children if Rona came anywhere near her.

The sun was just coming up, the sky dotted with a few clouds. Would the snow ease off a bit today or would it start again? Jolie looked at her children struggling to walk through the snow, which was up to Gable's knees and nearly at Vita's waist.

But she had no strength to carry either of them, with the bag on her shoulders and trying to lift her legs through the snow. All they could do was keep walking.

Every now and again Jolie would turn and look behind her to check that Rona wasn't there.

'My feet are wet,' Vita said eventually. She had been so focused on lifting her legs to get through the snow that she hadn't spoken much. But wet feet were a good thing. If Vita was complaining that she couldn't feel her feet, then Jolie would be seriously worried.

Jolie kept repeating the directions on a mantra, desperately looking for a shape in the distance that would be the trees Rona had spoken of.

But there was nothing on the horizon. They were definitely going uphill as well, and Jolie could feel it in her legs.

'How much longer?' Gable asked again, and Jolie remained focused on walking ahead because if she dared to let her real emotions come through, she would scream and cry. She didn't want her children to see her losing the plot, so she started to whistle. It then turned into 'Heigh-Ho' from *Snow White and the Seven Dwarfs*, and soon the children were whistling and singing too.

Jolie squinted at the sun on the horizon and stopped.

'Oh my God,' she whispered.

'What?' Vita stopped and turned, as did Gable.

'Trees,' Jolie said, pointing to what looked like a cluster ahead of them.

'Oh yes,' Vita said as though trees were something totally special, and she was playing along with a game with Jolie. But Vita had no idea how special these trees were.

'Oh my God, oh my God,' Jolie said and began to move faster. 'Come on, you two, last one to the trees is a rotten tomato.'

They barely moved any faster, but arrived panting, wet, and cold and Jolie felt a whole lot better.

'Now we head up there,' Jolie said and pointed to the mountain where it opened up to the right. 'We walk that way.'

'My feet,' Vita said and this time Jolie heard some distress in her voice.

She bent down and put the rucksack on her chest and told Vita to get on her back. It was instantly uncomfortable, but Jolie ignored the discomfort.

After they had been walking for another ten minutes, Jolie was out of breath, her thighs burned from lifting her legs high to get through the snow, and her arms were strained from holding Vita.

'Let's just rest,' Jolie said, feeling a prickle of fear run through her. They had been walking for long enough, which meant that if they had to turn back, Vita would be in a lot of pain with her feet, which were beginning to freeze.

Jolie stretched out her leg and it connected with something hard. She bent down and began pushing snow away until it revealed a fence.

'The fence,' Jolie whispered. 'Okay, it's not far from here. We need to turn left a bit more and it should be up there.' As Jolie looked further up the mountain she could see the tip of the shack. Her heart exploded. They would be safe for a little while.

Once they reached the shack Jolie could see how the snow had fallen so thick around the doorway there was no way they would be able to open it.

'Right, children, time to start digging.' Jolie began to use her gloved hands as a spade to quickly move the snow away from the door. The children got involved straight away, even though Vita looked freezing.

'Okay, I think that's enough.' Jolie went to the door handle, praying it would move and wasn't locked. She turned the handle and it began to turn and then the door opened outwards.

There was just enough room for them to squeeze through.

'In you go,' Jolie instructed and closed the door behind them. There was a plank of wood, which served as a lock, and Jolie lowered it, which secured them in the shack. Then she looked around. There was set of bunk beds built into the wall with thin mattresses on them. A small fire grate to the right of that. Opposite on Jolie's left was a small counter that held a gas stove. Jolie went over to it. No gas anywhere that she could see. She went over to the fire. There was a small wicker basket with some kindling and a few logs. If the lodge had become condemned, because the mountain was dangerous, then who knew how long this shack had been sitting empty? But at least they were a little higher now and away from Rona.

'Okay, let's get this going.' Jolie found the matches in her bag, arranged the kindling, and got a flame going. She waited a few minutes, the children watching patiently by her side, and then, when the flame was big enough, she laid one log over the top. She knew they needed to burn carefully to make them last.

'Right, let's get these boots off.' She put Vita on the bottom bunk and removed her boots and socks. The socks were drenched, and Vita's feet were pink and raw-looking.

'We'll heat them slowly. Don't get too close to the fire,' Jolie warned. She placed the boots near the fire and laid the socks beside them. Already, the small space was heating up. If Jolie had felt claustrophobic at the lodge, then she had no idea how she would feel now, here in this room that was about twelve by twelve feet, no bigger than their shed at home.

'Now what?' Gable asked, sounding so much like a grumpy teenager that Jolie had to laugh a little. Gable eyeballed her and then a small grin appeared on his face.

'You're the man of the house. You make sure that fire doesn't go out, for a start.'

Gable slipped his boots and socks off and crouched down next to the fire.

Jolie felt a literal weight off her shoulders now that the rucksack was on the floor. She rummaged through it, taking out the blankets and laying them on the bottom bunk. She looked at what else remained in the rucksack: the rolling pin and the small number of snacks and the water she had brought.

'Shit,' she whispered under her breath, but the shack was too small and her word echoed around the small, cavernous space.

'Mummy,' Vita scolded.

'Sorry,' Jolie said. But it didn't matter how much apologising she would do from here on in, nothing would help her now – she had forgotten Pooky bear. She had thought he was in the bag, the way it had felt on her back, so squashed against her spine. But then she remembered that he couldn't be. She could see him in her mind's eye, in the bedroom.

She took out the snacks and drinks and laid them on the counter. She would need to monitor them and stop the children from helping themselves. They had just about enough to feed them for three days. One meal a day. But Jolie was certain they wouldn't be in there for three days. She was focusing on getting home.

But how? No one had a clue where she was.

There had to be hope. There was always hope.

Jolie rolled up a sweatshirt and propped it under her head for a pillow, she lay down next the fire and closed her eyes.

Jolie sat up, looked around the room. She must have fallen asleep. She hadn't meant to. Vita was lying on the bottom bunk, playing with her hair, singing to herself. Gable. Where was Gable? Jolie ran to the door and saw the lock had been lifted up.

'Oh, Gable,' Jolie panted as she pushed open the door. A cold wind swept in. She peered outside, but couldn't see him. She pushed her feet into her snow boots and ran outside. She walked around the side of the hut. Nothing.

She heard a bang. She carried on walking round and there was Gable, in his boots and coat, taking logs out of a black wooden lidded box next to the side of the shack.

'Gable. You scared me. I didn't know where you were.'

'You said I was the man of the house and not to let the fire go out. There are only two logs in there. We'll need more for tonight. So I came to look for more, and there are some here – look.'

'Well done, darling.' Jolie bent down and took four logs, Gable carrying another four. Gable closed the lid with his leg and they turned to walk back to the door. As they turned the corner, Rona was standing right in front of them. There was dried blood on her face. She looked possessed.

'Hello, Jolie,' she said quietly and ever so subtly glanced down at Gable. Jolie didn't think twice. She dropped all the logs except the one she had rested on the top, which she was holding with her right hand.

'Gable, get inside,' Jolie commanded. Gable stood still staring at Rona. 'GABLE, GET INSIDE,' Jolie shouted. And this time he ran. Jolie walked over to Rona, holding the log above her head.

'I will smash your skull in,' Jolie said through gritted teeth.

'But why?'

Jolie spat out a laugh. 'Because you wanted to kill us, Rona. You had duct tape and rope in your bag. You lured me and my children to this mountain under the pretence of helping. What more do I need to say?'

Jolie heard Rona let out a pitiful laugh. 'Ah, just like your old friend Martina. So feisty. You never were back then. If only she could see you now.' Rona looked up at Jolie.

Jolie narrowed her eyes. 'You know.'

'Oh, Jolie, you're so naive, always so trusting. Never really questioned anything. Yes I know. It wasn't a pretty ending for her. She was begging for mercy just as she toppled off the ledge. So many dangerous places around the mountains, wouldn't you say?'

What was Rona saying to her? Did she know what had happened with her and Duncan on the off-piste mountain that day?

'What are you saying, Rona?'

'I was the one who was with Martina that day she disappeared. I was the one Duncan instructed to make sure she was dealt with.'

Jolie's face contorted with confusion. 'You? And Duncan?'

'I worked for him, for the first three years. Until he left after Martina starting making trouble for him. And you, Jolie, you got to walk away, whilst I was the one who had to deal with the problem. And what did you get to do? Make your money and leave when it suited you. For a while, I presumed you and Duncan had left together. Do you know how . . . messed up it's been for me? All these years living with the mess in my head? Having to remember what I had to do?' Rona hit her head hard as though she were trying to dislodge whatever memory she was referring to. But Jolie gathered it was to do with Martina.

'Did you kill Martina? Is that what Duncan asked you to do?' Jolie realised that Duncan wouldn't have done his own dirty work.

Rona hit her head again harder this time. Her face began to crumple like a small child's. Jolie didn't need to hear her say it. It was there, in her eyes.

'I knew it, I knew you were a liar. From the very first day I met you, you made my skin crawl. Martina was my friend.'

Rona looked shell-shocked.

'Ha!' Rona spat. 'You didn't care about her, Jolie; you only cared about yourself and making money. You couldn't see what was happening, what Duncan was doing to her.'

'I understood it in the end, and that is all that matters. When you told me that Duncan was coming for me, I knew you were lying. Because I knew Duncan was never coming back here. And it was you. You did it; you killed her, didn't you?'

Rona put her hands over her face. Her whole body was trembling.

'Get up and get out of here now.'

Rona began to stand up. 'No one will ever find you, you know.' She laughed as she half walked and tripped her way down the mountain. 'Good luck freezing to death.' She called over her shoulder.

'You come back here and I'll kill you, Rona!' Jolie shouted. She watched and waited until Rona was out of sight, and then she hurried back into the shack and locked the door.

'What did you do?' Gable said.

'Mummy, what happened?' Vita was asking. Jolie noticed what was in her daughter's hand.

'Pooky?'

Gable looked at his sister.

'Yes, I packed it in my rucksack. You left it and I knew Vita would want it.'

Jolie raced to Gable, fell to her knees and pulled him in to her. 'Gable, you are a beautiful, beautiful boy.' She kissed his cheek and Gable shot his sister a look and they both laughed.

'Now, we all huddle around the fire. Stay very still, very close, and do what Mummy says.' Jolie sat down and crossed her legs. Clutching the log. She wasn't sure what was going to happen, but all she could do was sit and wait and pray.

Jolie wasn't sure how many hours had passed when she heard the roar of a skidoo. She grabbed the log tightly and pushed the children back behind her.

'Don't move,' she hissed.

She heard sobbing. It was Gable.

The engine stopped, and she heard voices. Spanish accents.

Jolie's heart began to race. There was a loud bang on the door.

'*Hola*,' they began to shout. 'If you are in there, please open the door. This is the police.'

At the sound of that word, Jolie's whole body deflated. She rushed to the door and opened it, seeing a black skidoo with *Policia* written on the side, and two men in helmets and official-looking badges on their snowsuits.

Jolie couldn't believe her eyes, as her children joined her at her side.

'How did you know we were here?'

'Your husband contacted us; he thought you might be in danger. He was able to locate you with that,' he said in his Spanish accent, pointing to Pooky.

'I'm confused.' Jolie said. 'How?'

'We were able to locate you by that GPS.'

Jolie shook her head in disbelief. Pooky. She remembered how Idris had told her that they would never lose Pooky again. This was why; he'd only gone and put a GPS inside his daughter's favourite toy so he would indeed never be lost again.

'Good old Pooky,' Jolie said, the tears falling hard and fast, as she was now unable to hold in any more of her emotions.

41

RONA

TWENTY YEARS AGO

The sun was out for now but it had snowed last night. There was evidence of it all the way along the sides of the mountain.

Martina had been edgy when she got in the car. Rona knew she'd taken something. She was always on something.

But Rona didn't care. It was better if Martina was topped up with whatever drug she had from her new dealer, the rival supplier who was pissing Duncan off so much.

It had taken Rona some time to convince Martina to take a drive with her, to meet Duncan to try and come to some arrangement. She had been so angry and had hidden herself away for a while. Eventually, when Duncan arrived for his next visit, she came around. And here they were.

They had been driving for about half an hour when Rona recognised the curve of the road, knowing she would be approaching her favourite spot soon.

'Oh for goodness' sake.' Rona began to slow as she approached the spot where she could pull in to enjoy the magnificent view of the surrounding mountains but also the severe drop below, which thrilled and scared Rona in equal measure.

Martina had been dozing. She sat up and opened her eyes.

'What is it?' she asked.

'Damn car does this sometimes. It needs a minute to cool down. I really ought to get it into a garage.'

'Didn't it occur to you to do that before you drove us halfway out to the middle of nowhere?' Martina said groggily. She was always so self-absorbed, so God damn rude. She had no idea that she couldn't just go around saying anything she wanted that came into her mind. But Rona was beyond telling her now. What was the point? It would all be over soon, and she could wipe her hands of Martina Acosta.

Rona pulled the car to a halt and stepped out.

'Oh wow, it's glorious. We were lucky to get to my favourite spot,' Rona called and watched as Martina grew curious and began to stir inside the car.

'But you'll need to help me with something. Put your coat on and come outside,' Rona called.

She turned just enough to see out of the corner of her eye that Martina was slowly moving, grabbing her coat from the back seat and pulling it on.

Rona heard the sound of the passenger door slamming and the crunch of snow boots on fresh powder as Martina approached Rona at the ledge.

'Cil del món is top of the world, but look where we are,' Rona said. 'It just keeps going up; it's never-ending.' Rona held out her hands.

'Yeah, it's great,' Martina said, sounding less than impressed.

Rona turned around and looked at Martina.

'Be a little more thankful and appreciative of where you live,' Rona said.

'I don't listen to that sort of crap, Rona. You must know that by now.'

'There's not a lot you do listen to is there, Martina?'

Martina snorted.

Typical, thought Rona. *Even in her final seconds, she's still full of herself.* And with that notion fresh in her mind, Rona took a swift step to her left, placed two hands on Martina's back and thrust her forward. At first, Rona thought she hadn't pushed her hard enough. Martina reached the edge, where she teetered. Her foot spun so her body turned towards Rona. For a few fleeting seconds, as Martina was losing her balance before she toppled over the edge of the mountain, Rona took in the look on her face. It was one of horror, which Rona immediately began to convert into a core memory, and the word she screamed as she fell, would forever stay etched on her mind, and Rona would return to it over and over.

Mercy.

42

JOLIE

TWO DAYS LATER

Jolie leaned into Idris on the sofa, really feeling the softness of the fabric that he had picked out and not taking it for granted for one second. She was so happy to be back in London.

'So my obsession with not calling the children "kids" finally paid off,' Jolie said.

'Yes, my darling, as always, you were right.' Idris squeezed her shoulder. They had been home a few hours. The children were watching a movie in the snug. A takeaway was on order. Jolie couldn't have been more thankful. Jolie was seething that Rona had changed the text to Idris when she saw it on his phone, but luckily the word 'kids' had him on high alert.

Jolie knew that the phone hadn't been lost; it had been thrown away somewhere, smashed and never to be found again.

There had been time at the police station, a short stint at the hospital at Idris's insistence. Phone calls to Idris, flights were booked once the airline issues had been resolved, and then they were on their way. It was as though it had all been a dream.

'And I can't believe it was your idea to get the GPS put in Pooky,' Jolie said.

Idris let out a sigh. 'All right, you got me. It was Angie.'

'Of course it was.' Jolie stood up.

'Okay?' Idris asked. If he had been conscious of her behaviour before, he was going to be ultra-sensitive now.

'Just checking on Gable and Vita.'

'Okay,' Idris said in that tone, but she knew he would give her the space to do what she needed to do. Checking relentlessly on the children would be her new thing, but she had vowed she was going to get therapy this time for all that she had gone through in Cil del món. Enough time had passed for her to say she had lost a friend up the mountain. To admit a tragic accident had occurred that she could not have helped. Martina Acosta deserved to be remembered.

EPILOGUE

RONA

Rona stood in Barcelona airport, two brown suitcases at her side. They hadn't been replaced for twenty-three years. They were in good nick though, because she hadn't used them. They had been in the cupboard next to her bed, collecting dust.

She touched the side of her head where the bruise had formed.

The police had questioned her and held her for hours, but there was nothing they could do. Rona hadn't kidnapped Jolie, or hurt her or the children. Jolie had been free to leave the lodge at any point. Of course, there was no way she could, not in that weather. There was no sign of the tape or the rope. Rona wasn't stupid. The mountains were so vast, with infinite hiding places. The mountain had always been a good friend to Rona and would hold on to all of her secrets.

Rona had just been trying to help Jolie, she had told one police officer, who was impressed with her Catalan. Jolie had mental health problems, Rona explained. She had gone quite mad in the end.

She had been released without charge, although Corrine had a few words to say to her about using one of the lodges. But in the end, she just felt sorry for her. She was instructed to leave and Corrine wouldn't press charges.

Rona had been able to go back to her apartment where she started packing. She looked around at the home she had made these last few years, suddenly her apartment looked so welcoming now she was leaving it.

She looked into the corner of the room, where the chair and TV were. Mercy was hunched down in the chair. Rona noted the pink streaks in her hair. She really was very pretty; it was all such a shame that it had ended the way it did.

'You didn't get her in the end then,' Mercy said. 'You know you could have. You had so many opportunities. But with me, there was one and you took it.'

Rona smiled and nodded. 'That's right. I thought and then acted quickly and then just went for it.'

'It all happened so fast,' Mercy said.

'I know.'

'I called out. I asked for mercy.'

'You did. And that word has stuck forever. I'm sorry it happened. I had no choice. It was you or me. I do regret it and here you are, still haunting me every day. You've never let me forget. But now, Martina, it's time I let you go. I'm leaving Cil del món, the Pyrenees Mountains for good. I can't take you with me.'

Rona turned and picked up her suitcases and, when she was at the door, she closed it on an empty apartment.

'Madam, can I help?' the lady behind the desk at Barcelona airport called, thrusting Rona from her thoughts and into the present.

'Oh, hello, yes. I'm off to London.' Rona smiled. 'I'd like a one-way ticket to Gatwick airport, please.'

ACKNOWLEDGEMENTS

I visited Andorra in the Pyrenees between 2000 and 2001, and I worked as a chef in a restaurant. I was terrible at snowboarding and never caught the bug, but the scenery (and the shopping) was incredible. Years later, it just happened to be the perfect backdrop to my thirteenth novel. Cil del món is a fictional part of the Pyrenees, although there was a part of the mountain that was referred to as the Top of the World, which many people visited.

Many thanks to the brilliant team at Hodder for publishing this second thriller. Special thanks to Audrey Linton for your editing skills and for helping shape the story and characters. Thank you to all the lovely readers who buy my books and continue to support me in doing the thing I love most.

I am currently plotting my next destination thriller, set in a remote house here in the Highlands, where I live. Keep your eyes peeled!

Nina x

RAISING READERS

Books Build Bright Futures

Dear Reader,

We'd love your attention for one more page to tell you about the crisis in children's reading, and what we can all do.

Studies have shown that reading for fun is the **single biggest predictor of a child's future life chances** – more than family circumstance, parents' educational background or income. It improves academic results, mental health, wealth, communication skills, ambition and happiness.[1]

The number of children reading for fun is in rapid decline. Young people have a lot of competition for their time. In 2024, 1 in 10 children and young people in the UK aged 5 to 18 did not own a single book at home.[2]

Hachette works extensively with schools, libraries and literacy charities, but here are some ways we can all raise more readers:

- Reading to children for just 10 minutes a day makes a difference
- Don't give up if children aren't regular readers – there will be books for them!
- Visit bookshops and libraries to get recommendations
- Encourage them to listen to audiobooks
- Support school libraries
- Give books as gifts

There's a lot more information about how to encourage children to read on our website: **www.RaisingReaders.co.uk**

Thank you for reading.

hachette UK

[1] OECD, '21st-Century Readers: Developing Literacy Skills in a Digital World', 2021, https://www.oecd.org/en/publications/21st-century-readers_a83d84cb-en.html

[2] National Literacy Trust, 'Book Ownership in 2024', November 2024, https://literacytrust.org.uk/research-services/research-reports/book-ownership-in-2024